# SONS OF STORM

## FRANCESCA NOTO

Text Copyright © 2020 Francesca Noto
Cover Art © Rosaria Trivisonne 2019
Translation by Francesca T Barbini

First published by Luna Press Publishing, Edinburgh, 2020



www.lunapresspublishing.com

ISBN-13: 978-1-913387-02-0

TO MARCO, WHO ALWAYS FOUGHT BY MY SIDE;
AND TO MILA AND GIORGIA, ARROWS SHOT
FROM OUR BOW.

# Contents

"You are a child of the universe
No less than the trees and the stars;
You have a right to be here.
And whether or not it is clear to you,
No doubt the universe is unfolding as it should."

Max Ehrmann, *Desiderata*

# PROLOGUE

Richard looks out of the large loft window from the last floor of the historic UWS building. The window occupies the wall facing east. At this time of day, when the sun begins to carry out its descending parabola in the sky, the light is still strong; not the warm and majestic glory that envelops that room shortly after dawn, but he likes it anyway. He stands there, staring at the skyline wrapped in summer mist, over the green of Central Park. A slight smile touches his thin lips, offering a glimpse of unexpected kindness among the ravines of an ancient face, older than what, at first sight, those marked but sure traits might look, those greying hairs, those clear eyes full of deep awareness. Perhaps it is his eyes that betray it, so intense that few can support their gaze.

He waits. Waits and remembers. A Norse with a life as long as his can only live with memories. He begins to think that he is the last of his lineage, in a world that perhaps no longer needs him. He was the first to set foot in it, a pioneer by pure chance. Since then, too many centuries have overlapped. Too many conflicts have come and gone in his lifetime.

Is it time to close the games? No. It would not be his style. Besides, he knows he hasn't finished yet. He knows there is still someone carrying on the Norse bloodline, and that someone is relying on him more than he could have foreseen. That thought sketches a different grin on his lips, curling them, showing a white flash of perfect, white teeth.

He looks at the landscape. And he waits. Not long now. Is he so fond of his half-breed descendant that he cannot wait to find him at his feet? He thought he had already compromised enough with this young man, promising his father of things to come. After all, there are great expectations on him: it does not happen very often to see the first-born of the Phoenix and the White Rune grow. Then there's that other reason. An awareness made of incredible coincidences, but never accidental, in his name and in his lineage at the intersection of the primordial Nodal Point, where it all began. Even if the boy knows nothing now, who knows how long he will remain unaware of his true role in the story.

He looks away from the view in front of him, eyeing the loft door behind him. An abyss of time divides them, yet when they are together it does not seem so. Seventeen years. He still remembers, despite everything, what it means. The tumultuous period in which everything seemed possible, and at the same time so far away. The moment of impetuous passions, and even more impetuous loves. He remembers. He remembers as if it was the day before, not a thousand years, the smile and the look of Cressida after the Solstice night, and the fire they could ignite inside him.

The phone rings suddenly, distracting him from these thoughts. He moves towards the antique mahogany table and reaches for his phone.

"*Dick? I'm finally out. I couldn't take it anymore.*" The pleasant and warm voice of a young man, vibrating with adolescent tones, is on the other end of the line.

"Nate, there you are. I wondered when they would let you out. And so, another year closes ... Are you satisfied?"

"*That it is over? Immensely.*" The boy's voice melts into laughter. "*Can I come by? As soon as I finish with the goodbyes. Never ending!*"

He seems exasperated, like a chained wolf. And Richard smiles to himself knowingly. "I thought you wanted to leave right away. Aren't your parents at Maple Tree already?"

"*Since last week. But even if I start in a couple of hours, it won't make a difference. I'll be there tomorrow night.*"

"I wonder why you insist on a fifteen-hour journey by car when you'd need only three of them by plane ... Doesn't Rachel want to give you a quick lift?" He grins, already knowing the answer.

"*I love road trips. Even Mom and Dad have given up since I got the old Mustang. And anyway, I will not tell you where Rachel can shove her quick lift, out of respect for your age. I generally avoid throwing my soul up if I can help it. So, can I stop by? Will you be at home?*"

"You can. I'll be here," he grants, good-natured. That smile really doesn't want to leave him.

## CHAPTER ONE

"Nathaniel Gordon, you haven't signed my yearbook yet!" A merry voice reached him from behind like the ringing trumpets on judgment day.

*Shit*, he thought, rolling his clear but mismatched eyes, one green and one blue, a gift of his heterochromia. He hurriedly pocketed the mobile still in his hand. As expected, Kimberly Breckenridge was right there, about twenty paces away and rapidly approaching. She almost ran across the crowded courtyard of Trinity College, zigzagging among small groups of vociferous students.

Kim was one of the school's most popular girls, with blonde hair that shone under the June sun, framing graceful features and big green eyes. Nathaniel thought that she could have gone out with anyone, including Sean Davenport, the reigning champion of the swimming team who a few weeks earlier had pompously announced his admission to Stanford. But no, she spent the whole year running after him, the shy and lonely boy with few trusted friends, the boy with the different coloured eyes. He had kept his distance from her, amid general amazement. They didn't take him seriously when he said she wasn't the right one, that he wanted to wait for the person who would make him feel something really special. They could hardly believe him—that is, when they didn't engage in sarcastic and malicious insinuations.

"Are you off already?" she asked, stepping in front of him. The yearbook was pressed against the prominent breast under a blue T-shirt with the school's yellow coat of arms, *Labore et Virtute*.

Nathaniel nodded. "I have a fifteen-hour trip ahead, and if I want to get to Ocala by tomorrow night, I have to leave now." Actually, he had every intention of going home to retrieve his luggage and stop by Dick's place before heading off. But she didn't need to know that.

"Surely you've got time for coffee, goodbyes and my yearbook, don't you?" she pressed, tilting her head to the side with an irresistible smile.

Nathaniel sighed, resigned, then followed her to the cafeteria, where small groups of students lingered happily, yapping around the tables.

"Hey, look who's back—*Bright Eyes*. Weren't you supposed to head off pronto?" The jovial voice, coming from the line at the counter, rose above the buzz of conversation. Tall enough to stand above most of the other boys, with a rebellious tow-coloured mop, washed-out blue eyes and the wide face that made one think of latent Russian origins, Marcus Lerman was one of Nathaniel's few friends. They had already said their goodbyes, but he seemed to understand what had happened when he saw Kimberly. Nathaniel tossed him an annoyed look when he saw him grin in her direction.

Marcus was not alone. There was another boy with him, who had attended several classes with Nathaniel. He also seemed rather surprised to see him.

"Didn't you need to..." he started to say.

"No," cut in Marcus, amused. "*Bright Eyes* is staying a little bit longer, Zach. Aren't you happy?"

The other chuckled, seeing who Nathaniel was with.

When they reached one of the few free tables, Kim set the yearbook down and pushed it in front of him, with the sugary smile she employed to get what she wanted—although it hadn't made Nathaniel go out with her.

He shrugged, opening the album and looking for a pen in the old, worn down leather bag.

"So, Nate," Zach cocked his head to the side, watching him scribble something. "Will you spend another summer on that ranch in Florida with your folks? When will you get tired of shovelling horseshit and organise a coast to coast? We've been wanting to do that since the start of high school."

"You're the only one who keeps saying that, Zach," Marcus laughed, biting into his bagel. "Nate prefers to spend the summer between pompous riding contests for descendants of fallen British nobles rather than planning a cool-as coast-to-coast ride with us."

Nathaniel sighed, looking up from the yearbook as he closed it again, pushing it toward Kimberly. She stared at him dreamily for a moment: to many, his disquieting and intense look was as bizarre as it was alluring.

"It's not that I don't want to," he replied hesitantly, "but this year was already planned with my family. Next time."

"Damn right!" said Marcus, feigning indignation. "High school will be over next year. We could end up hundreds of miles away from each other, only meeting up during the holidays. It's the least we can do to spend that summer together somewhere."

Nathaniel started to get up. "I'd love to stay longer, I swear, but if I don't go I'll never make it on time."

"Here he goes again, with the precious act. Guys, tell him something!" Kimberly complained, with a melodramatic sigh.

"Something!" Marcus and Zach snapped in chorus before bursting out laughing.

"Very funny," she protested, scowling.

"She's right," Nathaniel chuckled. He nodded to his friends, gave Kim a rather awkward smile, and walked away.

*

He parked the Mustang under the elegant Upper West Side building where Richard lived and stepped out, activating the car alarm. Stopping at the wrought-iron gate at the top of the steps, he pressed the button on the old intercom. "Dick, it's me. I made it," he said when the man he thought of as his paternal grandfather answered him, opening the door soon after. Not that Richard looked like a grandfather. Since he had known him, he had always looked the same. He was just "Dick". His father, who had been adopted by him several years before, taking his surname, had also called him that.

When the doors of the elevator opened in front of him, the boy entered the cab, which was clad in shiny wood panels. He pressed the button for the top floor, peering at the reflection in the mirror on the back wall. He found himself in front of a tall, long-limbed teenager, with regular and slightly angular features, framed by short, rough black hair. On his ivory complexion, a trait of his father, the first June sun had caused a splash of freckles to appear. His own eyes stared at him thoughtfully.

He looked away as the elevator stopped at the floor with the gentle swing of hydraulic mechanisms, opening the automatic doors. Richard was waiting for him on the landing.

"They kept you more than expected, your friends," he began, patting him on the shoulder amicably before leading him inside the loft. "Come. Enter."

He had talked to him, as he often did when they were alone, in his native language. That Norse language that did not exist in other places of the world, secret and unknown, spoken only between covens, the territorial or family groups of the Waerne, and that Nathaniel had learned since childhood.

"Kim Breckenridge doesn't give up. And the boys would like to do a coast-to-coast," sighed Nathaniel, answering in the same language. He followed Dick into the kitchen and settled himself on a tall stool at the breakfast counter.

Richard poured himself a cup of black coffee from a kettle left to warm on the plate of the coffee machine and turned to look at him, a flash of good-natured fun in his eyes. "It doesn't seem such tragic news to justify that desolate air, Nate ..." he commented, after a moment. "Perhaps, all things considered, you should give the girl a chance, if only for the determination she has shown." He chuckled, seeing his nephew rolling his eyes in exasperation. "And I don't see what's wrong with a trip with your friends. You could just do it, without asking a lot of questions."

The boy sighed. "There's nothing wrong. It's me, perhaps, who's wrong," he finally groaned.

Richard took a sip of coffee, leaning on the island in the middle of the large kitchen. "And what's wrong with you? Let's hear it."

Nathaniel seemed to shrink as he crossed his arms over his chest. "You know what's wrong. Another year has passed and nothing has happened." He shrugged. "And anyway, I don't want to lose three months of training at the ranch, maybe with some of the passing European masters, to make a stupid coast-to-coast."

"You're seventeen, Nate," Richard said after a while, kindly. There was no paternalism in that voice, nor was he taking him lightly. It was the awareness of someone who knew the value of time well. "I know you would like to burn off the stages and have answers, but in these things there are no certainties. Your father was twenty-six years old when he reached the maximum awareness of his potential."

"But my mother was empathetic since childhood, and her power manifested itself spontaneously," he objected.

"Yes, but only when it was necessary did it reveal itself for what it really was," Richard pointed out with a knowing smile. "Everything happens when it must, believe me." He looked at him straight in the eyes and shook his head softly. "These seventeen years of yours will never come back, Nathaniel. Don't waste them."

The boy listened to him silently, nibbling at his bottom lip, a thoughtful look on his beardless face. Finally, he snorted softly. "You make it sound easy. You think I should behave like any other boy of my age... go out with girls I don't really care about, just so I can boast, spend my holidays with friends and worry about school. But the truth is that I spent my life feeling everyone's expectations on me and I'm afraid that they're wrong. That none of the skills that are expected of me will ever manifest. And that I will remain in a limbo, useless, forever. The boy of the prophecy, the son of the warrior of the storm ... an illusion. A lie."

Dick left the cup of coffee on the island's surface and approached him, putting both hands on his nephew's shoulders, straight and wide, typical of a competitive rider. "Listen to me. Stop being melodramatic and throw those doubts out of your head," he declared, his voice firm and sure, his light and magnetic eyes fixed in those of the boy. It was impossible to ignore him. "You are the son of Sven Gordon and Lea Schneider. You are first and foremost the fruit of their love. Keep this in mind and you will know that you are special. You would be even if your latent abilities never revealed themselves." He smiled, seeing the boy's eyes widen in dismay at that hypothesis so unacceptable to him. "We are all called to fulfil a mission in this world, only some know it better than others. Don't be impatient. Your path will be revealed to you at the right time."

Nathaniel opened his mouth as if to reply, but closed it again, saying nothing. He simply nodded, a slight smile softening his features, dissolving the doubts from his face. Dick could be convincing. And besides, it was no accident that he always went looking for him when something was wrong.

"Good boy. That's the spirit," laughed the man, affectionately gripping his big hands on his shoulders. "And now go if you want to get to the ranch by tomorrow. Or we'll both get an earful from your parents."

## CHAPTER TWO

He staggered as he advanced along the cracked concrete of the half-empty parking lot behind the *Rose Tattoo* bar. He wasn't drunk, maybe a little tipsy. Completely capable of looking after himself. It was just that the world had taken a strange angle. The street, in the deceptive sunset light, seemed tilted and sparkled in a bizarre way.

*The fucking Earth's axis has shifted and I haven't even noticed,* he thought vaguely, panting and carrying a not quite steady hand up to his face, made pale by his albinism, to move a tuft of hair so light as to seem threads of white gold.

*Where is my bike?* Further on, for sure, because he still couldn't see it. Maybe between the old mud-and-blood-coloured Buick and the wreck of the Dodge pickup that once—many aeons before—must have been beige. He snorted, swallowing a breath of air that smelled of old urine and rubbish left to soak in the sun. He forced himself to push back the vague idea of retching as he leaned against the back of the shabby Dodge—you could have carried out a stratigraphic study of the layers of dust and dirt on it. No, he wouldn't do it in that parking lot. He was sure of that. He would be on his way south, leaving Richmond behind, and goodbye to all of you. He straightened up with a grunt of protest and focused his eyes, so clear as to seem transparent, in the open space beyond the parked cars. Yes, he remembered well, the bike was there. But something was not right.

"Hey you! What the fuck are you doing? Don't touch my bike!" A growl rose in his throat, coagulating in those aggressive words, aimed at the man intent on stealing his Sportster, a bit shabby but still working.

The man almost jumped up, looking up at him. At first he seemed worried at that interruption, but as soon as he fixed his eyes on the young man he relaxed his tense shoulders and allowed himself an amused grin. Another guy, in all likelihood his mate, moved away with deliberate slowness from a street lamp a few meters from there, which added its sick yellowish beam to the amber shades of the sunset, unable to light much of the shadows that stretched ravenously at the corners of the parking lot.

"Is that so?" said the man by the bike, bending his head to the side with the sly and innocent air of a cat caught stealing. "And what if I do, Snow White?"

The boy didn't waste time. He closed the distance in a few quick steps and, before the stranger could even understand what was happening, he lifted his hands quickly, grabbed him by the hair and suddenly lowered his head, slamming the man's face against his raised knee with brutal timing. The revolting noise of the nasal septum being crushed was followed by the victim's incredulous groan. As the man collapsed to the side, dazed and in pain, the boy pushed him, away from the Sportster.

"I think I will do *this*," he said soon after, planting the reinforced toe of his boots in his ribs with a dull thud. The thief cried—if he had even contemplated getting up again, at that further aggression he thought better of it, moving away on his knees and elbows, covering his broken face with his hands. Dark rivulets of blood filtered through his fingers.

It could not have been more than a handful of seconds.

The boy turned to face the accomplice, who had only moved a step away from the streetlight, and stared at him, motionless, his eyes wide and incredulous. Everything had occurred so fast that he didn't even have time to realise exactly what had happened to his mate.

"Do you want some too, or are you going to fuck off with your friend?" The boy growled, a threatening flash in his disturbing blue eyes, reminiscent of the icy and transparent depths of a glacial crevasse.

"Stay calm, dude. Calm, okay? We don't care about your bike, we're leaving," said the other, looking worried as he approached his friend and tried to help him get up.

He watched them stagger toward the row of parked cars behind the bar. From time to time, the unhurt man turned to look at the albino nervously, fearing that he would pursue them to finish what he had started. But the boy didn't move. He stood there, next to the old black Sportster with a scratched hull, staring at them as they walked away and disappeared behind the vehicles.

Above him, the street lamp flickered, dying, giving him even more the impression that the world was rolling slowly, like a trawling boat on a restless sea. His mouth had the sour taste of hangover and adrenaline. His arms trembled. He had wanted, for a long and intense moment, to reach them and hit again, again and again, until he could feel the metallic smell of blood. Until it covered his hands. But he remained motionless and waited for that twisted desire to pass, as well as the nausea that gripped his stomach. He blinked, trying to focus better, and fumbled in the pockets of his leather jacket, one so old it had probably seen Woodstock and was old even then. He had never been able to get rid of it. It would just fall off in tatters, one day or another, and then he would stop wearing it. He closed his shuddering hand on the Sportster's keys, pulled them out and got on his bike. The engine started on the third attempt, growling and panting until it began to roar with determination—enough to convince him to remove the trestle with his boot, held together by a couple of rounds of black adhesive tape, and selecting the gear to exit the parking lot.

He left behind the yellow lights of the *Rose Tattoo*, taking the interstate south. He didn't know why he went that way; it was an idea like any other, born of instinct, and he had decided to indulge it. The sky grew darker and the first stars had already appeared in the east. The colours of the sunset turned to reds and purples on his right. He let himself be guided by the hoarse and laboured song of the engine, the old Sportster between his thighs like a lover too big for him, expert and fiery, the view that at times blurred. Bent forward on the wide tank, he felt the wind whipping at his face of an almost unnatural pallor, his hair as clear as snow, whipping his cheeks into splintered strands.

Like many times before, he was leaving behind his own story, hoping to start over, that it would be better. He would not go back. He had left behind a childhood and an adolescence growing up between several homes in Queens, the squalid recurrence of uncertain foster families who soon got tired of him and his mess, the endless succession of social workers and shrinks trying to understand what was broken in his head. For years they had tried to understand what no one but him seemed to understand. And then, once he turned eighteen, he had signed a form and had gone his own way. He had begun then to leave behind sleazy motels and complicated relationships, precarious jobs and hostile brawls and gazes. He was tired of being considered *different*, moving on the razor edge of a life that he didn't understand. Belonging was not for him—he had never had that experience. This he knew.

As the speed increased and the shiny black tarmac seemed to sway like a snake, a sinuous and immense black mamba that was lost in the darkness on the horizon, he felt tears marking his cheeks.

Perhaps he was not destined to find what he had always been looking for. Perhaps he was wrong, as they had always painted him.

In front of him, the road floated, exploding in indistinct bubbles. He felt the rear wheel suddenly slipping, sliding from below, the excessive speed betraying him. He tried to regain control of the Sportster, but even his old and impetuous lover failed him. The world became a chaos of colours and lights and shadows and, for a long moment that seemed to last forever, he realised he was suspended in the air, his arms spread out like wings. Gravity no longer existed, and he hung upside down in an overwhelming eternity. He had the time to think that maybe he had wanted it. That maybe closing the game like that was better, before everything really became unbearable.

Then the wings broke.

Fade. Dark.

# CHAPTER THREE

Nathaniel had been travelling for a few hours. Inside his Mustang, the notes of a cover of *Rawhide* made the old speakers vibrate. A half-smile danced on his lips, revealing irregular incisors, while the deserted street and the last warm lights of the day reminded him why he preferred fifteen hours of car travel to three locked up in the belly of an aeroplane. At times, he seemed to find his rightful place only like this. Travelling alone, in the middle of nowhere. Some cities behind, some in front of him. And in the middle, just the road.

He recalled the conversation he'd had with Richard as the song faded, giving way to the news. When he'd heard him speak with such conviction, and with all his Norse charisma, he couldn't have help but agree with him. It was as if Dick knew certain things, as if he had lived them and now presented them as facts. But the doubts remained, malignant and rooted within him. And he kept asking himself: would he be worthy of his inheritance? Or was it all a big mistake? Technically, even if he had never manifested any ability connected to the blood of the Norse, nothing would have changed for his parents and for the little coven of Silver Springs. If the verses he had heard repeated since childhood had turned out to be only an old musty prophecy, they certainly wouldn't stop loving him. But even that awareness would not save him from disappointment. And he didn't want it to go that way. When Lea, his mother, told him how bad her adolescence had been because of the empathic abilities she had to manage without a guide, he felt envious of her. Because, in the end, his adolescence was getting ruined too, but for the opposite reason.

*"And lo, Valoisa and Valkea will give birth to a son who will be the ruin of the Ancient One.*

*Be wary of them, for Thurs' final triumph is undermined in the glory of his rebirth.*
*Awaken the Nodes. Fear the storm and its warrior."*

The words of the prophecy, etched into his memory, once again came to mind, as if to mock him. It had always been his father, the storm warrior, Valoisa the Luminous. But what about him? Was he supposed to be the ruin of the Ancient One? According to who, when the circumstances had never happened, had never showed?

He was so immersed in those gloomy considerations that at first he didn't notice the twisted mass a dozen meters to his right. The Mustang headlights hit it in full soon after, and Nathaniel slowed down. Under the dark trunk of a tree by the side of the road, cut out like a black silhouette against the dark tones of the background, he managed to focus more clearly on what looked like a motorcycle, bent by the violence of the impact in a brutal acute angle. The front wheel rolled in the grass a few meters away. Nathaniel hit the brakes in a flash of consciousness that closed his stomach in a vice: the accident had just happened and, on that empty road, no one had seen its aftermath until then. Except for him. From the crashed bike rose a thread of black and oily smoke, which dispersed between the leaves of the tree. A few tongues of flame, listless, crackled in the dry grass.

The boy approached the guardrail, occupying the emergency lane not far from where the metal barriers opened in a gap bent towards the outside, a broken line of twisted sheets. He stopped the Mustang, keeping the engine running, and let the headlights illuminate the disturbing scene a few meters away.

Of the old Sportster, crashed against the tree, there was very little left that was easily identifiable, apart from the rear wheel deformed and tilted upwards, a piece of the handlebars and the dented tank. Around it, fragments and debris seemed to indicate an explosion had just happened. But it was the figure, motionless in the tall grass, which suddenly grabbed Nathaniel's gaze.

"Oh God ..." he murmured between his teeth as he realised he was staring at the remains of the rider, laying there against the darkness of the unkept field. And he was not moving.

Although he felt his stomach closing up in knots and his legs going soft, he shook off his morbid contemplation and jumped out of the car, moving quickly forward.

He looked around at area, but there was nobody in sight. The road he had chosen was among the least busy on the east coast, particularly at night. Never like that moment he found himself regretting his choice, as he realised the uncontrollable trembling that came from his hands. Still, he pushed back the sense of inescapable impotence taking hold of him, quickly bypassing the Mustang and heading for the gap in the guardrail, running past it, straight to the figure spilt to the ground. Meanwhile, his hand was already rummaging in his jeans pocket, looking for his mobile.

The rider lay on his side awkwardly, his light hair mixed with blood that, by contrast, was so dark as to seem black. The face was not visible, pressed against the crushed grass and covered with ruffled tufts of hair and by a torn shred of a leather jacket. Nathaniel was grateful. One leg, stretched out on the grass, was grotesquely bent; the same could be said of the arm protruding from under the body, the pale, dirty hand clawing at the grass. The boy suddenly saw the white of a broken bone jutting out from a tear in the black leather of the jacket, just below the rider's elbow, and he was forced to swallow his own bile, praying that the feeling of warmth at the top of his stomach and the tingling that stung his palms were not the symptoms of an imminent fainting fit or the fact that he was about to vomit. He felt his head spinning.

"Oh God, oh God, *oh Christ...*" he stammered, anguished, his breath rasping in his throat. He kneeled to the ground, making the dry grass crackle and a few twigs of low bushes twist beneath him. He mustered a deeper breath and put the mobile to his ear, after pressing a speed-dial button.

His father answered at the second ring. "*Nate? Is everything all right?*"

"No!" He found himself shouting. But more than a scream, a croaking vent came out of his throat, like the squeak of a broken bellow. "Nothing's all right! I'm on the road to Ocala, Dad, and there's been an accident, there's a motorcyclist..."

"*Did you have an accident?*" On the other side of the line, the voice of his father became immediately higher and more excited, interrupting him as soon as the word *accident* had reached his ear in all its alarming concreteness.

"No! No, it wasn't *me*, Dad!" Nathaniel said quickly, struggling not to tangle his words in his haste to explain. "A motorcycle. It crashed off the road, there's a man... he's here in front of me, I don't even know if he's still breathing..."

"*Have you called for help?*"

Something had changed in Sven's tone. He could tell. He inhaled a deep breath of air that tasted of metal, gasoline and blood. "No, I called you," he simply said, as if it were something obvious, and there was nothing else to add.

"*All right. We're coming. You remember how it's done, right? It's been a while, but it's still the same procedure. Do it now, let me find you. We'll be there right away. And stay calm.*" There was a brief pause, broken only by the metallic and alien rustling of static in the line. "*Everything will be fine, Nate. I promise you."*

His father couldn't know how much those words had made him feel, as tears of relief filled his eyes. He felt so confused and stunned that he could have burst out crying. But he bit his lips and forced himself to remain calm, despite that feeling of dizziness growing more and more intense, of the tingling that had become a warm, constant vibration, now, like burning needles buried deep in the skin. His ears were buzzing. "All right, Dad... come quickly. I... I'm here," he managed to say, before hanging up.

The mobile slipped from his trembling fingers, ending up in the grass. He tried not to notice the revolting smell that made its way into his lungs. Then he closed his eyes and did as he had been taught. He cut out everything else, concentrating on the inside of himself, aligning himself with what his coven called *kern*, the inner centre of perceptions, and channelled every feeling on that point. He focused on the tall, powerful figure of his father, on the warm tones of his reassuring voice, on his intense blue eyes, only one of which he had inherited. On all the details he could recall and on which he managed to focus his attention.

It was the simplest and most direct way he had to be found by him and by the other Waerne in Silver Springs. It was the best assurance he had, that he could always count on, wherever he was, on his parents and their companions and on their preternatural skills. He had learned that kind of exercise since childhood, for obvious reasons of defence. With an effort, he received a vague mental backlash that told him that the attempt had been successful.

When he was certain that he had given his parents a chance to connect to his *quantum track*—or so Rachel had called it when she tried to explain the principles behind the specific ability some Waerne had— he shook his head slowly, trying to clear his thoughts and regain calm. But the strange sensations he was feeling did not seem to abate. On the contrary, they grew louder and louder.

He found himself staring at the broken and bent figure of the biker in front of him. Instinctively, without even fully understanding what he was doing, he carefully leaned forward and stretched a hand towards the man's neck, trying to place his fingers on the skin just below the jawline, which stood out among a Rorschach test of blood and black streaks of dirt and mud. He wanted to check that his heart was still beating, if there was still something left to do for him, or if he had summoned his father and the others without a valid reason.

At that moment, he realised that the man was actually a teenager, perhaps close to his age. Suddenly, the contact of his fingers on the other's skin triggered a storm. He couldn't tell if the heartbeat was there or not, because that initial idea lost all importance, while every thought was swept away from his head in a violent and incomprehensible flash. Nathaniel heard a hoarse lament rising in his own throat, while the feeling that his skin was crackling under the onslaught of an unstoppable energy became stronger. The moan became a cry of pain and dismay as he leaned forward, his other hand descending on the lifeless body of the injured rider, unable to avoid it. He clung to him so as not to fall completely, but that contact only had the effect of heightening the flames burning in his chest.

That hot ball he felt below his sternum reached his brain, blinding him with a white flash, almost as if someone had punched him in the face. And then it descended into his arms, meeting the subtle vibration that made his skin quiver in an unbearable way. When he dared to open his eyes, struggling to focus through a veil of tears and a chaos of acid-green bubbles exploding in front of his eyes, he started, incredulous at seeing his hands surrounded by a pale light that seemed to emanate from within them, making his skin translucent.

It happened faster than his mind could cope with. Below him, the rider gave a convulsive jerk, almost as if he had just been shocked by a defibrillator. Soon after, Nathaniel began to feel the energies flowing from him, a violent torrent which poured from his stomach into his arms, and then down into his hands, vanishing at the point of contact between him and the injured young man. His eyes widened in dismay as he realized that he could do nothing to stop that vital life-bleeding. Shortly thereafter, he began to hear, as if through a water screen, an animal and inarticulate moaning.

*Nnn ... nnnnnnn ...*

That sound rubbed jarringly against his eardrums, a nasal growl that didn't want to stop. Insistent, distressing.

*Nnnn ... nn ... nnnnnnn ...*

*Let it stop, damn it, let someone shut it up!* he found himself thinking, closing his eyes again.

"*Nnn ... nnnnnnn ...!*" It took him a few slow, clumsy seconds to understand that it was he who was uttering that gurgling and infinite moan.

It hurt. His heart throbbed fast against his ribs, and every beat was a painful blow, every breath burned like liquid fire in the lungs. And he could not stop it. He could not force his own muscles to take his hands off the young man's body lying on the grass. It was as if the impetuous current that connected him to the wounded rider chained them together without escape.

He felt his head spinning, and he had time to wonder if it was body under him was stealing his strength, in the middle of the vortex of thoughts that crowded his mind. A mind now in a state of total alarm; if he had to imagine it, he would have visualised it as the control room of a thermonuclear power station melting at the core: a blaze of bright red and flashing lights. Would he suck up enough energy to kill him?

A hand closed on his trembling shoulder. A solid and firm grip. Reassuring. And then a hug wrapped him, supporting him.

"Shhh ... it's all right, Nate. It's all right ... follow it, don't fight it. I'm here now, nothing bad can happen to you."

"Dad?" His voice was suddenly released, in a distraught, croaking sob.

"We are here. Everything will be fine..."

He heard, a little further away, his mother's kind voice. And he was overwhelmed with relief.

"Let him go, now, son," Sven said. "You've been good ... he'll live."

He didn't understand; he had been good at doing what? But he did not have the time or the strength to ask, because the world began to swirl worse than before, and then suddenly he fell over. Sinking in the dark.

# CHAPTER FOUR

When he awoke, the first thing Nathaniel saw was the wooden beam that crossed the sloping roof of his room at Maple Tree Farm. *I'm home*, he thought gratefully, lying on the bed, enjoying the moments of ephemeral quiet. He had the feeling that even a banal gesture like moving a hand would break that calm. There was too much to deal with out there. He filled his lungs with the air of the small attic, which smelled of dusty wood and old honey. The placid noises of the ranch and the insistent chirping of birds entered through the half-open dormer window.

What happened? There had been a deep contact between him and that injured boy, the broken motorcyclist from the accident. He knew this. It was everything else that escaped, with dramatic certainty, his knowledge and memories. He really had no idea what had happened in those few minutes between the phone call to his father and his arrival with the others. However, the idea that finally his latent powers had awakened throbbed inside of him, and that thought was enough to make him want to face anything. He closed his eyes for a moment, reliving calmly the memories he had of the scene. The energies that had flown from his hands at an impressive speed, sucked up by that tormented body that needed it. Had it been him? Had he *healed* him? If so, it meant only one thing: he must have inherited his father's abilities. Sven was a healer too, among the most powerful healers among the Waerne. Could this mean that he would also start to develop the power to control storms?

"You're going too fast now."

A gentle voice brought him back to the present. Nathaniel opened his eyes and looked towards the half-open door in the room. "Mom ... how many times have I told you not to look into my thoughts without permission?" he protested, scowling.

Lea laughed, opening the door completely and stepping forward with long, graceful strides. A little over forty years old, she kept the slim and agile figure of a young girl. When they rode together, Nathaniel was always willing to bet that if she wanted to, she could leave him behind without the slightest effort.

Lea sat on the edge of the bed, extending a hand to caress his cheek. "How are you? It must have been quite shocking."

He sighed, trying to prop himself up on his elbows. "Yes, it was. But I would like to understand exactly what it was," he admitted, frowning. A straight wrinkle formed in the middle of his eyebrows, the same one his father had every time something worried him.

"I think you've already figured it out," his mother replied, coyly. "You healed that boy. You saved him with these hands of yours," she said, holding them in her own, the big and nervous hands of her son.

Nathaniel swallowed, settling himself better on the cushions behind him. "So ... has it happened?" he finally murmured, looking for his mother's green eyes—the other colour of its unmatched irises. "In the end, it happened?"

"Did you have any doubts?" Lea chuckled. "It was just a matter of time. Just waiting for the right opportunity to wake up."

Nathaniel looked at her. Hesitating, this time, before speaking again. "And now?" he managed to whisper.

"And now you will learn. As we all did before you," she replied with disarming simplicity.

The boy remained silent for a while. Then he searched for his mother's gaze again. "What about him? The rider ... how is he?"

"Better now. Your intervention was decisive. We are quite convinced that he would not have made it, had it not been for you."

"Actually, I didn't do anything consciously," he objected. "It was just chance that I touched him and unleashed ... whatever I unleashed."

"You think so? Your father doesn't. He says these things never happen by chance."

He shrugged.

"Anyway, he's out of danger. Now he just needs to recover and then we can learn more about him. There's not one Waerne in the Silver Springs coven that doesn't feel there's something special about him."

"Meaning ... he could be a descendant of the Norse people?" Nathaniel widened his eyes, surprised. In that light, the meeting and what followed took on totally unexpected, fascinating meanings.

"It's too early to say, Nate. But the general feeling is that he is not a common boy," she concluded. Then she returned to look at him. "Anyway, how do you feel? Are you hungry?"

Nathaniel smiled. "Now that I think about it ... yes, very. But I suppose I'll be subjected to an interrogation as soon as I step into the kitchen…" he grumbled, rolling his eyes. If he had really awakened his dormant abilities, the barrage of questions was guaranteed. "But, if Aunt Rachel has made her apple pie, I don't think Ashur's third degree will stop me from getting out of bed."

Lea laughed. "Come and see for yourself."

*

The barrage of questions, and even the foreseen third degree by Ashur, the veteran of the group, did happen, but not as much as Nathaniel had feared. More than anything else, his extended family wanted to make sure he was fine and that there were no negative consequences from that sudden manifestation of his abilities. The legacy of his blood had awakened. Now they would all work on it.

In the end, they let him eat in peace—Rachel's apple pie, as he had hoped, two large slices with a very sugary cup of coffee—and Ashur just assured him that they would soon resume their talk and workouts. The others slipped away, realising that, eventually, he needed to breathe some normalcy, in a sense. However *normal* was not the adjective that could define the Silver Springs coven, or his family members. Even his mother made the excuse of having to move a couple of horses and walked away. Only Rachel remained with him, chewing apple pie in front of him with that mischievous look that had earned her the nickname of pixie, years ago, and his father Sven. He had only sipped a black coffee without eating anything, looking thoughtful and presaging a serious talk. Or important. Or serious *and* important. He had remained quite silent, and Nathaniel had recognised on his angular face, made up of clear and defined lights and shadows, which he had partly inherited, that special weariness of when he used his abilities to heal someone, because he *had* done. Only this time, his son had participated in the miracle.

"That boy … he's weird," he said suddenly, in no uncertain terms, placing the empty cup on the old oak table. Rachel peered at him without speaking.

Nathaniel shrugged. "That's what Mom said too."

"Only she didn't have the chance to feel his emotions, his thoughts. It was only a vague intuition, similar to the one that everyone else has had when they saw him. But with us … with you and me, there was a different contact," Sven pointed out, fully attracting the attention of his son.

"I agree that he feels weird," Rachel interjected as she swallowed the last bite of her pie. "And, like the others, I had this feeling even just by getting close to him. But it could simply mean that he is one of us, I am fairly sure. It wouldn't be the first time that a potential Waerne ends up meeting their peers in a series of circumstances that have the appearance of chance. I wouldn't be surprised if it was the case. For you and Lea it was the same, at the time of the last crisis..."

"It's not just that," Sven said. And he looked straight at his son. "You ... what did you feel?"

Nathaniel hesitated, surprised by the question, by the seriousness with which it had been asked, by the intensity of his father's volcanic and magnetic gaze. "I ... I don't know exactly. It was all very chaotic." He shook his head. "It was as if somehow he had asked me for help without speaking. I didn't know that. I just felt I had to get close ... it was instinctive to look for physical contact, and then ... everything happened."

Sven nodded. "I know. The first time it feels like that." He raised his hands slightly, big and nervous like his son's. "But I wanted to know if you had felt something special about him during that contact."

Nathaniel thought about it, but finally shook his head. "I don't know. I can't remember much. Why do you ask me that?"

Sven sighed. "Because when I healed him, I felt a strange sensation. Almost ... of danger, but without really being able to define it," he admitted, after a few seconds of uncertainty. "I don't know why, but it came from him, of this I am sure. And it's not the only thing that makes us wary."

Nathaniel moved his two-tone gaze from his father to Rachel, perplexed. "What else is unusual? Well, beside his skin colour..."

Rachel smiled. "No, it's not the fact that he's an albino. But he has several marks on him. Old scars ... and one, right above the heart, resembles *Thurs' thorn.*"

The boy's eyes widened. "Do you think he's..." He broke off, dropping the thought mid-sentence. As if the simple naming of the Fjandar, their natural enemies, could be enough to make them come back, destroying the balance that had lasted for almost twenty years: from the time before its birth, and from the last nodal crisis, resolved precisely by the intervention of his parents, in the shadow of that old, dusty prophecy.

"It could also be a coincidence," his father interjected reassuringly. "It seems that he's been through a lot; those scars on him could simply indicate a difficult life. It could be a scar like any other, or maybe the Fjandar put that sign on him, and this would make him a servant of Thurs."

Nathaniel listened to those words, becoming serious. "Are you saying that they could have planted him on my way?"

"It's unlikely," Rachel replied. "It would make no sense, on their part, to try to infiltrate a boy so young among us without imagining we would notice his mark, or that we wouldn't be able to reveal his possible secrets."

"So," Sven said, answering the unspoken question he read in his son's eyes, "it is perhaps possible that he was a servant wanting to get out of one of their congregations, and for that they tried to eliminate him."

Nathaniel nodded. It made sense. "Well, if that were the case, at least now he would be safe," he replied with a small sigh, looking at both of them.

"We'll keep an eye on him, but it will be enough if he talks to your mother to see if we can trust him or not. So, yes, I would say that now he can feel safe, if it is safety that he seeks."

"Yeah," Nate muttered with a little grimace, considering that if that boy was going to lie, he would be in trouble even before he had time to say *shit*. Trying to deceive a potent empathic like his mother was an impossible task, as he had learned very early in life.

## CHAPTER FIVE

Another whole day passed before the mysterious boy woke up, by all accounts displaying extraordinary recovery skills. After all, Ashur had stated from the beginning that he seemed to show all the signs of the accelerated healing abilities typical of berserkers like himself.

The coven masters of Ocala and Florida had in the meantime been notified of the presence of a potential Norseman of an unknown—perhaps untrained—class, or indeed of a subservient escaped from the control of the Fjandar. For the time being the orders were to await his recovery and to discover more about his identity. The Maple Tree group, therefore, took care of him and waited for him to be well enough to face the dialogue. Nobody had talked about an *interrogation*, nor did they want to define it in those terms yet, but Ashur, as always, was suspicious. Not even the others, apart from maybe Rachel, the incurable optimist of the group, seemed very convinced. That sign on the boy's chest had put the group on alert.

Nathaniel felt confused about the whole business. It was he, after all, who had helped the boy and got him to the ranch. He felt responsible, though not for the possible risks his family could have run if the guy proved to be a danger. Looking back, as he galloped home that afternoon along a country track, he was not worried about his own people: he knew everyone's worth and abilities. It would take more than a single subservient, however strong, to create problems. In reality, the restlessness he felt was for that boy. What would happen to him if he turned out to be a Fjandi? Still, something told him that it wasn't the case. An instinct perhaps derived from the deep link that there had been between them. Right then he understood the extent of his father's question from the day before, *"You ... what did you feel?"*. He tightened his fists on the reins, straightening himself into the saddle. Gornil, his grey stallion, broke into a trot, coming out on a tarmac road that would lead them to the ranch in a matter of minutes. He had felt no danger. If anything, some undefined but concrete affinity. The more he thought about it, the more he began to convince himself that their meeting was not down to chance. And not in a negative way either.

He sighed, shaking his head as if to chase away all those thoughts that filled his mind, questions and doubts that he couldn't yet answer. He stopped the horse in front of the gate at the back of the estate, leaning forward to open the latch and pushing the white-painted wooden door. Unlike the heavy Clydesdales that were raised on the ranch, and the mighty Western Friesian of his father—Raido, who had more than one secret to hide—Gornil was a slimmer, lighter horse, showing the typical traits of the thoroughbred. Quick and snappy, a born jumper, it seemed made for the boy who was in the saddle. And together they had won several awards in the last few years. The notorious "pompous riding competitions for descendants of fallen British nobles", as Marcus would say. Nathaniel smiled thinking about his friend. Now that the legacy of his Norse blood had manifested itself, he had the impression that the famous coast-to-coast would not be so easy to organise. He caressed Gornil's neck, then, touching his hips with his heels, pushed him to cross the lawn towards the stables at the back of the farmhouse. Once there, Nate dismounted, leading the horse inside by the reins, speaking to him in a low voice, as he always did. And although he had never achieved the kind of extraordinary mental link that existed between his father and Raido, he and Gornil had nevertheless developed a deep bond.

As he unsaddled it, he saw Rachel rushing up to him.

"Nate! We were looking for you. Didn't you hear the calls?"

The boy frowned. "Ah … I'm sorry, Rache, I think I left the mobile in my room this morning."

"Never mind, it doesn't matter: the boy woke up … and asked for you." The enthusiasm and urgency in the young woman's voice were obvious.

"For me?" Nathaniel repeated, dropping Gornil's saddle on the box's gate, and turning towards her.

"That's right. He hasn't talked a lot, and to say he's wary is an understatement. But then he suddenly asked where the boy from the accident was. We didn't think he was ever conscious that night, but somehow, he saw you. And he knows you saved his life."

"All right, let's go then!"

They hurried back to the farmhouse.

"It's best if you talk to him," Rachel explained, using the back entrance that overlooked the large rustic kitchen. "He closed up like a hedgehog with us, and we couldn't get a thing out of him. But maybe it will be different with you."

"I hope so. Since he asked for me, it could be a good start."

When they entered the living room, they headed to the stairs leading to the upstairs rooms, where the rest of the group had gathered.

"How about you take your phone with you next time you go out with Gornil?" his mother began, unamused, one hand on her hip and the other waving his son's smartphone in midair.

"I know, my bad," he hurried apologetically. "Rachel told me he woke up," he changed the subject. Impatient, he turned his gaze on each of those present.

They were all there. His parents, Rachel by his side, and then Ashur, tall and thin, leaning against the doorframe that led out onto the corridor, his sharp, ageless features framed by short silvery hair, his hard, icy gaze fixed on the younger of the group; and of course the Heinlains, the landlords, Kenneth and Charlene, brother and sister, among the best friends of Lea and Sven, and their mentors when they had joined the Waerne in the midst of the nodal crisis of eighteen years earlier. To Nathaniel they were like a close aunt and uncle.

It was Kenneth himself who spoke, countering the impatience of the seventeen-year-old. Around fifty, with greying brown hair and amber eyes that could read deeply and calm any restlessness, he was the seer and the diplomat of the group. Yet, from what Rachel had said, it seemed that his magic had not worked this time if he couldn't even establish a relationship of trust with the mysterious boy. "Indeed. He woke up a few hours ago. And he seems to be better than we would have expected," he said, with a half-smile. "We could have told you hours ago, if ..."

"... if I had my phone with me. Got the memo, Ken, can we move on?" he moaned, rolling his eyes.

"All right. Did Rachel tell you that he looked for you and that he seems to remember you?"

Nathaniel nodded firmly. "What have you discovered so far?"

"He doesn't look like a subservient," Ashur replied, unfolding his arms and spreading them out in a vague sign of surrender. "That's what we all thought. He doesn't seem to have any knowledge of our world, Fjandar or Waerne. And if he has any special abilities, which we are almost sure of by now, he keeps them hidden and has never talked about them to anyone."

"And that sign on his chest—Thurs's thorn?"

"He knows nothing about it. For him it's just an old scar that he can't even remember. And he's sincere," his mother explained, reaching out to return the phone.

"Oh..." Nate felt a powerful sense of relief at those words. "So he's not a Fjandi ... there's no reason to fear him."

"It would seem so," his father conceded. "But we don't know anything about him, not even his name. After a while he must have felt under pressure, because he asked to be left alone and stopped talking. Not even Kenneth managed to get something else out of him."

"But he said he wanted to see me," said Nathaniel. "So can I go to him, right?"

"You have to," Kenneth said. "You're the only one who can get some useful information out of him, or at least convince him that we just want to help."

The boy grinned. "Leave it to me." Something told him that this was his job, in all that weird business. And he had never felt more ready. *Finally*, he thought, his head almost turning with enthusiasm. *It's my moment*. How long had he waited for this? He stuffed his mobile into his pocket and headed for the stairs. He turned to the group, after a couple of steps. "Hey ... No eavesdropping, are we clear?" Then he disappeared up the stairs.

Once outside the room, he knocked softly and, without waiting for an answer, opened the door a crack, peeping inside. "Hi, am I disturbing you? They told me you asked for me."

The rustic bedroom was similar to all the others on the ranch. Not too large, with whitewashed walls and the ceiling crossed by the wooden beams of the roof. Simple furniture, in dark wood, and a window ajar from which came the warm afternoon light and the scent of Charlene's rose garden.

The guest was half seated on the bed against the back wall, propped up by a pair of cushions. He wore a black sleeveless shirt, too big for him, that left his unnaturally white arms bare, except for the signs of spiked black tribal tattoos that, starting around the biceps, climbed up to his shoulders. The angular, marble-like face recalled the superimposed layers of hard ancient schists; it was framed by disarranged lunar tufts of hair, almost camouflaged against the white cotton of the pillowcases. He had pale blue irises that seemed transparent. Clear mirrors. Cold as ice.

They looked at each other as Nathaniel slid into the room, closing the door behind him. Eyes like glacier water focused on eyes different from birth. And for a while there was only that look between them. The silence continued and they seemed to study each other, trying to understand something of the strange, subtle interlocking of destinies that had brought them together in the most improbable manner, on an almost deserted road that wound southward. Finally, the young albino nodded.

Was that nod a 'yes, he had asked for him'? Or 'yes, he was bothering him'? Nathaniel hoped for the first one and moved over to the bed. He did it as he would have done with an untamed colt, trying to evaluate the acceptable distances, the behaviour to hold. That the other seemed suspicious was a fact. Scared? No. But wary, without a doubt. And he could understand that. He was in an unknown place, among equally unknown people, without knowing how he had ended up there after an accident from which he had awakened unharmed. And those people, moreover, had asked him many strange questions. No, certainly not to blame, if he had decided to keep his distance and stop talking.

Nathaniel chose to trust his instinct and behave naturally. He pulled a wooden chair from under the small desk, placed it beside the bed and lowered himself on it. "Oh, the very thing I needed. Sorry, but until ten minutes ago I was out riding and..." He broke off, shrugging his shoulders and slightly spreading his arms. "Well, here I am." He paused. "I'm Nathaniel Gordon. Nate, if you like. They all call me that. And you?"

"I'll tell you. But I swear that if you start laughing, I'll kick your ass, *Nate*."

Nathaniel's eyes widened. He had not expected him to answer him so directly. The other's voice was low, rather deep for a boy who showed little more than his age. A voice like that would have been better on an inveterate smoker. Or to someone more inclined to long silences than to speech. In any case, Nate shook his head, hurrying to reply. "Laugh? Why should I?" He smiled, raising his hands in a gesture of surrender. "I care about my ass, it's fair to say. So what's your name?"

The other sniffed slightly, wrinkling his nose. "Winter."

Well, actually, he was right. Living with albinism and with a name like Winter ... Nathaniel frowned. "Seriously, Winter? As in *Winter is coming*?"

The boy looked at him deadpan. "As in *Winter I'll kick your ass*."

There was an air about him that made Nate understand that he had to choose his next words very carefully. "Maybe whoever gave you that name wanted to be poetic ..." he tried.

Winter sighed. "I don't mind it. Even though it was given to me by a hippy with her neurons burned since Woodstock who ended up managing a foster house in Queens."

"It's cool," Nathaniel smiled. Somehow, he had the impression that the gap between them had been bridged. "So, just Winter?"

"Winter Garner. But it's not my father's surname. I've never met him."

"And you're from New York. Awesome, I live there too. That is, a little there, and a bit here, but above all there," he smiled, frankly. "By the way, did they tell you where *here* is?"

The other nodded. "Florida, Ocala. Although I still don't get how I got here from where I was before. And never mind that after the accident,

I expected to wake up at least in a hospital. If waking up was in the cards at all. Instead..." He looked at him. Careful, cautious. It was clear that many things made no sense to him.

Nathaniel hesitated, nibbling at his lip. "Well, there are a lot of things to explain..." he admitted, looking at him sideways. "But I can tell you that you are safe here. From whatever you were running away from..."

"And who says I was running away from something?" Winter interrupted.

"Ah ... no, I was just saying ... Were you running away from something?"

The other snorted. "From myself, mostly," he finally mumbled. "But I certainly didn't see this coming."

"As I said, you're safe here," Nate continued, with the most comforting smile he could muster. He widened his arms. "The ranch belongs to some family friends. I've known them all my life. It's like an extended family. Good people..."

"What the hell are you, Mormons?"

Nate's eyes widened and he burst into laughter. "What? No, not Mormons..." *Way stranger*, he thought, amused. "I just don't know how to explain the whole thing to you."

"Well, you can start from the beginning. I don't think I can move from here, in any case," Winter commented with a grimace, barely spreading his arms in a movement of exasperation. "I'm unharmed after an accident where I could have killed myself, but I cannot get up from this fucking bed without feeling faint. Just to add something to the list of quirks that you can maybe clarify for me."

"Maybe. Can I ask you a question, first?"

The other arched a thin white eyebrow, broken in two by an old scar. A silent invitation to continue.

"Why didn't you ask these questions to the others, when they came to talk to you?"

This time, Winter didn't hesitate. "Because you are the one who saved me."

# CHAPTER SIX

"Hold on, Nate, hold it." Winter's voice seemed more surprised than dismayed, but had certainly changed tone. "Tell me again ... Did you really heal me just by *touching* me?"

Nathaniel nodded solemnly, looking straight into his eyes. He didn't need his mother's skills to understand that what he was telling Winter had upset him. Which was expected, of course. What he couldn't tell was whether the boy was just incredulous and confused, or if there was also a sort of conscious curiosity in his transparent eyes. As if he were not so surprised to find out that there were people in the world with certain skills. But maybe that was just wishful thinking on his part—the hope that he really was one of them. He would have liked to have a peer with whom to share those situations and emotions.

In any case, he had decided to tell him the truth. It seemed that Winter also shared in the legacy of the Norse people. It was clear that he had no family to go back to, and no close connection. A lonely young man, with a difficult past, who had admitted being fleeing from himself. It wouldn't be the first time that the Waerne became a shelter and a family for such subjects.

They looked at each other once more. It was obvious that some kind of connection between them had been established. With that suspicious caution that seemed to distinguish him, Winter seemed to have decided to give Nate some form of trust. "So, does it mean that you touch people and ... heal them?" he asked, a straight wrinkle between his eyebrows. No sarcasm, no disbelief, this time. He was just trying to understand.

Nathaniel shrugged. "In theory, yes. Actually, you were the first one I healed. But ... yes, that's it. And there are others of us who can do it. Even better than me. My father, for example. I inherited this gift from him."

The other frowned, settling himself better against the cushions—hands folded in front of him on the sheets, he fiddled with a smashed metal ring he wore on his thumb. "Okay. So you're not the only one," he grumbled.

He was taking it quite well, considered Nate. "No. There are several people, all over the world, who have special abilities. And I'm not just talking about what I can do. They are different skills, but all ... well, special." He smiled at him. "My family is like that. My parents, and others. We are the coven of Ocala, but there are others such groups. Here in Florida, in the rest of the States and beyond. We are connected to others in a worldwide network. We try to find those like us who don't know about us, so that they can be trained to put their skills to good use and without becoming a danger to themselves and others. Other than that, we live among the people, trying to lead a normal existence, as far as possible."

Winter cocked his head. "In short, I ended up in the X-Mansion..."

Nathaniel burst out laughing. "Not exactly ... I mean, maybe my father *could* look like Magneto, but ..."

"When are you going to introduce me to Professor X?"

"I know, it sounds crazy. Anyway, you can call us *Waerne*. It means "defenders". Our history seems to date back to the Viking age in Europe ... or at least, the first testimonies of our existence come from there. It could even go further back..." He paused. "There are so many things to tell that I doubt I can do it on my own. But we can explain everything," he reassured him. "There's no hurry though. Are you hungry? Let's take a break and get a bite."

"I can't remember the last time I ate," Winter admitted, rubbing his flat stomach.

"Okay, then. Tuna sandwiches—there should be an industrial quantity in the fridge. What do you say?"

The crooked smile on the other's face became more pronounced. "Sure."

*

If the others were surprised at how quickly a bond had formed between the two boys, they didn't show it; they just went along with it. It seemed that the mysterious young man trusted Nathaniel, pointing towards an uncomplicated resolution of that story. Nathaniel had asked them to watch from the sidelines for the time being, and they had agreed. As the afternoon light turned to the warmer shades of the sunset, the two remained locked in the room, devouring tuna sandwiches and washing them down with iced Coke.

After the initial cautious perplexity, it seemed that Winter had accepted with surprising simplicity all that Nathaniel had explained. Even the wildest of things. So much so that after a while, Nate decided to investigate further. "Maybe I'm wrong, Winter, but it seems to me that what I'm telling you isn't much of a surprise to you." He couldn't be sure, but he had decided to follow a hunch. "Am I right?"

The boy stirred uneasily on the bed. For a few moments he didn't look up, then peered sideways towards Nate. "It's just that ... everything you're telling me seems to make certain things clearer now. And it's strange, really weird that we ended up meeting, and that it was you who found me. And saved me. Nothing seems more like a simple coincidence." He raised an eyebrow, and that half-smile on his pale lips took on a sarcastic fold. "And I doubt you can call me crazy, since you're the one spinning the revised X-Men story."

Nathaniel chuckled. "I don't think you're crazy. I think you're right. I stopped believing in coincidences a long time ago. And the others also agree that ours was not a casual meeting." He paused, looking for Winter's restless look. "Do you think you have any special skills, then?" he finally tried.

Winter stared at him with a sort of strange solemnity this time. "I ... I don't know," he murmured first, then tightened his jaw. "I know how to defend myself."

Nate said nothing, waiting patiently for him to add more.

"And what's so special, you'd say, in knowing how to defend yourself?" The other grumbled at last. "The fact is that no one has taught me. I've always been able to do it. And quite well, too."

"Do you mean that you fight instinctively? If you must, you just react, like it was muscle memory?"

"Yes, something like that. You've explained it better than me." He smiled, but there was a cautious hesitation in the sharp edges of his face. "The first few times happened when I was young, with the older kids in the place where I lived. I was an easy target for the way I looked. They stopped tormenting me after one of them ended up in the infirmary and stayed there for more than a week." At that point, he fell silent, pensive. He was on the brink of adding something but instead remained silent, shifting the attention on the glass of Coke resting on the bedside table. He took it and brought it to his lips, emptying it and grinding the remains of an ice cube between his teeth.

Nathaniel raised an eyebrow. He had the impression that he was hiding something, but decided to let it be. "It must have been hard. I mean ... living as you have lived."

"Certainly, this *special* thing, as you call it, has not helped me find an adoptive family. Who wants a troubled and aggressive kid? And I got into difficulties more than once," he said, wrinkling his nose in a small grimace.

Nathaniel couldn't help but notice that his septum was marked, a little crooked, as if it had been broken more than once.

"For one reason or another, I have always found myself in a fight. And almost always the last one standing." He shrugged. "When I lost, I recovered quickly. Perhaps that's the other strange thing about me. I ended up in the infirmary or in the hospital many times, but always had a quick recovery. Doctors never knew how to explain it. They would give a prognosis of fifteen days, and I was back on my feet in half that time."

Right then, Nate nodded enthusiastically, a flash of understanding in his eyes. Apparently Ashur had hit the mark on their guest's abilities. "Of course. Rapid regeneration, just like a berserker. And also the fact that you can fight without anyone teaching you to. We should talk to Ash. He's a berserker. They are our front-line warriors, so to speak," he explained, infused with the idea of having discovered what kind of class the mysterious boy belonged to.

"Ash? Berserker?" Winter grumbled back, both suspicious and perplexed.

"Yes, Ash. Ashur, that tall and grumpy guy, grey hair with the sergeant's face. Grouchy at first glance, but in reality he's ..." He thought about it. "Grouchy," he resigned himself, giggling and shaking his head, before hurrying to add, "But one of the best teachers you can find, if you're a Waerne. Do you know what I mean?"

Winter nodded. "I hope you're not too serious about him shouting orders. I have ... problems with authority, let's put it that way."

"I had imagined it. But I bet that when you get to know each other, you'll get on just fine. I think you are a bit like him."

"We'll see. Hey ... you talked about "front-line warriors". Why do you need them?"

The question had arrived in the end. Nathaniel turned the empty glass over in his hands, making the ice inside rattle softly. "Because there have been wars," he replied sincerely. "And because we have enemies."

Winter looked at him, tilting his head slightly.

"We call them Fjandar, a Norse word that stands for "adversaries"," Nate explained, barely gesturing with the empty glass. "Waerne and Fjandar have always been opposed. They have similar abilities to us, but many are corrupted descendants of the Norse, or have obtained their abilities from entities of another world, which they would like to bring into ours, the Jötnar, the frost giants of Nordic mythology."

The other just nodded, becoming more serious.

Nathaniel had noticed that part of the explanation, hinting at parallel realities from which long ago the Norse had come into our world to mix with men, and from which other less benevolent entities could also arrive, had been among those that Winter seemed to have accepted with more nonchalance. As if they were a normal thing, when in reality it was usually the moment where a newcomer would be fully shocked. The idea that Winter was hiding something took root in Nate at that point. For the rest, he had seemed sincere. Certainly not hostile. Deciding to trust his intuition, he continued in his explanation. "They, our adversaries, are convinced that the advent of the Jötnar would lead to Ragnarök, the end of everything, according to Norse mythology, and at the same time a new beginning. According to the Fjandar, this would lead to a new order where those like them ... and like us, should no longer hide but reign over on humanity."

"And you think it's bullshit, and try to stop it, I suppose," said Winter.

Nate had begun to recognise the quiver of sarcasm in his low, scratched voice. "More or less," he said.

"So, if I were one of you ... you'd like me to fight on your side?"

"Actually, there has not been a major confrontation for about eighteen years," Nathaniel said, looking like someone who would prefer a different scenario. "Since the last attempt by the Fjandar to open an alpha-class portal and bring a Jötunn into our world has been thwarted." And here he smiled. "Stopped by my coven, by the way. And by my parents."

Winter chuckled, leaning back against the cushions and stretching slightly. "Listen to you boasting. I bet you weren't even born yet."

"No, in fact. I was born the year after," muttered the other. "And I've never seen a fight worthy of the name. Things seem to have been quiet. It happens. Sometimes decades pass between one nodal crisis and the next..." He noticed the puzzled look of the boy and hurried to explain. "We call them that because the portals from which the Jötnar could arrive, carrying the Ragnarök in our world, are also called Nodal Points. And when they are activated, they are usually trouble."

Winter remained silent, listening to him, a serious expression on that tense and angular face, pale as snow. He seemed attentive now, interested. "But since then there have been no nodal crises."

"Right. And so, well ... it's not like there's a lot to fight for at the moment, apart from a few border clashes between the covens, or something like that. In any case, no one would force you to do anything. The Waerne are not a militia; they are first of all a family. They try to help each other and those who are like them, because they know that it's not easy living with a skill without being able to tell anyone." He smiled. "It will be so for me, now that I have discovered my potential. And it can be like that for you too, if you wish. You will not have to run away from yourself anymore."

Winter nodded.

"Our enemies tend to corrupt and indoctrinate their servants," Nathaniel continued, sighing. "They are often part of gangs; they cause trouble, they create problems. The last few clashes were all about things like that. And ... well, as you can imagine, they rely on feelings of revenge, anger and the will to abuse those who are like us, to attract them on their side."

"The dark side of the Force ..." Winter grinned, amused. "Do they have cookies too?"

Nate smiled, shaking his head. "I doubt it. But I'll tell you who has cookies: Aunt Rachel. And I swear to you they are the best biscuits on planet Earth!"

## CHAPTER SEVEN

It had been a little over a week since Winter's recovery and his first chat with Nathaniel. Since then, the boys' relationship seemed to have taken a fluid and natural direction. There was a sort of elective affinity between them, one of those friendships that knew how to prosper, evolving in the best way, playing on a trust that didn't need words or assurances to exist.

Everyone in Maple Tree Farm could see that and they let it be. With the others, Winter remained wary, typical behaviour of someone with a difficult childhood and a tormented adolescence, without adults to guide him. However, Nathaniel's mediations were paying off. They were all more or less certain that sooner or later Winter would open up with them. Besides, he was not the first difficult teenager they had been forced to deal with. Ashur had lived a similar situation in his day. Who better than he to understand the boy's behaviour? Everything pointed to the fact that he was a potential berserker too. And they found out soon after, when the veteran, who had heard about the boy's fighting ability, wanted to test him.

The last rays of the sun cast long shadows on the whitewashed walls of the ranch. Some industrious bee was still buzzing around Charlene's rose garden, but it was jasmine and honeysuckle that filled the air with their sweet, inebriating scent at that time of day. A scent that almost went to the head, speaking of ancient secrets, of sensual abandonment.

They stood on the lawn behind the main building, in that makeshift arena that had seen other Waerne measuring against each other, including Nate, who was now perched on a fence as a spectator. That same grassy patch that had seen Ashur and Sven clash, eighteen years ago, to reveal the true nature of the storm warrior.

Ashur was still there, despite the passage of time, more aware than he had been then. More of a teacher and a mentor for the son of the

Phoenix than he had been for Sven. And now, he had that boy in front of him, that unresolved mystery out of nowhere, miraculously torn away from death.

"So, boy. You said you could fight," the berserker urged him, watching him with a coldness that seemed to be part of him as much as his physical features. "Show me what you can do."

In front of him, Winter moved cautiously, his clear gaze fixed on the man as if to study him. He seemed aware of having a veteran fighter in front of him who had seen many clashes before. A very different opponent from the ones in his usual street fights. Yet, when he snapped, without even wasting time to look for a guarding pose, he did it quickly and forcefully. It was so sudden that not even Nathaniel, from his vantage point, saw the movement with which the boy had stepped forward.

He feinted a left hook to Ashur's ribs, when in fact his real intention was to reach him with a devastating right uppercut to the jaw. He moved with such speed and fluidity that Ashur's eyes widened for a moment, not expecting such a sure and aggressive reply. He dodged it in any case, barely, while the boy's fist cracked the air with a hiss before the berserker had completely closed the distance. Using the greater body weight and experience to creep into the open gap in the young man's defence, he immediately grabbed him in a firm grip at the waist and threw him on the ground with no apparent effort.

Winter landed on the grass with a gasp, winded; yet he didn't seem ready to surrender to the punishment imposed by Ashur. Nathaniel heard him laugh, as if that situation was natural enough to amuse him, despite being worst off. Then, with a thrust of his back and the skilled positioning of his right knee between them, he freed himself from Ashur's grip, showing that he had more strength in his muscles than his nervous body let on. Instead of getting up again, he continued the fight, wrestling on the ground.

Nathaniel noticed it as he observed the training—if one could still call it training—with a growing sense of amazement and restlessness. There was an instinctive and wild abandon in the way Winter fought. A natural necessity that had the taste of a twisted joy only to be found in that violent outburst; a satisfaction and a realization that nothing else would have been able to give him.

It took Ashur a while to handle that explosion of almost uncontrolled aggression, and not before suffering a split and bleeding lip. He finally had the best, blocking Winter to the ground with his face pressed into the grass and his left arm bent behind his back. "You know what you have to do now, don't you?" he suggested, leaning slightly over him.

In response, the boy tried to rebel again, raising his shoulders and the back of his head in an attempt to hit him in the face. Ashur moved back just enough to turn that desperate attempt harmless, and with a hoarse laugh, he pushed him hard on the ground, his free hand coming back to crush his gaunt cheek in the grass.

"You are combative, *Hveitwulf*, I grant you that. And you get by very well, given you're self-taught," the berserker admitted. "But I have too much experience for you. Accept it, it's normal."

Although he was holding him in a painful grip, Nathaniel realised the unusual kindness in his voice. He sounded satisfied. That was the tone of a master who had finally found a worthy student to whom pass on his art. And he became certain: Winter must have been born with the abilities of the berserkers. Those two were alike.

As for the young man, he finally seemed to accept his defeat and understood what Ashur wanted from him. He tapped the palm of his right hand on the ground, two or three times, as he would have done on the tatami of a gym, to declare his surrender and make the opponent desist from the attack. The berserker left him free at once, rising in a fluid motion and taking a few steps back. He brought his thumb to his split lip, arching an eyebrow when he saw the blood. He passed his tongue over it. "Look at that. You can fight," he conceded, with a crooked, amused smile.

Winter had got up and was loosening his shoulders, still aching from Ashur's brutal grip. At first, he looked at him with an almost ferocious expression on the sharp features. Then he pulled out a smile that curled his lips, wildly, revealing the white incisors. "What did you call me, before?" he asked, the lean, sculpted chest rising up from breathing fast.

"*Hveitwulf*. It means white wolf in the Norse language," Ashur replied nonchalantly.

Winter seemed to understand, as Nathaniel had also understood, that somehow the old warrior liked him. That initial mistrust was beginning to yield. And besides, from the smile on his lips, it was clear that now that the fight had taken place and they had measured each other, the boy liked him too.

Nate jumped off the fence, approaching the two. "Well, now that you know each other better ... it's my turn, Ash, right?"

The berserker looked at him with a sly grin on his face, hardened by time and fights. "It's your turn, yes." He nodded towards Winter. "Against him".

Nathaniel looked at the boy and realised he should have kept quiet.

*

The training went rather well. Maybe Winter had decided to go easy on him, unlike he did with Ashur, or perhaps, all things considered,

Nathaniel had learned enough from the berserker to be able to defend himself even from a more skilled and capable opponent. In any case, when Ashur left them alone, they lay on the grass catching their breath as evening fell and the first stars lit up in the sky.

Winter turned to Nate and offered him one of his usual crooked and ironic smiles. "You're not bad. Did you learn from the berserker? It looks like his style."

"Yes, I learned from him. He's been teaching me for years, and ... well, I suppose I have to take it as a compliment given that it comes from the one who made Ashur bleed at his first fight!"

Winter chuckled and shrugged as he leaned forward, hugging his knees close to his chest. "I told you I'm good at beating people up, even though no one taught me," he said, looking at him sideways. "I learn fast, anyway."

Nathaniel looked up at him, frowning. "So you're one of those types who get blood out of turnips whenever you want, huh?"

Winter laughed out loud. "I don't think so. I've always sucked at school."

"I said *when you want*. It seems obvious to me that you've never cared much about school." Winter didn't bother to deny it. "If you really are so quick to learn, you must try to ride," Nate suggested, with a thrill of enthusiasm in his voice. "I could teach you."

"You're not talking about bikes, are you? Or women?" he said, arching his scarred eyebrow, sly. "Riding as in ... horses?"

Nathaniel laughed. "Does it seem so strange? Horses, yes. Would you like to try, tomorrow? And you can show me how easily you learn."

Winter grinned, laying back down, his arms spread out in the freshly shorn grass which smelled of green and things that grow. "Sure, why not. We'll see what you can teach me."

Nathaniel turned to look at him with a bit of calculated cunning, this time. "But in return you must teach me to fight your way."

"Ah, I should have known. Nobody gives you anything for nothing in this life," he commented jokingly.

"It's a fair exchange," Nathaniel said.

"It seems to me," cut in Winter chuckling, "that learning to fight hard could be much more useful in life than knowing how to stay on the saddle. But sure, let's say it's a fair exchange."

Nate gave him a playful kick. "What an asshole. You'll see. The day will come when knowing how to stay on a saddle will save your ass, and then you will be forced to thank me, and I will hold it against you for life." He shook his head and stretched, nursing his aching muscles. "Come on, let's go back now. I'm starting to get hungry," he said, standing up in a fluid, agile movement. He spontaneously extended his hand to the other, with a broad and friendly smile on his adolescent face.

Winter hesitated for a moment, as if he had not expected it. Then he grabbed it and let Nate help him get back on his feet.

For a moment they lingered under the purple lights of a sunset that had given way to the summer night. A strange awareness made its way into their consciousness. Something had brought them together, and there were no more doubts about it. Nothing happened by chance.

# Chapter Eight

*The grey concrete of the courtyard is not very different from the grey of the sky. The same shade that leaves no room for hope. Beyond the orange metal gate that encloses it lies a road with trees raising their dry and dark branches against the falling November rain. Freedom seems so close, and yet unattainable. He tried to escape several times, but never succeeded. Not for too long, anyway.*

*He tightens his pale fists around the cold bars. In there, everything feels like a prison: from the curfews to the rules he can barely endure, to the precarious relationships.*

*He hears them coming, behind him, even before they speak.*

*"Look at him. He knows he'll not get out of here until judgment day," says a sarcastic voice.*

*He turns slowly. There's three of them. He stares at them with hatred.*

*"Stop looking at me like that, monster. You're making me sick," says another.*

*"I heard somewhere that even among beasts runts like you are abandoned at birth. I bet the same thing happened when the monkey who gave birth to you saw you," snickers another.*

*Laughter follow that statement.*

*"Leave me alone."*

*"Oh, the freak dictates orders … Otherwise what happens, freak?"*

*He doesn't answer. He rushes forward without a sound, with the speed of a silvery and unnatural flash. Taken by surprise, his target falls to the ground on his back under his weight. The boy cries out, unable to stop, when he straddles him and begins to punch his face repeatedly with a violent, delighted abandonment. "Ground and pound, son of a bitch."*

*The other two, shocked by that unexpected reaction and unnatural speed, spring into action, trying to help their friend, who is getting the worst of it despite being at least three years older than his attacker. They try to grab the boy by the arms and remove him from the one lying on the ground, whose face is split and bleeding and does not move anymore. "Leave him be, monster! What the fuck are you doing?"*

*In response, he growls like a wild animal and turns against them, freeing himself effortlessly from their grasp, slipping between their fingers with overwhelming ease. He floors one of them when he tries to grab him, exploiting his inertia and lever of the arm to make him roll on the hard cement of the yard. When he throws himself upon him with extreme satisfaction, the third boy stares at him in horror, as if he was a creature vomited out of some hell, then turns his back and runs.*

*Two adults eventually step in to detach him from his victim. They drag him away, writhing like a possessed man, shouting and struggling, until he finds himself in the isolation room he knows so well. Narrow and dark, with the metal door against which he beats his fists until the blood comes out, shouting until he no longer has a voice. And until he has the impression that those narrow walls will close in on him and crush him.*

*

"Winter! Winter, wake up ... it's a dream, just a bad dream ..."

It was Nathaniel.

The boy stared at him with wide eyes, the T-shirt glued to his back by the icy sweat, his fingers clinging to the tank top of his friend. "What...?" The voice hoarse, as if he had really shouted, not only in the dream. He realised that he was clutching the other's garment and let go, embarrassed, trying to look away. Yet his presence there gave him a strange, unexpected feeling of comfort. He was so used to waking up alone in some sleazy motel room, after one of those nightmares, that having someone beside him, instead, brought a bizarre relief that melted the knots in his muscles and warmed him up inside the bones.

"You were talking in your sleep. Then you shouted. You must have had a nightmare," Nathaniel explained, sympathetic.

The first light of dawn filtered into the room through the shutters. In the stables behind the farmhouse, a horse neighed. From somewhere beyond the fence, amidst the patch of trees that ran along the pasture, a nightingale sang improvised and melodious twitterings. For the rest, everything was immersed in the silence that preceded the day.

Winter sighed, looking away from Nathaniel, uncomfortable. "Yes, a nightmare," he voiced. "Sorry if I woke you up."

"Nah. I was already awake, actually. In fact, if you don't want to go back to sleep, we could go out riding," he proposed, with the enthusiasm of someone who had not thought of anything else since the day before.

"Dawn is one of the best moments, and then there's nobody around."

"You're truly obsessed with riding..." Winter snorted, dissipating the residual tension that clung to him along with the sweat of the nightmare. He shrugged. "Let's do it."

*

When Winter said he was a quick learner, he had not exaggerated. There was something surprising, almost alien, in the unnatural ease with which he instinctively adapted to new things. Nathaniel realised that immediately when he saddled one of their Clydesdale mares—English style, as was the tradition of Maple Tree—explaining how to mount it and giving him the first tips in the wide sand field not far from the stables. The bay mare was quiet and reliable, perfect for a beginner, but the boy got the impression that Winter would have had no issues even with a livelier specimen. He was riding Gornil and, seeing Winter and his horse trot around the circle, while giving him some suggestions on how to handle the mount, he found himself envious of the simplicity with which he seemed to absorb his advice and put them into practice with a stunning physical grace.

"I didn't think your *fast learning* was at these levels," he admitted with a grin. "I think it's one of your special abilities. I don't know what the others will say, but I've never seen anything like this in my life. To do what you are doing now took me weeks when I started riding."

Returning the mare to the pass, with an ease that had nothing of the novice, Winter shrugged his shoulders, a crooked and defiant smile on his lips. "I told you. Shall we go out?"

Nathaniel was barely restraining an impatient Gornil, eager to run on the country tracks surrounding the ranch, still wrapped in a light morning mist. "First let's see how you gallop," he said, chuckling. "Though I'm sure you'll be just fine."

*

The sun had risen above the low hills, flooding the sky with reddish reflections and erasing the haze of dawn, when the boys stopped at the bottom of a pasture, after an hour-long ride. They led the horses to a watering hole, then tied them to a fence a short distance away, leaving them free to graze the grass wet with morning dew, sitting nearby to catch their breath.

"So, what do you think?" Nathaniel asked curiously.

Winter allowed himself one of his cautious smiles. He didn't seem to know how to smile in any other way. It was as if it remained broken in half, as if he had never learned how to do it properly or learned too late. "It's not like my old Sportster left on the road ... but I have to give it to you, it's exhilarating."

Nate laughed as he stretched out on the grass, leaning on his elbows. "Are you comparing it to a motorcycle ride? Seriously?" he objected, amused. "It's *way* better. And sooner or later I'll hear you admit it. But I'm afraid your annoying ability has just turned our deal upside down."

Winter raised an eyebrow. "Why?"

"I didn't teach you anything. You've done it mostly by yourself. I doubt it would be the same if you were to teach me to fight your way."

Winter laughed in a way Nathaniel had never heard before. Warmer and fuller, sincere.

"So? I like challenges."

"Thank you so much for the trust," Nathaniel said sarcastically. But then he laughed too, turning his gaze to the summer sky. "Let's start today."

"Fine by me."

They remained silent for a while. Then Nathaniel spoke again. "How old are you?"

Winter looked at him, with irises so clear they seemed transparent. He frowned. "Don't you know? Haven't you seen my documents?"

"Yes, it says you're twenty-one. But I don't believe it."

"Are you suggesting I carry false documents?" There was a tone of amused curiosity, in his voice. Almost defiant.

"Do you?" Nathaniel urged him.

Winter shrugged nonchalantly. "I'm nineteen," he finally admitted. "Almost twenty. But you must be twenty-one for a lot of things. So..."

No matter how much his curiosity niggled at him, Nate didn't ask how he had gotten fake documents. Perhaps he preferred not to know it, nor feed the restless interest that the most rebellious and arrogant side of the other provoked in him. However, it didn't mean that he couldn't direct his curiosity elsewhere. "Even if you're not really twenty-one, it's been a long time since you've lived alone, right?"

Winter stared at him in silence for a few moments. He looked away to rummage through his jeans pocket, pulling out a shabby pack of cigarettes. He lit one and breathed deeply. "As soon as I turned eighteen, I signed up to leave the family home. I had tried to escape from it for fifteen years." He had taken on a sarcastic tone, like the half-smile that danced on his lips. "But, as it turned out, I had to learn to get by long before then." He shrugged. "I still remember Juniper's face—the former hippie, the one responsible for my name—when I told her I was leaving. *'You're a smart boy, you could graduate, we could help you go to college ...'*" He laughed softly. A bitter laugh, which should never have come from a young man's throat. "At *college*. That crazy Wiccan. Only *she* could think of something like that." His smile softened slightly. "I think she was the only one, in all those years, to see some kind of potential in me. And I also think I've done everything to change her mind."

Nathaniel looked at him sideways. He didn't know how far he could push it without risking to break the instinctive and natural camaraderie that had been created between them. However, he wanted to know him better, and Winter seemed in the mood for confidences at that moment. More than he had ever been since they'd met. "What did you do, then?"

"I started travelling. I'd stayed in a place to work for a while, then a bus, destination wherever, or as far as what I had in my pocket could take me." He smiled. "I've spent the last year and a half like this. At times something would happen and I had to run for it."

"And your bike?"

"The old Sportster? Ah, that came later." Winter took another drag from the cigarette, turning his transparent eyes to the clear blue, veiled by mist. He threw the smoke out of his nose, slowly. "I won her in a bet, back in early spring."

Nathaniel looked at him with badly repressed admiration. The respect he had for Winter grew by the second. That boy was less than three years older than him, but he seemed to have already done enough to fill a movie. Not that his life had been easy or pleasant, this was sure, but he had somehow managed to react, had found a way to go. That road that had finally made them meet.

Silence returned between them. And this time it was Winter who broke it. "I could buy us some drinks one evening. We could drink together in the parking lot of the bar. Or in the car. Or in the middle of the countryside, or ... wherever. It wouldn't be bad."

Nathaniel understood on the fly, with an instinctive intuition that surprised him in his concrete intensity, that this was Winter's attempt to be accepted. To offer him his friendship and his trust in the only way that tormented and lonely boy knew. Because, perhaps, before then he had not had the opportunity, the desire or the courage to offer it to anyone.

"It wouldn't be bad at all," he agreed. A full smile—the first as he could recall—appeared on the angular features of Winter's face at that, and the feeling of having done the right thing rewarded him instantly.

# CHAPTER NINE

A cool northerly breeze swept the parking lot of one of the local bars, taking a can or a greasy bag of fast food swirling in a merry dance. The boys were sitting on a low wall that divided two commercial lots just outside Ocala, on Silver Springs Boulevard. Nathaniel's old Mustang was parked a few meters from them, along with other cars. They had eaten something at a nearby diner, and then Winter, as promised, had bought a few drinks from an off-licence next to the bar, rather crowded on that Friday night. Nobody seemed to have minded; not that Winter had mentioned it, anyway.

After a couple of beers, thrown down more to show Winter it wasn't his first time—although it was—Nathaniel felt as if the world around him had lost stability. The wall was pitching like a boat in the middle of gale-force winds, and the edges of his vision moved and stretched beyond his control.

"Don't tell me you're drunk already ..." Winter giggled, taking a sip of beer from his glass bottle.

Nate looked at him sideways, and saw him waving and flickering too, with that faded and messy hair, his features even sharper under the halogen light of a nearby lamppost. "I'm fine," he retorted, and suddenly the whole situation seemed so absurd as to snatch a little gurgling and lost laugh.

"Yes, of course. But let *me* drive us home."

"Pfff ... if they stop us, I bet they'll say you have more alcohol than blood in your veins. Not sure it's a good idea," Nathaniel said, raising an admonitory finger and waving the empty bottle in his other hand. The drops of condensations made it slippery, and it fell on the asphalt at their feet, crashing into pieces. "Oops ..."

"They'll say what they want, but if you drive we'll certainly end up in a ditch ... not sure that's any better." He looked at him, arching a pale eyebrow in amusement. "You've never drank before, have you?"

"Not true. And not fair at all. Making these allegations about me ..." Nate frowned, his words twisting his tongue in a funny way.

"Then it means that you can't hold it. Which is possibly worse!"

"And what's wrong with not holding a drink, huh?"

Winter laughed even more, but soon held back. "There's nothing wrong with it," he concluded instead. He seemed about to add something, but the cackles of a small group of guys heading from the bar to the cars shut him up. They were staring at them, amidst a choir of coarse laughter. And that was enough to make Winter stiffen.

A strange awareness, as if the emotions that the other was experiencing reached him in waves, pervaded Nathaniel, and he felt the change instantly. That feeling, sharp as the thorns of a porcupine, penetrated effortlessly beyond the light stupor of the drink.

"What the fuck are you looking at?" Winter's harsh voice rose all of a sudden, crashing the surface of tranquillity into shards.

"Winter ... just ignore them. They're not worth it," Nathaniel tried, stretching one hand towards the other's arm. But he shook it off.

"Where did you get out from, the circus?" one of the guys cried, gesticulating broadly. It was obvious he was drunk. "Better if you listen to your boyfriend."

"If you get back to him, he'll give you a consolation kiss," added another, with a crooked grin, making the others laugh. "Isn't that what you want? I can read it in your face, snow queer."

Winter didn't answer. He took a step forward, and every gesture he made exuded a sense of obscure threat. The small group stopped laughing. They spread out in a semicircle, the atmosphere turning foreboding.

Nathaniel felt it clearly. He slid off the wall, worried by this ugly turn of events, and a situation going out of control in a matter of seconds. And Winter was the natural catalyst of that negative energy. It was such an obvious sensation that it left him breathless for a moment. "Winter, don't..." he begged him, praying that he would listen to him, but also that he could remain standing without stumbling.

Winter didn't even turn around. A moment later, he was no longer there. He had moved so quickly to deceive everyone, including Nate. Only he had expected it and had already seen it happen. The others had not.

Within a few moments, a furious brawl erupted in the half-lit parking lot. For a long, endless handful of seconds, Nathaniel couldn't react. He stood still against the wall, the reflexes slowed by two lousy beers; all around him the air had thickened like molasses, while in front of him, a few steps away, Winter was grappling on the ground with the first young man who had spoken. The others were stunned at the speed with which the boy had come into action, but their amazement didn't last long. They rushed at him, while screams and curses filled the air. Nathaniel couldn't even distinguish his friend anymore.

He had seen him fight, and knew how strong he was, but they were too many for him. And even if the whole mess had been his fault in his furious need to fight, manifested in blatant hostility like a beacon of danger to the rest of the world, he couldn't let them take him. "Stop! Leave him alone!" he shouted, raising his voice above the chaos of the melee. He pounced on one of them, the closest, grabbing him by the shoulders and trying to remove him from the pile and especially from Winter. His friend was still struggling on the dusty tarmac, beating and kicking and biting with the usual joyous, crazy abandonment, despite having two guys assaulting him, and a third who tried to kick him at every possible opportunity.

"You're in six against one, cowards!" Nathaniel snapped as the guy caught in his arm lock tried to wriggle free.

"Get off me, kid! Your asshole friend went looking for it. He deserves a lesson!"

They were more or less of the same size, though the boy had to be a few years older than him. He managed to hold on to him until one of his mates intervened, grabbing Nate by the shirt and making him lose his balance. He ended up on the ground, a few meters away, scuffing his elbows on the asphalt and leaving the first layer of his skin on it.

He got up again, furious. He stared at them as they kept on hitting Winter. And while his chest rose quickly under heavy breathing, he felt something growing inside himself. Perhaps it was the alcohol and the effect it had on his inhibitions, but he'd never experienced such clear and intense emotions. So strong to fill his chest, so violent to give him the impression that the blood in his veins had turned into a luminous bluish energy which now filled the corners of his vision, making his thoughts sizzle in his mind. His nerve endings vibrated and crackled, overloaded. His heart throbbed aggressively against his rib cage, in rhythm with the rapid breathing. He realized that he was biting the inside of his cheek only when he felt the taste of blood.

He screamed. Suddenly he unleashed the powerful energy that threatened to kill him and left it free to expand with breath-taking violence. He heard a sudden snap of sparks, and his raven hair stood on his head. A pungent smell of ozone filled the air, making his eyes tear up. With a shocking crackle a blinding flash of lightning fell a few meters from them all, crashing into the parking lot wall and sending its pieces flying in a wild blast. The nearest street lamp flickered and died, its weak halogen light sucked into the darkness of the night. The thunder rumbled so loud and close to make the windows of the surrounding buildings tremble.

The boys, by then, had already scattered away from Winter, left on the ground with his arms still wrapped around his head in protection. They stared at Nathaniel with terror in their eyes. They looked at the broken and blackened wall, the signs left by the lightning in the parking lot. Then it started to rain heavily, a raging summer storm that nobody could have foreseen, so few were the clouds in the sky until a few moments before. They turned their backs and ran away. He stood there, his T-shirt glued to his chest from the water, his dark locks framing a pale face. His head begun to spin. He ran towards what was left of the wall, staggering, leaned over the edge and threw up.

He knew what had happened and was afraid.

A hand rested hesitantly on his shoulder, and he straightened up slowly after the last empty retching. He jumped with a hoarse curse, whirling around. Winter stood there, just as soaked under a rainfall that didn't want to stop, one eye swollen almost completely closed and a split lip. Nate stared at him in silence, panting, passing the back of his hand over his lips, desiring for something to drink to remove that sour and revolting taste from the mouth. Wishing that everything he had seen in the last few minutes had never happened.

Winter seemed uncertain, confused, and at the same time filled with admiration. "Did you ... do it?" he finally asked, his speech slurred by the swollen lip, the only open eye capturing the reflection of the farthest street lamp, the one spared from the fury of the electrical storm.

At that moment, all of Nathaniel's fear and dismay gathered in a dark core inside him, below his sternum. A core as heavy as lead, which smelled of anger. The hangover that had caught him seemed to have been burned away by that sudden and overbearing manifestation of uncontrolled power. "And you even have the courage to come and ask me?" he snapped, moving a step forward and pushing his friend.

Winter staggered back, eyes wide with surprise, a foot sunk to the ankle in the puddle created by the rain and a depression in the road. It was obvious that he didn't expect such a reaction. "What...?"

"Seriously? It's all your fault, you antisocial asshole! You and your damn fights! Why the hell did you need to worry about those idiots? Tell me! Why the fuck did you have to attack them?"

Winter seemed increasingly confused. He looked like he had just been slapped in the face by the most unexpected person. "But they had ...they had said ..."

"I don't give a shit about what they've said!" Nathaniel cut in, furiously. He stepped forward, and pushed him again. "Did you understand what just happened? What could have happened?"

"You ... you dropped that lightning. It was you, right?" he tried, and for the first time he seemed taken aback. As if someone had stolen his role and he no longer knew how to behave. If he wasn't the one snarling, cursing and beating people up, what would he do?

"It was me. And I could have killed someone. Do you understand now? I didn't even know I could do it until a few minutes ago. This too I inherited from my father, and d'you want to know something? I have no idea how to control it. I could have fried one of those guys. Sent him to the morgue. Do you have any idea what would have happened, then? And all because of your damn wish to fight everybody!"

"Nate ..."

"*Nate* nothing! Don't you *Nate* me, now!" Furious, Nathaniel walked away, heading towards the Mustang, splashing muddy water all around. In the parking lot the smell of burning still mixed with the pungent smell of ozone. Someone looked out from the nearby bar, but the wall of pouring rain had kept the curious away. A bolt of lightning that fell too close to the town, the likely explanation. Oh, but a dead body...

Nathaniel shuddered, more at the implications of that thought than because of the water-heavy jeans glued to his legs, and opened the driver's door. He got behind the wheel and locked his fingers on it strongly, hoping that his hands would stop shaking, hoping to regain control over the chaos that swirled inside him. He raised his glance towards Winter, who looked at him, still dazed, standing under a storm that was anything but natural.

"Get in here," he said, slipping the keys into the ignition and turning the engine on.

Winter hesitated for a moment, as if pondering on the idea of turning around to run away instead, to get out of Nate's life before causing him serious trouble. Then he seemed to shake off that restless stillness. He went around the Mustang and slipped into the passenger seat, closing the door with a strange shyness, noiselessly. He sank down onto the fake leather of the seat, wetting it with his soaking clothes. He looked straight ahead while Nathaniel moved into gear and exited the parking lot onto a still rain-battered Silver Springs Boulevard to return to the ranch.

Neither of them spoke a single word all the way.

## CHAPTER TEN

Nathaniel didn't sleep much that night. When they got home, everything had been silent as the household slept, so they'd just gone up to their rooms. Before entering his and closing the door behind him, Nate had broken the grim silence between them. "Wait."

He had stopped him there in the corridor, lit only by the pale and silvery rays of the moon that filtered through a skylight, and had stretched a hand toward his wounded face. Winter hadn't moved, letting him. He looked pensive, distant. In those transparent eyes, Nathaniel had managed to read, with impressive clarity, a sort of poignant melancholy. He had started to believe that he had become really empathic like his mother. It was strange, as if, since his abilities had been unlocked saving the life of the boy in front of him, everything had fallen into place. Perhaps too fast.

He had forced himself to banish the feeling of compassion that threatened to break the austerity behind which he had hidden since the parking lot incident, and touched his broken face with his fingers. "I'm not doing you a favour. I just don't want to be flooded with questions tomorrow," he had pointed out sternly, before narrowing his eyes and letting the urgent need to help him do the rest.

Winter had said nothing. He had simply remained motionless, waiting for the swollen eye and the wounded lip to return intact, as if those kids had never beaten him.

Nate had been amazed at the ease with which the healing had succeeded. It had been as natural as breathing and he hardly felt any consequences.

Then they separated, without a word more.

The night had passed slowly, the hours dragging on while the stars moved with unbearable calm in the quadrant of the sky. Nathaniel, after getting rid of his rain-soaked clothes, had stayed in his boxer shorts and put on an oversized grey sleeveless shirt that had belonged to his father. He had remained curled up on the windowsill of his dormer, watching the remnant of black velvet sky quilted with pale diamonds until the darkness of the night had left room for the placid indigo before dawn.

Only then did he allow himself to lie down, having decided that he would not talk about the events of the night before with anybody. He didn't feel ready to face something that, at the bottom of his soul, frightened him.

He had spent years hoping that such power would manifest itself. He had prayed to really be a Child of the Storm that everyone hoped for. But now, all of a sudden, Richard's words were clear: everything had changed suddenly, and he couldn't go back to the anonymity of teenage years, whose only worry was to disappoint his friends. He felt like he was in the eye of the storm. And a part of him hated himself for the new doubts it had brought with it.

He fell into a light and restless sleep for a few hours. The images of the brawl scrolled in his mind on a loop, so vivid as to seem real. Except that in the dream those kids didn't stop beating Winter, and he could only see his still form on the ground, curled up in a useless attempt at defence, the whiteness of his hair marred by the dense and alarming crimson of the blood that gushed from the curled edges of an open wound on his temple. The lightning suddenly broke that scene with a dry crackle. In that blinding glare, he seemed to glimpse twisted shapes, while screams of piercing agony pierced his ears.

Who had he killed?

He awoke with a start, his locks glued to his face from the sweat, the heavy breathing that shook his chest. Someone was knocking on the door.

He sat up, taking a few deep breaths, trying to pace the gallop of his heart against his ribs. He looked out of the window—it couldn't have been more than a few hours since he had fallen asleep. The sky was crossed by the delicate reddish tones of dawn, and when he glanced at the old digital alarm clock on the bedside table, he saw that it was just past six o'clock.

Someone out there knocked again.

"I'm coming, I'm coming..."

For a moment, he thought it was his mother, and that somehow she had managed to feel his agitation from a distance.

But it wasn't her.

It was Winter.

He looked as if he hadn't slept much either, and was already dressed in a pair of jeans, an old black sweatshirt with a hood that Kenneth had given him, and a pair of boots.

"What's going on?" Nathaniel began, breaking the awkward but persistent feeling that hovered between them.

"I couldn't sleep and I thought ... I don't know, maybe you wanted to take a walk." He hesitated, as if he had just thought of something to say only then. "Did I wake you up? Do you want to go back to sleep?"

The other rubbed one of his eyes, feeling it burn as if it were full of sand. "No, I wasn't sleeping," he lied. "Give me a moment."

It didn't take him long to slip into the small en-suite bathroom, wash his face and get dressed. There was something in Winter's attitude that gave him a strange uneasiness. He had no idea if it was the consequence of a newly awakened empathy; he didn't even know if it could evolve into something more defined, reaching his mother's potential. But he was certain that the boy was not there just to take a walk. There was a tormenting need in the depths of his light eyes. He gave off an aura of hesitant need for sharing - or at least that was what he seemed to feel. Perhaps it was it his way of apologising for what he had done the night before.

He bent down to tie the old blue Converse and walked past him to leave the room. The air seemed electric around him, trembling with a sense of ill-concealed expectation. "Let's go," he urged, walking along the corridor towards the stairs. "Do you want to go out riding?" he asked then, turning to look at him.

Winter shook his head. "I'd prefer not to."

Nathaniel didn't insist and shrugged his shoulders. He took the last steps down and looked around. There was nobody downstairs. Or maybe they were already busy with the chores on the ranch. In any case, the living room and the kitchen were empty. Nate took a look in the fridge, but then closed the door empty-handed. He hadn't decided whether the feeling in his stomach was hunger or nausea.

They stepped out of the door that led to the small backyard, through Charlene's garden, and set off past the white-painted wooden gate, onto a path that led to a spot of cypress trees. For a while they walked in silence. Nathaniel didn't know what to say, and he had the distinct impression that Winter wanted to share something important, and was looking for the right words. Or the necessary courage.

"I'm sorry for yesterday," he said in the end.

By the way those words came out, croaking and awkward, Nathaniel realised they must have cost him a lot. Maybe he wasn't used to apologies.

He shrugged, looking at him sideways. "Sure. Is that why you wanted to take a walk? To apologise?" he asked, a hint of curiosity in his voice, despite everything. Appeased.

He had been furious with him the night before, and he still thought he had reason to be, but he couldn't be angry now. There was something about Winter's attitude that made him look suddenly much younger than his age, lost. As if his usual bravado, the way he had to prove to the world that he was able to get by on his own, was only a form of defence. A wall to use as refuge, to hide uncertainties and weaknesses that it was better not to show.

"Not just for that. Though, yes, I want you to forgive me," he finally replied, nibbling on his lip.

Nathaniel said nothing as they continued to walk along the path. By now they were far from the border of the ranch, halfway between the open pasture and the thicker part of the forest, not far from the edges of the National Forest. They seemed to be alone in the middle of nowhere, while the sky cleared and the uncertain dawn of that summer day peeked out from behind the hills, flooding them with its warmth.

Winter slowed to a halt when they reached a stream, its edges suffocated by the tall grass. The path crossed it through an unstable bridge of damp planks, covered with moss. Nearby, a weeping willow leaned over the tiny course of water, touching the surface with the ends of its hanging fronds. He deviated from the path to reach the tree, slipping under the curtain of light green leaves. There he slid to the ground, his back against the rough trunk, the long legs gathered at the chest and his chin resting on the knees.

Nathaniel followed him, and sat on the grass beside him.

"When you asked me if I had any extraordinary abilities, I didn't tell you everything," began Winter after a while, his voice barely higher than the humid, silvery whisper of the small stream not far away, muffled by the thick green wall around them.

Nate looked at him, a shadow of curiosity in his eyes. "So there is more ... what can you do?"

Winter's transparent irises seemed lost, staring at nothing beyond the whispering branches of the willow. "I can show you, if you want."

Nate hesitated, wondering why it suddenly seemed that the atmosphere around them had become restless. However, in the end, he nodded. And waited.

He watched him standing up with an agile movement, and then, stretching a hand behind his back, slipped it under the light fabric of the sweatshirt. And then his eyes widened, and he stood up quickly, shaken more than he cared to show. Winter was holding a kitchen knife. He had it with him all the time, tucked into his belt. Nate wondered when he had taken it—perhaps before coming to his room, that morning.

Only then the boy looked up, giving him his usual little crooked smile, only sadder. "There is nothing to be afraid of. Really Nate, I didn't bring you here to hurt you," he murmured, in a low and calm tone.

Sincere.

Nathaniel cleared his throat. He must have looked really worried to elicit that comment. "It didn't cross my mind." *Yes it did.* "But ... what's that for?"

"For the tribute," said Winter. Then he took a deep breath, pulled up his left sleeve and placed the blade on his forearm, where other subtle and pale marks could be seen, old scars bleached by time.

It happened quickly. Before Nathaniel could do something to stop him, he had already made a thin diagonal cut that intersected the others. "What the hell are you doing?" he cried, trying to snatch the knife from his hand.

Winter dropped it in the tall grass at their feet. It didn't matter; he didn't need it anymore. He had done what was necessary.

The scarlet line stood out as an insult on the white forearm stretched towards the outside. The blood began to gush out in large shimmering drops, which rained downwards ... *without ever reaching the ground.* They frizzled in mid-air as if they had encountered a hot surface, disappearing in flashes of reflected light.

Nate stared at the inexplicable phenomenon with his mouth open. The air seemed to vibrate, swaying like in the summer when the heat forms faded mirages in the distance. Then it began to expand in front of them until it formed a swirling mirror with an opal surface, which had no defined colour. A slit engraved in the fabric of reality, like the wound on the boy's arm.

"And what is *that*?" Nathaniel's voice came out more croaking and upset than he would have liked.

Winter grinned, lowering the sleeve of his sweatshirt on the scratched forearm. The blood had already stopped flowing. "It's a door. Look..." Without hesitation, as if he knew what he was doing, he stretched out his hand towards the strange mirror that reflected nothing. It was like putting it into the fog. It disappeared, sinking into it. Then he withdrew it, unharmed.

"A door to where?" asked the other in a disbelieving whisper.

"I don't know. Another world, I think. Like the ones you mentioned when you told me about the Norsemen. I've done it before. I went in and came back. But I never had the guts to stay there." He paused. "It's been a while since I opened one. I wasn't sure I could still do it. But what you told me made me think, and I couldn't get it out of my head."

Suddenly, Nate understood why it had seemed to him that Winter had been hiding something from him. And why he had accepted with surprising ease his explanation of parallel universes, and the origin of the Norse. It was such a shocking awareness that it made him feel dizzy. "Are you saying you can go ... and then come back here? And that you opened these portals more than once?"

Winter nodded. "I used to do it as a child," he explained. "I often ended up locked in isolation, where I lived. It was a dark, narrow room. It scared me, and I didn't want to stay there. They'd leave me for hours. Then it happened. I don't even know how ... I just knew I wanted to escape from there, with all my heart. I think it was that ... along with the blood. I soon realized that blood was always needed to open those doors." He looked down at the wounded forearm, hidden from the sweatshirt fabric. "For a while, it was a refuge. I'd go there whenever they locked me up. Sometimes I thought about closing the door and never coming back."

"Why didn't you?"

"I've never seen anyone on the other side. And I knew that I couldn't have done it alone. Unbearable as it was, there was food on this side, and a roof over my head. It wasn't the loneliness that scared me; in the end I was alone here too. But I guess I was too afraid to die."

Nathaniel tried not to get too emotionally entangled in that confession, the sensations it carried. He focused on the opal mirror with a mixture of amazement and anxiety. He never expected to see anything like this in his life. And the implications of that discovery were breathtaking.

"Try it," Winter urged him. "Look inside. Nothing bad will happen. It's a nice place. Always the same, every time I saw it. I don't think it has changed over the years."

Nate hesitated. Then Winter grabbed his hand and took a step towards the portal. They crossed the swirling mist before he had the chance to react. For a moment, it was like being blinded by a milky, greyish screen. When the fog cleared, Nathaniel found himself looking at a landscape of hills covered with thick forests of conifers that climbed, dark green spots, towards a horizon of high mountains, bristling with icy peaks hidden by clouds. In the midst of a narrow valley shone the unmistakable sparkle of a river. There was no living soul to be seen, no trace of towns or cities. The air was cold and clear, clean, intoxicating. It was the world as it should have appeared when men had not yet conquered it. A virgin land, intact.

"See?" Winter said, with a small, hesitant smile.

"It's ... incredible," he admitted, a shiver travelling down his spine. He turned to look at the portal, which swirled behind them, opening onto the middle of nowhere. "You have the ability to open Nodal Points at will. That's what this is ... do you get it? Of course you do. You didn't even blink when I told you about them the first time. You already knew it, damn it. And I think I know what place this is." As he spoke those words, he felt his stomach knot between restlessness and excitement.

When Winter looked at him, puzzled, he still hesitated before continuing to talk. He knew his intuition could be the right one, but the consequences were out of his reach. Uncontrollable. "I believe you can open a portal on the world from which the Norse came. I can't be sure, and we'll have to talk about it with the rest of the coven, but—"

"No, wait," Winter suddenly interrupted, his smile disappearing from the sharp face. "I don't want to talk about it with them."

"But they *need* to know. It could be dangerous. Don't you understand? If the Fjandar knew about your ability, they would force you to activate a Nodal Point, to bring about Ragnarök."

Winter thought about it, looking diffidently at the opal split in the fabric of reality. "I don't know. Maybe you're right."

"Believe me, it's the right thing to do. And if you trust me—if you trusted of me enough to share this—I assure you that you can trust them too."

"What if they think *I'm* dangerous? What if they don't want me here anymore? If they think I could be a danger to you ... if they decide to lock me up somewhere so I can't cause any trouble ..."

His distrusting and distressed tone struck Nathaniel like a slap in the face. He sensed Winter's emotions in a direct and concrete way, almost like they were his own. He felt cut off, different and rejected, as Winter must have felt for years. Only in violence and transgression did he see a key to force his way into the system, to slip into a role that had been made for him since forever. All the way to that feeling of melancholy and relief at the thought of ending his life in a crash on the highway, rather than facing another hostile look, another word of condemnation.

"No," he murmured softly, taking a step closer. With caution, he put his hands on his shoulders; Winter flinched but didn't back away, so Nathan squeezed over the thin sweatshirt fabric, trying to communicate all he was feeling. "No, it won't be like that, Winter. When I said you would be safe with us, I meant it. Nobody will judge you for what you can do. You were born with this ability, and you're not to blame. All you need to do is trust in who knows more than you and let you lead, so you can learn to control it. You are not the first to go down this road, and you will not be the last. Believe me."

They looked into each other's eyes once more. In the end Winter nodded, sighing and loosening his muscles, as if a weight had just been removed from his shoulder. Perhaps no one had ever talked to him that way before.

"We'll tell the others when we go back. I've got something to share too." He had awakened the lightning and hadn't told them yet. He had certainly not set a good example.

Winter nodded, seemingly convinced, though a vague mistrust still danced in his colourless eyes. "All right," he said finally. He sat on the grass in the middle of the meadow where they had emerged, at the foot of the hill crowned by a thick forest. The shades of green were so intense to hurt the eyes. "Only ... let's stay here a little longer, OK? Just a little ... before going back."

Nathaniel agreed and went to sit next to him, bringing his knees to his chest and wrapping his arms around them. He could understand why Winter wanted to stay. There was something about the place that called to him, as if deep inside he recognised the land of the Norsemen. A strange wholesomeness sang in his blood. "*This is where you need to be,*" that song kept repeating inside of him. Without words, only with its intense light. He found himself smiling without really knowing why. "*Home. And your destiny.*" He turned toward the portal, which continued to vibrate and swirl, a sort of white noise in the background. Incomprehensible, but somehow perceptible. "And that? How will you close it?"

"We'll go through it again and then close it. I'm not sure how it works, I want it to close and it closes. It has always been like this."

"When did you last open one?"

"Many years ago." Winter seemed to think about it for a while. "After the last time, I thought it was better to forget about it. In the end, I would never have had the courage to shut the door behind me and start afresh in a new world. Not even when I realised that I could handle myself if I wanted to. Maybe I didn't want to find out that this world was the same as the other. That nothing would change for me. That people would have looked and treated me the same as before. So I decided to keep it as a dream instead of living it."

It was the deepest confession he had made to him so far. And the saddest. Nathaniel looked at him sideways. "But now you are no longer alone. You no longer need to imagine another world to feel good," he tried, with a smile.

"Yeah," he replied, but he seemed hesitant, not entirely convinced. "It's just that I can't get used to it," he finally admitted.

Nate started to answer, then he felt that something had changed. He frowned, his senses alert, a shiver of premonition pricking his skin. He looked around, but the landscape was identical. Nothing seemed to upset that austere valley, the reflections of snowy peaks cloaked in clouds, or the intense green of the coniferous forests that crowned the hills and the slopes of the distant mountains.

Then, all of a sudden, he understood. The wordless song of the portal, the vibrant interference of its presence: he no longer felt them. He whirled around, and so did Winter, perhaps alarmed by his sudden movement, or perhaps caught by the same awareness.

In front of them there was only the meadow, its grass waving slowly under a slight biting breeze. In the background, a patch of trees similar to firs. There was no trace of the opal mirror, the crack between parallel realities.

The portal had closed.

## Chapter Eleven

"What do you mean, *I can't reopen it*?" Nathaniel's voice was sharp, broken, a very young and scared little boy.

"It means what I said, Nate ... I can't. Reopen. It." There was a mixture of exasperation and tension in his voice. He had tried to make the portal reappear before them, but neither his blood nor his will seemed able to recreate the passage.

"You said you would close it once we went back. That all you had to do was to wish for it to close, and it would. So? Did you decide to close it? Did you decide we had to stay here?" Nate's accusation was not subtle. Part of him seemed convinced that Winter had trapped them in that unknown world—perhaps hostile—on purpose, so as not to have to talk to the coven and face the consequences.

Winter shook his head, looking straight at him. He kept a certain coolness, despite the situation they were in. "I've already told you. It wasn't me. I don't know what happened—it's the first time. It's stuck. Like a door locked on the other side."

Nathaniel understood this just fine. And that awareness was there clutching his stomach in an icy grip. "And now?" The question they both wanted to ask, but hadn't dared to do out loud.

Winter looked at him, removing his gaze from the latest cut on the wrist, still bleeding under the fabric of the sweatshirt pressed against it. He had realised that any further effort would have been useless, as well as harmful. "We'll find a way to get by," he declared, straightening his shoulders, a flash of determination in the eyes, "and to go back."

Nate blinked a couple of times, stunned, overwhelmed. Was it possible that the thrill of excitement he seemed to have felt in his voice was real? Possible that, for Winter, that absurd situation was turning into an exciting adventure, a looked-for opportunity?

He took a deep breath, trying to calm himself, to own the determination that seemed to emanate in waves from the other boy. He looked around. This world seemed deserted. From behind the mountains, an intense light suggested the presence of a sun about to rise in a sky of such an intense blue to hurt your eyes. It could have been early morning there too.

"We must seek help, a town. And I think we have the day ahead to do it." He looked up at Winter. "I don't know about you, but I don't want to be outdoors when darkness falls."

Winter agreed. "It seems cold now. The temperature could drop a lot during the night. And we have no idea of who lives in those woods. Yes, we need to find shelter. And hope that someone will help us."

"We need to find them first..." groaned Nate. He closed his eyes for a moment, swallowing dry. He was still struggling with denial. *It's not possible*, a part of his brain kept saying. *It's not happening, really*. A denial which would have turned into anger and into despair if he couldn't keep it in check. He grabbed at the strong rope of rationality, no matter how ridiculous it sounded in a situation so out of the ordinary. Of course, he had always known that there were other worlds besides his own. But to be inside one of them, unprepared and with only the company of a boy who had shown himself to be quarrelsome, unstable and with more than one problem of socialisation, it was quite another thing.

"All right. Okay," he grumbled at last, fists clenched against the hips, shoulders stretched in a rigid pose, like a martial artist. "Let's go. There is nothing else we can do here, and staring at that damned hill will not make the portal reappear."

Winter looked at him for a moment, seemingly pondering on Nate's sudden resolution. Then he just nodded, walking towards the bottom of the lawn. "Doesn't that look like a path to you?" he observed, pointing to their left, not far from a patch of trees and the gentle curve of some low hills. "If there's a road, it will have to go somewhere."

It was a start. And as he headed for the path, Nathaniel tried not to think about what would have happened on the other side when his coven wouldn't see them return. When the initial hypothesis of a longer than expected absence would become the awareness of a disappearance. He tried to recall all the survival notions that Ashur and Sven had taught him on their camping weekends and training in the National Forest and, further down, in the Everglades. He didn't really believe they would ever be useful to him.

He had no idea how wrong he was.

*

They walked for about an hour without speaking much, along what had turned out to be a dirt track, maybe created by the passage of men rather than animals. The grass grew higher in the centre, perhaps an effect of carriage wheels running at either side of it, and more than once Nathaniel seemed to notice in the damp soil the uncertain shape of hooves.

Eventually they reached what appeared to be the first trace of human presence in the place: a spring in between the trees that skirted the path, splashing into a watering hole carved in stone.

They stopped to drink, grateful for that cold and pure water, which tasted of mountain and minerals dissolved in its secular underground course.

"If this is really the Norse world," asked Winter, "what should we be expecting, d'you reckon?" He wiped his lips with the sleeve of the sweatshirt.

Nathaniel shook his head. "I have no idea. Richard—my grandfather—never spoke about it. And he's perhaps the only Norse left in our world."

"The first impression is that this place has never seen the industrial revolution. That, or we just ended up in an area with little population and factories."

"I hope we can find people," concluded Nate. "The watering hole bodes well. And ... hey, aren't those strawberries?"

They approached the edge of the woods. There were plants on the slope that led to the path, with the unmistakable serrated leaves, vividly green, whose stems bent due to the weight of small red ripe fruit.

Nathaniel took one off, bringing it to his lips cautiously. Then he smiled, narrowing his eyes in delight. "It's a strawberry. Honestly. This place seems more and more like a ... projection of our world."

It was strange to realise how grateful he was for that little treat. The strawberries were plentiful and they had an intense aroma he didn't think he'd ever smelled before. They picked up handfuls, proceeding along the path, staining fingers and lips with their juice. Their first meal in that unknown place, as far away from home as Nathaniel had ever gone. He wasn't sure what Winter felt about it, but he could tell he was as hungry as he was.

"I had never eaten strawberries so good," admitted Winter, licking his fingers.

"We'd better go on now," Nathaniel said, stretching.

"Wait. I want to take some more for later." Winter filled the pockets of his sweatshirt.

"Oh, come on, we'll need something more substantial than that."

"Are you going to start hunting like Bear Grylls?"

"I hope we won't need to. Rather, I was thinking of a town and something better to eat than a handful of wild strawberries."

"We'll see. I don't think they take dollars or credit cards, if you have one. And assuming they understand what we say."

Nate replied to the sarcasm with a dirty look. However, Winter was right. Even if they found a town, they would have several more problems to solve.

"No point in worrying about that now. Let's just go. If we don't solve one problem at a time, I think I'll go crazy," grumbled Nate in reply.

Winter started walking again, but he stopped after a few meters, stiffening suddenly. "Did you hear that?" he whispered.

"Hear what?" Nathaniel also stopped, straining his ears. And then he heard it. A rhythmic noise of hurried steps, the crash of sprigs broken in the passage, the dry rustling of the bushes. It came from the thick of the woods to their right, and it seemed to move closer and closer.

"Let's get off the road," Winter suggested quickly, running for shelter behind the trees on the opposite side of the track.

Nathaniel followed him, and they both stopped behind the huge trunk of an evergreen. After a moment, unsure, they peeked out towards the path. And they saw him.

He came out of the trees, out of breath, running. When he raised his head, they realized that he was a boy a little older than them. He had hard features, covered by a glossy and thin patina of sweat, framed by reddish-brown hair that went down passed the broad shoulders, and onto the middle of the back. One arm, strung with tense muscles, like a sprinter, was covered in fresh blood, which traced uncertain and zigzagging designs down to a fist clamped on a short blade, a kind of shining dagger with silvery sun reflections.

He saw them, and his eyes grew bright green, spangled with golden sparks. And as he ran towards them, Nathaniel found himself wondering, with growing dismay, where he had seen those eyes before and why he had the intense feeling of already knowing him.

The boy passed the escarpment that divided the path from the woods with an agile leap, and rolled beside them, crouching behind the huge tree. Gasping, his strong chest shaking from short broken pants, he shrank, lowering into thick bushes.

"Stay down ..." he hissed through clenched teeth, his voice hoarse. "They are coming."

Nate looked at him, dismayed. He understood him, but the boy had just spoken in a language he never thought he would hear outside of his coven. He obeyed, grabbing Winter by the wrist and pulling it down with him.

"What the hell are you doing? And what the hell did he say?" he cried. Suddenly, his eyes widened too. "You can understand his language?"

Nate nodded. "It's the language of the Norsemen." It was increasingly clear where they had ended up and in how much trouble they were.

The stranger put a finger to his lips, looking at both of them severely. There was no need for words to understand what he wanted from them. They fell silent, remaining motionless behind the shelter, waiting for something they didn't even know.

They began to hear the unmistakable sound of rushed steps. Heavy, metallic. They approached, breaking branches and moving forward towards them, through the woods. When they reached the road, after a brief moment when only indistinct and guttural voices could be heard, the steps began to move away again.

The boy dared to come out of hiding. And he uttered a sigh of relief. "They're gone. I was hoping that on seeing the road they would think I was heading north." He shook his head. "Anyone would go and seek help in Wunderbaar now. I thought about it too. But this road isn't safe." He pressed the nape of his head against the rough trunk of the tree, regaining his breath. Only then he looked at the boys again, perplexed, lingering longer on Winter, as if something didn't quite fit. "And who are you? What are you doing here, for the Nine Hells? Don't you know that the Jötnar have conquered most of the region?"

Winter just looked at him with a neutral expression, tense. He hadn't understood a syllable of what the boy had said.

Nathaniel swallowed. He had understood everything. And that single word the stranger had used, Jötnar, was enough to freeze the blood in his veins. He looked in those eyes that seemed so familiar, and tried to explain. "My name is Nathaniel. Nate, if you prefer. And he's Winter. He does not speak your language," he hastened to add, when the other made to address him, for some reason. "We are ... travellers." He chewed his lip hesitantly. "We came from far away."

The other, at that point, raised an eyebrow and nodded. "I can tell by your accent ... and your appearance," he commented, observing their clothes. They were different from his own leather trousers tucked into reinforced knee-high boots and a coat of raw wool.

Nate looked for the right words. "These lands ... do they belong to the Norsihir?"

The boy looked at him strangely. Then he nodded. "Yes. At least, they *used* to belong to us. Since the Jötnar began their invasion, it is difficult to tell where the borders are. This is becoming a no man's land." He paused for a moment, his stern expression adding years to his back. "I'm Reidar, anyway."

"Were they Jötnar—the ones from before?" asked Nathaniel. "The ones that chased you?"

The other boy gave a sharp nod. "Who else? They've been hunting me for a while. Hopefully this time I've lost them. Those fucking obstinate hunting dogs!" He gave no further explanation, and Nathaniel didn't dare ask, at least for the moment.

They remained silent for a while, during which time Reidar tore a flap of the greyish wool tunic he wore to make an improvised bandage to wrap around his injured arm. A tear on his biceps, not too deep at first sight, continued to bleed.

Nate hesitated. "I ... if you want I can give you a hand. With that wound, I mean."

Reidar frowned, puzzled. Then a flash of understanding lit his eyes, followed by an expression of relief. "Are you a *laege*?" He used the Norse word for "healer". Someone who had the ability to heal with their hands.

Nathaniel nodded, though it still made him feel very strange. But there, where they were now, that kind of ability was perfectly normal, and he knew it very well. Perhaps he wasn't even a good healer, considering that he wasn't a pure Norse.

However, the thought didn't prevent him from dealing with the laceration on Reidar's arm. What surprised even him was the speed with which the wound closed without leaving a trace, giving him only a vague tingling in the hands, and almost no fatigue. It hadn't happened that way, the first time, and not even when he had erased the bruises from Winter's face. He wondered if abilities like his own worked differently, better, in that world. But he didn't have time to think about it.

"You are good for one so young," smiled Reidar.

Now that the healing had taken place, that helping gesture, he seemed more inclined to trust them, though he kept glancing at Winter from time to time with a kind of vague suspicion. Or of perplexity, Nathaniel couldn't tell.

The boy stood up, and the other two did the same. "Where are you heading to?" he asked, focusing his green eyes on Nate.

He hesitated. A good question without easy answer. "Actually, we are lost," he finally admitted, deciding to trust that boy with the familiar air. He frowned, worried. "We are not doing great; we don't have supplies with us and we don't know where to go. You said that the road is not safe, towards the north." He took a deep breath, staring at him right in the eye. "Can you take us to the next town? Or a safe place to spend the night?"

Reidar tilted his head slightly, as if wondering what those two were hiding from him. It was true, but Nate didn't really know how to explain to him that they didn't belong to that world, and that they had no idea how to get back into theirs. So he merely looked back at him, waiting for an answer.

Eventually the young Norse looked at his healed arm, and nodded resolutely. "I'll travel away from the road, cutting through the woods towards Nivak. There is Niels Newth's farm near the valley, fifteen miles east of here. We could stop there for the night. He will not deny us a hot meal and shelter. Think you can do it?"

Nathaniel explained the situation to Winter. "I'd say we should go with him, and figure out what to do," he concluded.

The other nodded, peering sideways at the Norse. "Better than finding yourself in the middle of these woods tonight, in the cold, without a roof over our head and with an empty stomach," he grumbled.

"Then it's decided," murmured Nathaniel, and turned back to Reidar, in Norse. "We'll come with you. Thanks for your help".

Reidar nodded, a dry gesture. He added nothing else at that point. He turned his back on the other two and looked around as if taking his bearings. Then he walked in one direction, towards a path just visible among the dense trees, perhaps a path dug in the undergrowth by passing animals. He turned away from the road without looking back, and without waiting for Nathaniel and Winter, who exchanged a puzzled look and hurried to follow him.

## CHAPTER TWELVE

"You seem to trust him. Yet you don't know him." Winter laid in the hay, wrapped in the blanket of raw wool he had been given. As he had guessed, in those parts the temperature fell a lot during nightfall.

"I feel like I know him," said Nathaniel, intent on observing a patch of dark sky from the opening in the barn roof. He couldn't recognise a single star and the silvery glow that illuminated the night came from two twin moons. "He makes me feel safe. He helped us, after all, without asking anything in return."

"So far," objected the other. "And how can you be so sure? You are trusting your feelings, which doesn't seem enough to make a serious assessment of the situation."

"Ever heard of empathy?" Nate turned to look at him. "My mother can read people's thoughts. She can feel their emotions as if they were hers and can influence them. I don't think I inherited her ability fully, but a lot has changed now. And I *feel* I can trust Reidar." He paused and looked for Winter's transparent eyes. "Do you trust me? This is the main thing."

The other snorted. "Go to hell. If I didn't trust you, we wouldn't even be here now." He seemed to think about it. "Which makes me think that maybe it was a mistake anyway." But this time, a slight irony had accompanied his words. They looked at each other in the shadows and burst out laughing. Then, for a while, they remained silent.

They had reached the farm at sunset and, as the young Norse had guessed, Niels Newth—the grumpy owner with thick eyebrows and a fiery red mop—had welcomed them for one night, in the barn. Reidar, who seemed to know him and his family well, had remained to talk to the man even when Nathaniel and Winter had taken leave. The frugal but abundant dinner, served in the large stone kitchen of the farmhouse, had filled their bellies, and they had felt the tiredness from the forced march and all the emotions of that day weighing on their shoulders.

"Are you asleep?" Nathaniel asked after a while.

"Not anymore, Nate. Thanks! What is it?"

"Don't sleep. We have to decide what to do."

"The only thing we can do is to ask your Norse friend to find us a safe place to stay until we find a way to reopen the portal and go home."

Nate felt his head spin. He didn't want to think about what was happening right now at Maple Tree, the anxiety and anguish which his family must have fallen into. Winter had no one; he could hardly understand how much that thought was enough to make his stomach clench in a vice. "What makes you think anything will change, that you'll be able to reopen the portal if you didn't succeed today?" he murmured, not caring about the anguish in his voice.

The other turned to look at him in the shadows of the barn. His brow furrowed. "Fuck all, actually, but I don't think we have any choice. Or am I wrong?"

"You are wrong. This world belongs to the Norsihir. They have opened Nodal Points and travelled to our world for centuries. Perhaps even to them it's not such a common ability, but I can't believe that there is no one able to help us."

"What do you propose we do?" Winter kept looking at him with a raised eyebrow, somewhere between perplexity and restlessness. Maybe he knew where this was going and he didn't like it.

"I say we talk to Reidar. Tell him the truth and ask him if there is someone who can help us return home." Nate propped himself up on one elbow, as if to underline the decision he had made.

Winter, in turn, sat up and stared at him. "I'm not sure that's the right choice." He wrinkled his nose in a grimace. "You saw how he looks at me, right? He just needs to know that I open portals and I don't come from his world to freak out completely."

"Why does it all have to revolve around you, Wint?" Nate mumbled, spreading his arms. "All right, he looked at you oddly. They *all* looked at you like that. But you will admit that you are particular too, right? Maybe they never saw a person with albinism in their lives..."

"They look at me with suspicion. How would you look at someone you can't be sure is a friend or an enemy, but you're inclined to believe more the second option? That's how they look at me. And, allow me, I have some experience with fucking hostile looks. Didn't you feel it with your empathy?"

Nathaniel pursed his lips in a grimace. The young man was not entirely wrong, and he too had become aware of those wary looks on the part of all those who they had met. "Let's not get caught up in paranoia," he tried, finally. "We are in a place with different rules from those of our world. What I know about the Norsemen is that they have special abilities, compared to which those of the Waerne are at least watered down. And I know with the same certainty that they have opened portals to reach our plane of existence. Several times at least." He hesitated. "I don't know how they did it, if they were aware of it, or how many times it happened, but it has happened. And I'm sure that for Reidar it won't be an absurd thing if we tell him. Indeed, he could also give us a hand. Maybe he knows why the Nodal Point isn't reopening. Or he can point us to someone who will help us reopen it."

Winter sighed. "Damn, all right ... I haven't got a better plan, and I realise that you're keen to go back." He let himself fall back into the hay, which crackled under his weight. "You have a family to return to. Friends waiting for you. And they will be worried. I don't know how it is, but it doesn't mean that I don't understand how you feel."

Nathaniel's heart tightened, this time not at the thought of his worried family, but at how Winter had said those last words. There was something in his tormented melancholy that continued to strike deep chords inside him. "You have a place to go back to now," he repeated firmly. "Maple Tree can be your home, too. I promised you would be safe, and it will be so. Believe me, I will do everything to get us back there."

Winter had nothing to say in front of so much resolution.

To Nate though, he seemed to smile in the shadows. "Do we agree then? Will we talk to Reidar tomorrow?"

"Well, you'll talk for us both. I don't understand a word of what you say."

"Then it means you'll have to use your best skill."

"What—punch him? The Norse?"

"Idiot," mumbled Nathaniel, exasperated. "I'm talking about your ability to learn quickly."

"Oh!" Winter chuckled. "I've never tried it with a language."

"I bet you won't have any problems. In fact, let's start right away."

*

Apparently they weren't to continue on foot. Nathaniel had never seen horses as large as the ones Reidar was pulling out of the stables at the back of Newth's farmhouse. They were taller and more imposing than the Clydesdales that Ken and Charlene raised at Maple Tree, the thick, shiny black coats, the long, wild manes that fell well beyond their muscular shoulders. They resembled Raido, his father's Friesian, that Helhest with special powers who was also the gift of Richard, his Norse ancestor.

He walked under the fence, leaving Winter to stand there watching, silent and frowning, and approached Reidar and the enormous horses that he was preparing to saddle. "Do you want a hand?" he asked, giving the animals an admiring look.

"Sure you know how to handle it, *Smukoj*?" he retorted, gripping one of the saddles. It was a heavy, padded leather one with a comfortable look. "These are Helhestir; you need to know your way around with them."

Nathaniel didn't know whether to feel more surprised that Reidar had just called him by the Norse word for *Bright Eyes*, as his friend Marcus had done in his own language, or because he had three Helhestir. "My father has one," he replied simply, and began to saddle the second animal with sure gestures that came from experience.

Reidar seemed satisfied.

For a time they worked in silence, side by side. "Do they belong to Master Newth?" Nate asked after a while as he stroked the neck of the great mare to whom he had just finished fixing the bit.

"Yes. The one you have saddled is called Berkana. The other two are Jera and Vunjo."

"They're all runes names..." he remarked, thinking of Raido, his father's stalwart. He also had the name of a Nordic rune.

Reidar smiled and nodded. "You know more than I thought. The names of the runes are almost always given to the Helhestir. It bodes well for the development of their abilities. These three are young and have not yet manifested them."

"My father's Helhest ... he's called Raido." Nathaniel scratched Berkana's withers, which she seemed to like, and moved her great muzzle towards him, watching him with intelligent eyes. "Why is Master Newth giving them to you?"

"Niels was a good friend of my father." Reidar seemed to darken, his voice lost for a moment. "He watched me grow up and would never deny me a favour, especially after he thought he would never see me again. Because of the war, you know. However, horses know their way home. When we reach our destination, we will let them go and they will come back here."

Nate nodded. Now he understood the reason for the generous welcome they had received.

"Does your friend not like Helhestir?" asked Reidar, peering sideways at Winter. "Or maybe it's me who he doesn't like?"

Winter continued to watch them from the fence, serious.

"Don't worry about him. He's quite close. And he's worried. I am too, for that matter." Nathaniel chewed his lip, looking for the right words to say. "See, yesterday I didn't tell you everything about us."

Reidar changed expression. He looked suspicious and tense now. "Don't tell me he's *really* one of them."

"One of who?" asked Nate. "What are you talking about?"

The Norse hesitated, frowning. "I thought you were going to tell me that he's a half-breed Jötunn. One of those hybrid abominations born after their first wars of conquest..."

Nathaniel's dark eyes widened in surprise. "No! What are you saying ... of course not ... Winter has nothing to do with them." He turned to his friend, who kept watching them from afar, with no apparent intention of joining them. He wondered if he knew they were talking about him.

Reidar frowned. "You would at least agree that he looks like one of them."

"I don't know. I never saw a Jötunn," Nathaniel admitted, and this time it was Reidar's turn to look amazed.

"Are you kidding me, Smukoj?"

"No. The fact is that we ... me and Winter ... we don't really belong to your world. He opened a portal. A Nodal Point—do you understand what I'm talking about? And we ended up here by mistake, and now we can't go back because it closed." He had told him everything in one breath as if to get it out of his system, regardless of how it would be received.

The Norse looked at him with eyes wide with surprise. The emotions he was feeling—dismay, wonder, even a bit of incredulous admiration—were as clear as the sun to Nathaniel. If nothing else, they didn't seem hostile.

Reidar opened and closed his mouth a couple of times, unable to say anything. He turned to Winter, by the fence, who returned the look, something between the annoyed and the suspicious. Nathaniel hoped that he wouldn't pick a fight with Reidar. He gave him a warning look, which he hoped was clear enough.

"Are you telling me your friend is a *rejsend*? That you are world-travellers?"

Wonder leaked from Reidar's voice.

"If anything, only him," Nate explained, after a moment's hesitation. "But he's not trained to do so. From what I understand, it's a spontaneous ability, and we got stuck here by mistake. Only he can't bring us back home." He looked at him expectantly. *Please tell me you can help us.*

The other became more serious. "Now I understand several things. Your foreign accent, him not speaking our language. Your ignorance, the strange clothes." He paused. "It was a long time since we've seen rejsendir in these parts. Since they were born among our people. But this ... well, this changes everything. You are in danger. You *and* your friend, the one who looks like a half-breed Jötunn and knows how to awaken Nodes. If they knew..."

He didn't finish the sentence, but the implications of what had not been said were enough to tighten Nathaniel's stomach in a grip of icy concern.

"Tell Winter to come here," Reidar said after a few moments. "We'd better leave. I'll explain everything while we travel."

They all mounted their horses shortly after, waving farewell to Master Newth and his family and leaving the farmhouse behind.

Nathaniel briefly explained to Winter what he had discovered. Contrary to what he feared, his friend didn't close himself off behind a wall of hostility. He gave a vague, crooked smirk rather, and commented softly: "That moment has arrived, I think."

"What moment?"

"The one where I have to thank you for teaching me how to ride, and you can hold it against me for life."

Despite the situation being anything but comforting, Nate found himself laughing. Some of the anguish he felt disappeared, letting him breathe better. He was not alone in that strange story—this was clear, if nothing else. And it did him good to know that.

*

Reidar had led them into the woods that surrounded the narrow valleys between the hills and mountains of that region. He had picked a path through the trees, not wide enough to allow the three Helhestir to travel side by side. They proceeded in single file, the Norse leading the way on Vunjo, the long stride of the huge horse setting the pace of the journey. Reidar sat in the saddle, looking back and talking to Nathaniel. Behind them, Winter seemed to manage Jera, the filly that had been entrusted to him, without any problems, and quietly listened to the other two. Nathaniel had the distinct feeling that he had already begun to comprehend the language after his first and only lesson of the previous night, and that he understood something more about their conversations. Which was certainly good. It didn't look like they would be leaving anytime soon, the way things were going.

"The Jötnar arrived in our lands about half a century ago," explained Reidar, in response to a direct question, resting his left hand on the raised back of his saddle. "They likely used a spontaneous Nodal Point. And they began to conquer the lands of the Norsihir by force. They took our women because, from what we know, it is the only way their people can have heirs: they have no females, nor are females born from their hybrid unions. Their women are always those of the peoples they conquer." For a moment he darkened, full of bitterness. "Much of the Konnershild region has fallen since then," he concluded, shutting himself up again as he urged Vunjo to cross a fallen trunk across the path.

Nathaniel nodded, a silent invitation to continue the story. After a few moments, Reidar obliged.

"They established their dominion over the conquered lands and none of our armies has ever managed to take them back. They have a military and physical advantage over us, and only few of our koenigir have managed, so far, to oppose them. Koen Rurik, who rules over the Wunderbaar clans, is one of the few to have kept his borders firm and his lands safe." He turned back to look ahead, lowering his head under a branch that intersected the path. "Until now, at least."

He remained silent as they waded through a small stream, using a series of surfacing stretches of gravel.

Nathaniel turned to Winter. "Can you understand something?"

He nodded, serious. "Ask him why they were chasing him," he suggested, letting his horse side with Nate's in the clearing beyond the stream.

Nate did so and Reidar's face grew even darker.

"For almost a year, their warbands have begun to invade and pillage. Borders have become uncertain. *Everything* is uncertain. They were chasing me because they are looking for me." He paused, turned back to look at him. "Do you know what a lynnewulf is?"

Nathaniel shook his head, puzzled.

"A lynnewulf is a Child of the Storm. A Norse with the power to dominate lightning. They are very rare among us. Very powerful. Dangerous if not properly trained. And I'm one of them."

Nathaniel remained silent, his brain absorbing the concrete awareness of that information. A lynnewulf. A Child of the Storm. The gift of his father. The one he had discovered he owned, just two nights ago. His heart started pounding fast against his ribs. "I don't understand ... are they looking for you because you're a lynnewulf?" he managed to murmur, despite his dry mouth.

Reidar nodded. "The fact is that these new raids are not a real attempt at conquest or expansion. The Jötnar actually want to get out of here."

Those words only added to the feeling of anxiety that was stirring in Nathaniel's chest. "Are they looking for another world to conquer?" he asked, clenching his fists on the reins. "It's our world they want. I know. The Norsihir warned us a long time ago."

It was at that moment that he considered that fact for the first time. *A long time ago.* That world where they were seemed ancient. In a flash of intuition, he wondered if he and Winter had travelled in time, and not just in space. But he didn't have time to dwell long on that thought.

"Did the Norsihir travel to your world?" asked Reidar. "It must have happened a long time ago, then ... rejsendir have not been born for centuries among our people." He shook his head. "And the Jötnar aren't able to open Nodal Points, from what we know. Perhaps a half-blood would be able to do so if he inherited this ability from his Norse mother. But it is unlikely to have ever happened, considering the rarity of the gift. However, they believe that there is another way to open a portal."

Nate's eyes widened as his sudden agitation caused Berkana to pause, as if she'd sensed the boy's nervousness. Even Winter seemed to understand that something wasn't right; he could see it in his eyes.

"Sacrificing a lynnewulf," Nathaniel said, his eyes planted in that of the young Norse. "They want to use the power of the storm to reawaken the node, pouring the blood of a lynnewulf into a ritual of suffering and death. Right?"

It was Reidar's turn to stare at Nate in astonishment. "How do you know?"

"Because that's what their followers tried to do to my father in the world we come from," he explained cautiously. "He had refused to use his power to support them, and they tried to sacrifice him to Thurs to open the Nodal Point."

Reidar narrowed his green eyes. "Your father?"

It was clear what he was thinking, and those two words were enough to make Nate understand as well. He hesitated, swallowing hard. For a moment he peeked at Winter, as if looking for support for what he was about to reveal. His friend returned his gaze, seemingly understanding. He saw him nod. "Yup. I inherited the power of the storm from him. I discovered it recently." Before the Norse could say anything, he went on. "I'm not trained, and I can't control it, if that's what you're about to ask me."

Reidar looked more thoughtful, than surprised. "It must be the wyrd. I have no other explanation," he finally said. "Two Children of the Storm and a rejsend—who looks like a half-breed Jötunn." He looked at them with a serious and frowning expression. "If they found out what you are, you would be in as much trouble as I am."

Winter pursed his lips with a determined expression. "Trouble," he repeated, his pronunciation clear, hard but almost perfect. "We ... don't want trouble. We want..." he hesitated, searching for the words. "To go back home."

Reidar raised an eyebrow and peered at Nathaniel as the horses left the thick of the woods and moved side by side, increasing their gait in view of a wide valley enclosed by green hills. "Didn't you say he didn't speak my language?" he asked, curious.

"He learns easily," Nathaniel said shortly. "But he's right; we have to find a way to go home, to open that portal."

"And risk it being used by them too?" Reidar pointed out sharply.

"They don't need to know. And anyway, at the moment we have no idea how to do it. Winter has not been able to wake up the Nodal Point ever since we got here." Nate paused, squaring his shoulders and barely checking on the young Helhest who was swelling the muscles beneath him, determined to break at a gallop. "We ... hoped you could help us," he finally admitted.

Reidar looked at him for a moment, holding the horse in his turn. Then he burst into a bitter laugh. "Help you? And how? The only way I can help you is to try to get you to the Wunderbaar safely. Keep you away from them, before they somehow get back on my trail. Nothing else."

At that point, he gave voice to his mount, pressing his heels against his muscular hips, and the stallion lunged forward, passing from a canter to a full gallop, down towards the valley, its heavy hooves lifting lumps of grass and muddy splashes. Nathaniel and Winter exchanged a look. There was nothing left for them but to follow him.

## CHAPTER THIRTEEN

The bivouac fire, in a clearing between what looked like huge oaks, cast its reddish reflections on the moss-covered trunks, on the raven-coloured mantle of the horses tied a little further away, and on the faces of the three boys, all wrapped in rough blankets. They had eaten some of the supplies Newth had stashed in the Helhestir saddlebags. And now, using those same saddles as cushions, Nathaniel and Winter just lay there, exhausted after the long, almost uninterrupted, day of travel, while the young Norse carved into a knot of wood what seemed to be a female figurine.

"By tomorrow, if all goes well, we will reach Nivak," he said. "It's a fortified city, so far untouched by the conflicts. And even if it makes the journey longer, it's the best route for reaching the territories of Koen Rurik's clans. We'll be safe there."

Nathaniel looked at him, the shadows of the fire forming dark pools between his features. "Once there, what will we do?" he asked, disappointed. In the end, his hope of finding a way back home had turned out to be an illusion. Reidar's solution was similar to what Winter had proposed the night before. And that was not a solution, as he saw it.

The Norse shrugged. "I don't know. I suppose you'll find accommodation there." Perhaps he also realised that he had been harsh, because he hastened to add, "I can't help you, Nate. I have no idea how to awaken a Nodal Point, and I don't know why Winter can no longer reopen it. I'm sorry."

Winter, who had looked at Reidar in hearing his name, frowned. "Speak ... of them," he tried. "Jötnar. Why do you say I look like Jötnar?"

It was the first direct question he had asked, as he had mainly listened throughout the evening. Nathaniel realised he had made incredible progress and that if he kept improving like that, he would not need an interpreter for long.

Reidar darkened. "You look like the half-breeds born out of their conquests and violence," he explained. The dancing shadows from the bivouac reflected off his face, making his expression angrier. "Even if you are not one of them, you will not be able to prevent the Norsihir from looking at you with suspicion. Although they have Norse blood in their veins, the Jötnar sons have always rejected it. After all, they were born and raised in the conquered territories, and they are the only descendants that our enemies can have."

Winter asked Nathaniel for help in understanding some of the words. He seemed troubled. He thought about it, struggling to articulate his feelings. "If they see me, then ... do they want to get me too?"

Reidar sighed, his hands still carving the figurine. "It's likely. It is also why we must avoid them, for that and for the fact that they are looking for me. That war band you've met, it's not the only one on my trail."

"So, it's possible that we'll meet them again," said Nathaniel after a while.

The firelight cast rust-coloured reflections in Reidar's green eyes as he lifted them. "This territory is not entirely safe. There's no certainty we can avoid them from here to Nivak, or beyond. But the further we are from the border and from the battle front, the further we'll be from danger. That's why I'm travelling fast," he explained.

"What I'm trying to say," pressed Nathaniel, "is that maybe we should be armed. You are, after all." He pointed to the short blade at Reidar's belt, tucked into its reinforced leather sheath.

"Until we reach Nivak, you can't really arm yourself, unless you fancy cloth slings and river pebbles, or a knotty branch ... And they would do little, I assure you." He frowned. "In any case, I wouldn't recommend you let one of them coming *that* close to you—their ugly snout could be the last thing you see. No. Your best defence will always be lightning against them. Aren't you a lynnewulf?"

Nathaniel sighed. "I told you, I just found out. I'm not trained. Anyway, if I used it against them, they'd find out that I am like you."

"Better than getting yourself killed so you *won't* let them find out, don't you think? As for the lack of training, it can always be remedied."

"Why? Are you going to teach me?" As he said that, Nate felt a thrill of excitement growing in him.

The young Norse nodded. "Let's reach Nivak first, then we'll see what can be done." He remained silent for a while, turning the figurine between his fingers, freeing it from some thin curls of light wood. He watched her in the firelight with a slight melancholy smile.

"Who is she?" It was Winter who broke the silence, his deep and hoarse voice articulating those two simple Norse words. He looked straight into Reidar's eyes, his own so transparent that the flames coloured them of an eerie red.

"Reika, my sister," he replied hesitantly, without taking his eyes off Winter. His face had become unreadable. "I lost her two months ago, along with the rest of my family, when the Jötnar attacked our lands. My father fell in an attempt to save us, but they caught us and brought us back. Reika didn't inherit the power of the storm from him and, when they realised it, they separated us. They took her west, to make her a slave so she can bear their bastards. Maybe hoping that one of them will be born with the gift of the storm of my family." He paused, pursing his lips. "As for me, they knew I was a lynnewulf, and that's why they kept me alive. It was their biggest mistake." The tone of his voice was flat, impersonal. As if he wasn't talking about himself or his family. But it was obvious that it was a form of self-defence, perhaps the only one he had left in order to move on.

"You ... manage ... escape," Winter urged. He seemed to have understood the whole story without problems.

Nathaniel looked from him to Reidar, with some apprehension. "Maybe he doesn't want to talk about it..." he whispered in their mother tongue. But Winter merely looked at him, before returning to the other boy, waiting for a reply.

"Yes. I managed to escape." Reidar didn't hesitate this time. "They were furious at not being able to capture my father alive, and I was the only opportunity they had left for that damn ritual. My family is one of the few in which the sign of the storm has continued to manifest itself in each generation. We know of no other family in the lands of the Norsihir. At that point, they had everything to lose and I had nothing. I would have died, taking with me as many of those dogs as possible, rather than allow them to awaken the Nodal Point through my blood. This made the difference in the end."

A flash fleeted in his eyes, while the shadows on his hard features became deeper. Anger, revenge. Nathaniel felt those feelings right inside himself. His jaw clenched in surprise. The empathy was getting stronger and stronger.

"Now rest," the Norseman finally said. "We leave at dawn."

And no more words were exchanged for that evening.

*

Nivak's walls seemed to be made of black and shiny obsidian. Reidar explained how the rock had been extracted from the surrounding quarries and worked by artisans skilled in runic magic, an art handed down for generations. Winter and Nathaniel found themselves admiring the fortifications as they passed the east entrance of the town on a road winding uphill. It was almost sunset, and the coming and going was minimal. Nivak was preparing to close the huge gate-doors for the night, hoping in their strengths and the extra protection of the runic symbols wrought in its metal. Yet, none of the guards stopped them. A nod from Reidar was enough to allow them entry.

"Do they know you?" Nathaniel asked, joining him once the paved road became wide enough and opened into an almost empty square. A row of open shops stretched under the long arcades, lit by warm lights.

"Yes. My family is from here. We still have a dwelling within the city, although in recent years we have come here less often, and almost only for my father's business."

It took a while for them to reach their destination, wandering along the alleys of the fortress, up stairways with wide and low steps that seemed made for the passage of horses, even those as huge as those mounted by the three. The streets were almost empty now. The only noises were coming from the houses made of stone and of that glassy-looking substance of every bizarre sparkling colour; they were perched on top of the other, linked by arches and suspended bridges. Voices, chuckles, jingles of crockery; the cry of a newborn baby and the gentle, low melody of a lullaby; the warm light emanating from the closed windows. Passing by as they climbed towards the oldest and most perched part of the town, Nathaniel realised that those warm and welcoming lights came from globes of a crystalline material of rock, in which they seemed to move and dance like fireflies.

The Norse stopped in front of a gate opening on a courtyard. The overgrown vegetation gave it a wild and deserted appearance; a kind of purple ivy had climbed up the walls of the house, rendering its façade almost invisible and ending up merging with the very side of the rocky hill behind it.

"Come," Reidar urged them, dismounting to open the gate.

After entering the courtyard and leaving the horses below a canopy from which curls of green vines protruded dark and intense, Winter whispered to Nathaniel: "How the hell did he open that gate? It was barred."

"I think he drew a symbol on the lock. Could have been a rune, or something similar."

Winter remained puzzled at that, while trying to imitate Nate in removing Jera's saddle. The horse, however, was more focused on grabbing the hood of his sweatshirt with his teeth, yanking it with gusto.

Nathaniel tried not to laugh at the bizarre scene. The young Helhest seemed to have taken her rider to heart. "Here everything works differently. We will have to get used to it, the way things are," he murmured, stroking Berkana's powerful neck, scratching at her withers and thanking her softly in Old Norse. The mare turned her face to look at him, her dark eyes sparkling in the sunset light.

She was so similar to Raido, his father's horse, that he felt his heart tighten in the grip of nostalgia.

After he had finished freeing his Helhest from the harness, Reidar took a sack full of fodder from the saddle and emptied it into the manger in front of the three animals. "Come. Let's get inside," he called them almost brusquely.

Nathaniel looked at him. That place seemed to darken his host's mood. Not surprising, considering what had happened to his family. *Who knows how many memories he has of them in this house*, he thought as he pushed away the anguished feeling that the absence of his own family had insinuated into his soul. He could not afford to give in to despair. Together with his friend, he crossed the courtyard and followed Reidar inside the house.

"He did it again," Winter whispered, noticing how the Norse had opened the heavy wooden door of the house.

It was true, Reidar had traced what looked like a sign on the door, which had opened with a click. He pushed them inside, preceding his guests in a large entrance hall.

"What are they, runic protections?" Nathaniel ventured.

Reidar nodded. "How much do you know about runes?" he asked as he approached a big globe on one side of the entrance.

"Very little, and mainly theory. Not many of the descendants of the Norsihir, as far as I know, has this kind of ability," he admitted.

Reidar seemed to focus on that opaque crystal globe that sparkled in the last lights of the sunset. Long shadows lurked in the corners of the hall, a prelude to the upcoming night. He moved his fingers, touching the convex and soft curve of the object, drawing a sign on it.

The same warm glow that Nathaniel had seen inside the windows he had just walked by, spread inside the sphere. A pleasant light cast out the shadows.

"This was a simple rune. Those for the doors and gates, a little less so, but I've been trained to use them since I was a child. In any case, I've always used them in my family's home, so it shouldn't surprise you that I'm so quick," he explained. "Doesn't it work that way, where you come from?" he asked then, with genuine curiosity.

Nathaniel shook his head. "No, it's all very different with us. We had to come up with other solutions ... Very few have skills similar to yours, and they don't use them often."

Reidar observed him with a mixture of interest and perplexity. Then he nodded without asking more and led them into the two-storey house.

"You can sleep here," he said, inviting them to enter a spacious room on the ground floor. He lit more of those opaque globes, illuminating the environment, and pointed to a smaller door on the other side of the room. "If you go through there, you will find the hot springs at the bottom of the stairs. It's a pleasant place. In any case, I'll be upstairs." He looked as if he wanted to say more for a moment, then concluded: "See you in the morning."

He left with them the last supplies received from Niels Newth two days earlier, before leaving the room and closing the door behind him.

Alone, the two looked at each other for a moment.

"I have the feeling that this house is not good for his mood," Winter said, with a hint of sarcasm.

"It was his family's house," remarked Nathaniel, giving him a reproachful look for what had seemed to him an unkind thing to say. "How would you feel in his place?"

"I have no idea," he cut short, with a defiant smirk.

It made Nate instantly regret asking him, because behind that bold expression, which by now he had learned to recognise, he suddenly felt an intense bitterness which went to tear his soul with its claws.

He looked away, trying to hide the burning embarrassment that had seized him, and focused on the room where they would spend the night. The high-vaulted ceiling, crossed by a beam of light wood, was lost in the darkness. The furniture was also made of wood. Nathaniel noticed one ornate desk full of drawers leaning against a wall, with a chair positioned in front of it; a big wardrobe that turned out to be almost empty, except for a few items of old male clothes; and a bed big enough to sleep three. The stone floor was covered with soft carpets, and on the walls symbols of constant changing colours could be glimpsed, seemingly coming to life under the light of the spheres runic, as if they wanted to tell stories in an unknown language.

"Nate, come and see!" Winter's hoarse and deep voice, echoing and a little distorted, made him turn towards the little door in their room.

It was open, and a strange pale, silvery glow poured in, splashing onto the floor. "Winter?" he called, approaching.

"Come on!"

His voice came from within the passage, and it seemed far away. Nathaniel stopped in the doorway, peered inside and felt his eyes widening in surprise. A staircase, carved into the live rock, descended, penetrating into the depths of the hill on which Nivak was perched. The walls and ceiling of the passage, and even each of the steps, seemed to be quilted with stars. Whirling flashes, in the dark, filled the air, illuminating it with a dreamlike glow.

"What the hell...?" His voice bounced off the walls of the passage, distorting and turning back several times. "It's crazy..."

"And you haven't seen anything yet. Come on down!" Winter urged him, laughing, from somewhere at the bottom of the steps.

Carefully, almost as if fearing that the steps were only an illusion of lights and shadows, he began to descend, placing a hand on the wall to his right: it was cold, a little moist, but solid. The light fleeted randomly on the polished, dark stone. At the bottom of the stairs, the passage opened into a large cave, lit in the same way. Winter was kneeling beside a low, regular pool of crystal-clear water. The effect of the lights played beneath the surface, generating silvery reflections that made the pool resemble a round mirror. From the water rose a light veil of steam, and a thin stream ran out of the tub, digging a path between the polished rocks of the floor and disappearing with a slight gurgling in the depths of an opening.

"It's the hot springs Reidar mentioned," said Winter, touching the surface with the tip of his fingers, fascinated. "This place is incredible."

Nathaniel approached, astonished, a slight smile on his lips. He knelt beside Winter and in turn immersed a hand in the water. A pleasant warmth enveloped his fingers, while a series of concentric circles quivered around them, breaking the mirrored stillness.

He heard his friend standing up. Then a rustling, and saw his black sweatshirt landing noiselessly on the polished stone floor. Nathaniel watched him as he shed his sneakers and jeans, revealing a dry and athletic body, the skin of a diaphanous whiteness that, in that strange underground cave, took on as many unreal shades as those on the surface of the water. His eyes went up, along the slender and taut legs, over the skin at places irritated from the too many hours spent in the saddle. They paused for a moment on the thorny tribal tattoos chasing each other on his torso, up to the shoulders and arms, telling in their own way, stories of urban and post-modern rites of passage; and on the scars that marked that milky skin, telling other stories, more grim and secret: that network of subtle signs inside the forearms, and the most recent scratches, by now almost vanished, those of the tribute that had opened the portal, but that had not managed to unlock it again. And the old burn on his chest, into which the coven of Maple Tree had read the dark omens of the rune of Thurs; not surprisingly, because it was just what it seemed.

And yet those marks could not hide what, in the eyes of Nathaniel, was becoming an incontrovertible fact: he was beautiful. Of a wild and extraordinary beauty, alien and careless. And he seemed aware of it to the point of showing it off with a sort of natural arrogance. "What are you doing?" he whispered finally, looking away and feeling stupid for asking.

"What does it look like? Getting rid of the dust from the journey," replied Winter with a hoarse laugh. He finished undressing and entered the water, using a series of steps carved into the side of the pool. He sank to his neck with a thankful sigh, then he dived completely only to emerge several seconds later with a spray, the white hair glued to the sides of his face. "Why don't you come in?" he urged, going to sit on a step on the other side of the hot spring, his back leaning against the smooth wall and his arms spread out on the edge of the pool. "If I were you, I wouldn't wait one more minute." He pressed the back of his neck against the polished end of the tub and sighed with pleasure. "You don't know what I'd give for a cigarette right now. I guess I'll have to get used to the idea of quitting."

Nathaniel hesitated. There was, in the movements of the other young man, a sureness that threw him. A sensual and wild grace that, somehow, was making him feel inexplicably embarrassed. He had never felt this way during the countless times he had shared the men's locker room at school with friends and other students, and he tried to drive away that feeling, especially as Winter was looking at him with an air that seemed both fun and mischievous.

Maybe he had imagined everything. He shook his head, getting rid of his clothes with  nervous tugs, before entering without further delay in the warm spring water, inside the rocky side of the hill where Reidar's house was set like a strange, austere jewel. He immersed himself quickly, settling on the opposite side of Winter, staring at the vaulted of the large cave, with its sparkling light effects, light blue and ethereal. "Do you also think that we will never go back?" he asked after a while.

Winter sighed. "I don't know. But we certainly don't have many alternatives at the moment, except following Reidar up to that place where he wants to take us. What was it called? Wunderbaar?"

Nathaniel nodded. "I'm worried. When I think about the situation we got into, I can't not be," he murmured, looking for Winter's transparent eyes, which were looking back with a vibrant intensity now. "We should never had crossed the portal the way we did. Nobody knows where we are. They haven't even seen us leave the house."

Winter wrinkled his nose in a grimace, as if those words bothered him. But then his expression softened. "Listen ... don't think about it now. There is no immediate solution, but I haven't said that I'll stop trying," he tried to reassure him, calmly—unusual even for him. "We need to know more about this place. How it works. If there is a way to allow me to reopen the portal, we will find it."

He smiled then, a bold and convinced smile that, by now, Nathaniel knew, hid a very different fragility. He couldn't smile back. Not fully, but he nodded, trying to be brave. On one thing Winter was right: there were no immediate solutions.

They remained immersed in the small natural pool for a while, relaxing, relieving muscle soreness, speaking softly in the Norse language so that Winter could continue to learn. He could already sustain basic conversations.

"You don't know what I'd give to have your quick-learning ability," commented Nate as he came out of the water, recovering the clothes left on the floor. "Some of my school subjects would stop giving me nightmares."

Winter shrugged, emerging in turn from the tub. "I still need to make a mental effort—and I feel it. I prefer it when I have to learn something physical," he replied, amused.

"Yes, but I bet it's always better than banging your head on pages and pages of Maths and Chemistry formulas," he muttered back, walking up the stone staircase that led to their room.

"I never had to bother," Winter admitted, following him. He laughed softly. "I left school before graduating."

"A genius thrown to the winds. What a waste," Nathaniel joked, turning towards him. His eyes were on him. Clear and sparkling, the eyes of a predator. Without even knowing why, he blushed and ran up the last steps, pushing the door to re-enter the room. He opened the wardrobe, then its drawers, looking for something that could pass for a sheet of fabric. Finding what he needed, he wrapped it around his waist, grateful, casting a curious glance to other clothes inside. They didn't look very different from those of the Norse. "You think Reidar will be annoyed if we take a change of clothes?" he said, hoping that Winter wouldn't detect in his voice the emotions felt before. "If this stuff fits us, that is," he added, with a sigh.

"Well, I really fancy clean clothes, and if we have to stay here we might as well start dressing like the locals, right?" Winter began to fish among shirts, jackets and trousers. He didn't seem to care about his own nakedness, of which Nathaniel, instead, continued to feel fully aware.

After a while, they found enough comfortable clothing to be satisfied. They ate of the supplies that Reidar had left them before lying exhausted on the huge bed, protecting themselves against the cold air with what looked like a feather-filled quilt. It was dusty and with a vague hint of mould, but warm. Any attempt to chat failed as they both gave in to sleep—inevitable after a long day of travel and the warm and relaxing bath. Winter didn't wake up screaming, as had happened a couple of times even in the last few days. It was Nathaniel who woke up, towards dawn, when the first blades of thin light leaked from the closed shutters, dancing insistently on his face. He frowned, wondering for a moment where he was, and realising that he wasn't in his bed, neither in New York, nor in Maple Tree Farm. In the handful of seconds that his brain took to remind him that he was in a universe away from home, he also noticed the pleasant warmth which he felt, given off from the body huddled against his. He remained motionless; he even stopped breathing while the awareness of the gentle weight pressed against his back became powerful and concrete. He felt Winter's warm and regular breathing on the nape of his neck. His knees pressed in the hollow of his own. He had wrapped a white and tattooed arm around the chest, squeezing him gently. They lay there, tight and snug, like two spoons inside a drawer. No nightmare, no tears. No soft cry into the dark. Only that unconscious search for a contact. Nathaniel sighed. He crouched better in that bland and dreamlike embrace, letting his muscles relax once again. And he returned to sleep.

## CHAPTER FOURTEEN

A thick fog enveloped the base of the hills, pouring out into the valley and hiding the treetops. The humidity in the cold morning air stuck to the skin, wetting the hair of the travellers and the thick mane of the Helhestir, threatening to change at any moment into thin rain. The sky was dark, gray and thick with low clouds.

Another whole day had passed before they had resumed their journey. Reidar had let them rest, and then had led them to the Nivak market. Among shops sunken under the arcades of lava stone and outdoor benches, they had stocked up with supplies for the road and weapons. Thea young Norse had had no problem paying for them, while Nathaniel and Winter had only been able to thank him, devoid of money as they were. Now they both sported a short sword at their belt, similar to that of Reidar, and bows and quivers hanging from the saddle of their horses.

"Don't tell me you can even use a bow ..." laughed Nate, when Winter had tried one out under the small, sharp eyes of a bearded and wary merchant—a man who had kept on staring at him as if he had feared a short hand shot on his part. Moreover, Reidar's fears had turned out to be true: people were wary of Winter, considering him one of those half-breeds born from the conquests of the Jötnar. He was trying not to show it, but Nathaniel could tell that the situation was making their host unsettled. It was just as he had feared: another world, but the same hostile and wary looks towards Winter, who, in turn, answered to the uneasiness in the only way he knew, with bravado and boldness. At least this time Winter was not reacting with the usual aggression towards those who doubted his intentions.

Winter had ignored the merchant's dirty looks and had laughed in return, focusing only on Nathaniel. "And why shouldn't I?" he had replied, as if it were the most natural thing in the world. "There was this guy, in Rutland, fixated with bows. I worked for him for a while, and he taught me."

"And in three days you became better than him, I bet."

"Something like that," Winter had replied, unperturbed.

The weather had changed overnight—another night that the two boys had spent hugging each other in the only bed in the room, without saying a word about it, as if it hadn't even happened—and when they had left Nivak, the following day, the sky was already threatening to open up in a sudden downpour of rain. It hadn't improved in the early hours of travel, but this had not prevented Reidar from continuing to journey northeast, at a good trot, taking advantage of the less uneven terrain and wider roads that extended along a valley tamed by the presence of men, between cultivated fields and verdant pastures. To their right, the fog slipped through the trees of a dense forest, erasing its contours.

"What's the plan?" asked Nathaniel, pressing his heels against Berkana's shiny and raven sides to increase her gait and flank the young Norse on the left. It was not Gornil, but in those few days of travel he seemed to have reached a good link with the huge Helhest.

"We continue northeast," Reidar said, turning slightly to look at him, his pale eyes clouded over like the sky above them.

It seemed that the stop in Nivak had made him gloomy and thoughtful. Nate had no idea how many memories that place could have awoken in him, but in any case it didn't seem to have done him any good.

"I'm hoping to leave the valley and the gully between the slopes of the Groebjergen ahead behind us by today." He pointed to the rocky and cloaked hills of fog that could be glimpsed at the bottom of the valley. "I want to stop for the night in a mining village to the north. We shouldn't have problems if we keep this pace."

Nathaniel nodded.

Winter, a few meters behind them, picked up the pace to reach them. "How long till we get to Wunderbaar?" He asked, barely holding the filly pawing restlessly beneath him.

"If we keep going without stops, five days. Maybe six, to be safer," replied Reidar, glancing at him. "What's wrong with Jera?" he asked, noting his difficulty in controlling her.

"I don't know. She's ... scared," Winter replied, trying to calm her. He didn't have time to add anything else. As infected by the restlessness of his mount, the other two Helhestir began to get excited.

"They are afraid," said Nathaniel, with a sudden urgency. He searched for Reidar's eyes, as if his horse had managed to transmit him what he felt. "And I think we should trust their ... Oh shit." There was no need for him to say anything else, or to indicate what he had seen.

Reidar and Winter turned towards the thick trees to their right, on the other side of the fields capped by mist. Amid the grey that veiled the dark green of the conifers, a group of equally grey figures had appeared. They were still far away, but Reidar had no doubts about their nature, not even for a moment.

"Jötnar," he growled between his teeth, "and they have shapeshifters with them ... We have to leave. Now. Follow me!"

The young Norse planted his heels in Vunjo's flanks, making the horse spring forward in a rush and steer him towards the bottom of the valley. And yet, it was as if time had slowed down to a stop.

Nathaniel stared at them with a twisted mixture of horror and curiosity—a handful of greyish figures on the edge of the forest, creatures that came from an early age, in the stories of his coven, he had identified as the most fearsome enemies of his world, those to keep far away at any cost, those who, without a tight control of the Nodal Points, would have brought Ragnarök to Earth. They were still far away, but he could distinguish certain details with impressive clarity. Some of them were on foot, others were riding what looked like giant white felines; everyone had a stature and a tonnage out of the ordinary, and suddenly it was clear to him why they had the name of the giants of the frost of Nordic mythology, and why people looked at Winter suspiciously: apart from their proportions, leonine features, and the fact that they wore protections that sparkled like white gold in the milky light of the day, they shared with him the diaphanous pallor of the skin, the colour of the hair, which they wore long and twisted into complicated motifs on the shoulders, and the glacial glow of their eyes. For a moment, looking at his friend, he felt inside the certainty that people's suspicions were real, and that he was indeed a half-breed born of that lineage. But he didn't have time to fully flesh out that thought, as right at that moment Winter gave a start and leaned forward on the saddle, dropping the reins to bring both hands to the temples, with a hoarse moan.

"Winter! What's happening?" With difficulty, he managed to lead a nervous and pounding Berkana alongside Winter's Helhest, while he had bent forward even more. "Winter! Look at me! What's happening to you?" he snapped, unable to hide his concern and fear, ringing out loudly in his voice.

"In my head ... it's ... in my head!" he moaned, hands pressed against the temples and an expression of suffering and confusion on his face, so pale as to made one doubt he was even alive.

Nathaniel reached for Jera's reins, trying to grab them. "Reidar!" he shouted, looking for the Norse and realising with dismay that he was already a fair distance ahead on the path which led to the hills. "Winter is sick. Wait!" His voice broke when he realised that one of the imposing Jötnar, riding a huge cat, had stepped forward at the head of what seemed to be a platoon. And despite the distance between them, he understood instantly that his eyes were focused on Winter. He shouted something incomprehensible to his companions, raising an arm, and the group set off charging like a single entity, the riders in arrowhead formation behind the leader and the foot-soldiers further back.

"Move!" cried Reidar, his stallion rearing up mad with anger at having been restrained. It seemed clear that he wanted to put as much distance as possible, and in the shortest time, between him and those riding the shapeshifting creatures. "They saw him! They want him!"

That awareness hit Nathaniel's brain full on and made him jolt as if hit by electricity. They wanted Winter. That Jötunn's gaze he had already noticed didn't leave any doubts. They had seen him, thought of him as one of their children, and they wanted to take him back. By force and against his will, if necessary.

"Winter! Can you hear me? We must leave immediately. Come on! Please!" He tried to shake him and got nothing but a hoarse groan in response as the boy staggered on his saddle.

It would have been useless to grab Jera's reins to drag her away. It was clear that he would have fallen at the first attempt at galloping, and at that point it would have been impossible to save him from the incoming Jötnar. With them, a storm front came too. A cold gust of wind hit him, while the rain began to fall in a violent roar.

There was no time.

He could escape.

Or he could stay.

But he had no choice, and he knew it: he wouldn't leave him to them. He dismounted and Berkana didn't wait: leaping forward past Reidar's stallion, she headed towards the bottom of the valley. Nathaniel tried to grab Winter's filly by the reins as she became more and more nervous. If nothing else, she seemed to have realized that something was wrong and that her rider was no longer able to lead her. But she rolled her eyes and sidestepped as the boy approached her to try to mount on the saddle. Winter swayed, falling forward on the animal's mighty neck.

"Oh, no ... no, *damn it*!" Nathaniel moaned, suddenly feeling, like a cold river in his veins, all the terror of the Helhest. If he couldn't get himself onto the saddle and lead her away from there, their escape attempt would soon be over.

He took a deep breath, trying to calm himself. He knew very well that his fear would also be transmitted to Jera. Instead, he had to exploit his empathic abilities to their advantage. He tried again to approach her from the left, this time managing to grab the reins. He prayed that she wouldn't start again, or worse, that she wouldn't decide to rear up or run away.

"Come on, Jera, I just want us to leave ... together," he panted as he clung strongly to the saddle. He felt her pound the great hooves on the ground, raising splashes of mud. She chewed the bite, staring at him with a sparkling, dark and frightened eye, but stood there waiting for him. Nathaniel slipped one foot into the stirrup, which Winter, now unconscious, had lost, and settled himself on the Helhest. Clumsy, awkward and with his heart in his throat, but he had done it.

He barely had time to tighten his arms around Winter's body before the mare gathered like a steel spring under him and snapped forward, releasing all the energy of the mighty muscles in a wild gallop. The boy gritted his teeth, grabbed the knob of the saddle and the thick corvine mane, praying that he had enough strength in his legs to stay on the saddle while supporting his friend. He had never galloped so desperately and messily in his life.

Before him, Reidar was now reaching the end of the valley and the gully between the rugged rocky hills that he had aimed for from the beginning. Berkana was on the verge of slipping into the passage. Nathaniel realized he was too far behind, and when he dared to cast a quick glance over one shoulder, he saw that the pursuers were gaining ground. The Jötnar riding the felines, guided by what seemed to be their leader and which, by now he was sure, must have done something to Winter, were opening up in a wider formation, like a fan, preparing to surround him.

*We will never make it*, he thought, as a sense of dark despair penetrated his bones as coldly as the furious rain that was whipping them, a wall of water making it difficult even to figure out which direction to take.

The sudden pungent smell of ozone made his eyes water. He felt a violent shudder and, if he hadn't been so soaked, he was sure he would have felt the hairs on his body stand on the back of his neck. The vibrant rattle of lightning announced itself behind him: a blade of sulfurous light that split the sky in two and struck among the pursuers, suddenly scattering them. The deafening roar of thunder shook the ground, so close that lightning had fallen, and stifled the screams of fury and pain of their adversaries.

Nathaniel looked up with difficulty and saw Reidar at the entrance of the canyon, a clenched fist on the reins of his pounding Helhest and the other raised and vibrating in the air. And he understood.

A warm thrill of admiration and relief filled his chest. The lynnewulf was fighting for them. He would have liked to do the same, but he just tightened his legs around Jera's hips, urging her with his heels to increase her gait. Behind him, another spike of lightning cut the air into a snapping crack, illuminating the valley, darkened by storm-laden clouds, for a moment. More screams, along with the rumble of thunder. Nathaniel didn't have time to turn around, but he was sure that one of the pursuers must have been hit.

He risked throwing a glance over his shoulder only when the Helhest began to cover the last stretch of the path before the rocky gorge, raising splashes of mud and murky water under its hooves. The Jötnar on the back of their big cats were scattered and tried to regain cohesion, while those on foot were regrouping. But their leader didn't seem to have suffered from Reidar's attacks, and he kept pointing straight at him, leaning over the neck of that sort of gigantic lion that he mounted. Nathaniel felt his gaze on himself, like cold splinters of poisonous ice. Suddenly, he saw him lift an arm, stretching his fingers forward, claws charged with malevolent intentions.

"Oh, shit ..." he groaned, leaning forward, squeezing the unconscious Winter and praying that his filly could run even faster. He knew something bad was going to happen. Moments later, his hunch came true.

A series of sharp whistles seemed to surround him, and then the mud around him and between Jera's paws began to rise in a sequence of rapid explosions, as if a string of shrapnel had been shot down over them. He heard the Helhest neighing in fury and pain, a high-pitched, almost human sound that knotted his guts and, immediately after, a sudden pain tore at his left arm by the shoulder, ripping a hoarse cry out of him. He looked and saw what seemed to be a large shard of crystal planted in his flesh, at the biceps. A dark, liquid stain spread rapidly around the epicenter of the impact, soaking the rain-soaked sleeve with a thick heat.

He cursed between his teeth, suffocating a groan in his throat. As he galloped, it seemed to him that the splinter dug further into his arm, wrapping itself in turns of barbed wire and nails. He forced himself to focus on the increasingly strenuous attempt to remain on the saddle and to hold Winter's lifeless body against him. His thighs and calves burned with a tormenting fire, and he began to fear that his legs would betray him, and that his muscles would stop obeying that desperate need for resistance. He hardly realized that he had reached the mouth of the passage between the rocks, and he understood this only from the fact that the Helhest's hooves began to resonate with the force of hammers on the bare stone, instead of sending back the dull thud to his ears and the vague suction of the muddy ground.

"Don't stop!" He seemed to hear Reidar scream behind him, which he had passed without even realizing, in that desperate race. "Whatever happens, *don't stop!*"

Then he felt again the violent tension of the lightning that was discharging on the ground, and the echoing bark of thunder was followed by something much more frightening: the roar of boulders that crashed. He didn't dare turn around this time; he continued to gallop, sobbing now without restraint at the pain and terror he felt, gripping the mane of the filly.

They raced along the rocky canyon, the reverberation of the earth trembling around them, the dark and deep sound of the landslide that chased them. The air movement hit them hard and Nathaniel leaned further forward, pressing his wet cheek against Winter's back for a long moment. He was surprised by the vivid intensity with which his senses sent him broken and neat scraps of that single, ephemeral instant: the spherical glitter of raindrops amid the long and wild mane of the Helhest, reflecting the enraged sky and the glow left by lightning; the wet and slippery leather of the reins between the fingers, the rough texture of Winter's shirt under his cheek mixed with that of rain and wet fabric, the smell of his skin, the same that he had felt as he embraced him, in the Nivak's house.

He closed his eyes as time seemed to expand out of proportion and lose consistency. He clung to the placid and reassuring memory of that moment. *I will not abandon you. I won't let you down*, he thought forcefully, opening his eyes again. With a cry of determination and pain, he straightened his shoulders, forcing his tired muscles into a last effort. In fact, he didn't even know where they were going, but he knew he couldn't stop. Reidar had said so, and he would do so.

After a few hundred meters, as the rain began to subside, turning into a light and constant drizzle, the passage seemed to widen, the bottom covered with rocks giving way to a grassy stretch and less steep sides, covered with bushes and vegetation. Jera, exhausted, began to slow down, and Nathaniel indulged her, just as tired. His arm throbbed, and when he tried to move it he realized how stiff it was. He gave up almost immediately, fearing he might make the situation worse as he felt his stomach knot with nausea. He looked around. For the moment he was alone; of Reidar there was no trace. Suffocating the dismay that this awareness had caused him, and trying not to think of the feeling of loss and anguish that gripped his guts, he finally let the Helhest walk, gasping for breath. The pursuit, if nothing else, seemed concluded. He had an idea that Reidar had crumbled the entrance to the gully between the rocky hills, closing the narrow entrance and preventing the passage of the Jötnar at their heels. He didn't want to give a voice to an obvious fear: what if the young Norse had been caught in the landslide? What would he and Winter do, alone? That caused an avalanche of other thoughts. He looked down at Winter and pursed his lips in concern. He tried to shake him with his right hand.

"Winter ...? Winter, can you hear me?"

Nothing.

With an anguished sigh, he looked around again. Maybe he should start looking for a sheltered place to stop and wait for Reidar. Because he would come back. He would join them. He repeated it several times, like a mantra, until he could at least convince himself.

"Hey!"

A thin, urgent voice. It seemed to come from a thick tree a little further on, to his right.

"Hey, you! This way!"

## CHAPTER FIFTEEN

Nathaniel frowned, turning to the caller. He prompted his filly forward and saw Berkana amid a tangle of brambles and bushes. A thin, hooded figure held her by the bit, and the mare looked calm and poised. And, as if that presence gave off a reassuring aura, even Jera seemed to calm down and approached without fear. From under the glossy rain hood, in the shade of the trees, a little boy's face rose up, peering at him with a pair of glittering grey eyes like the heart of flint and full of curiosity. He could not have been more than twelve or thirteen.

"Who are you? What happened to you?" he asked, his voice low and a little hoarse, but melodious. The Helhest that he held by the reins seemed to appreciate that tone, so much so that he lowered the little muzzle on his shoulder, rummaging with his lips in the folds of his coat. The boy raised a hand to gently rub her rain-soaked forehead, but he didn't take his eyes off Nathaniel.

"We are ... travellers. A group of Jötnar chased us. There were three of us, but my other companion stayed behind to stop them."

The boy tilted his head to the side, a few tufts of red escaping the edge of the hood. "You're hurt," he remarked, with a small grimace on his young, freckled face. "Your Helhest is hurt and your friend doesn't look well either."

He had a stronger accent than Reidar's, a more rustic and direct speech. Even Nathaniel could tell the difference.

He inhaled, then smiled a little. "I think you need a safe haven, where those odious giants can't find you. Come on, follow me. I'll bring you there."

Nate's lips tightened, shaking his head. "I can't. My friend wouldn't find us and I need to know what's happened to him. There was a landslide at the entrance to the passage that leads from the Nivak valley to here."

The other frowned, snorting. "*Of course* there was a landslide. There was lightning coming down like there was no tomorrow. Your friend is a lynnewulf, isn't he?" he commented, wrinkling his small, upturned nose. "No wonder the big, stinking white thugs are chasing you."

Then he blinked a few times, focusing his gaze on Winter's lifeless body. "By the way, why did you take one of their bastards with you?"

"He's not one of their bastards," growled Nate. "He's just ... Winter."

The red-haired boy looked at him perplexed. "Oh, well. And I'm *just* Cress. And who are you?" he asked, bowing his head to one shoulder, with an impertinent smirk.

"Nate," he replied, before feeling the need to reiterate. "I'm telling you he's not one of them. We are rejsendir ... me and him. We have nothing to do with this world." It wasn't really the truth, but the boy didn't need to know it .

Cress raised an eyebrow barely darker than his hair, and a surprised but also amused expression appeared between the shadows of the hood. "Of course we hear of strange stories of late," he said. "But if that's not a half-breed of the Jötnar, I'm no longer a heks."

Nathaniel had no idea what he meant, but he didn't have time to ask. From behind a formation of rocks at the entrance to the clearing, an excited sound of footsteps and broken branches caught his attention. Instinctively, he turned in that direction, his right hand coming down to tighten the hilt of the sword tied to his side, a rush of adrenaline that stretched his muscles ready to spring.

"Nate! Smukoj, are you okay?" Reidar's voice. Unmistakable.

He slumped his shoulders, relaxing, the torrent of overwhelming relief making his head spin. Only at that moment, as he staggered away from the saddle and his legs threatened to give in under his weight, did he really realise how exhausted he was. He clung to the long, soaked mane of Jera with his healthy arm hand, the other stiff and abandoned along his side. "Reidar!" he called in turn, the relieved tone clear in his voice. Even the young Norse looked exhausted and limped on the right side. He was on foot.

He approached the tree patch and stared first at Nathaniel, looking seriously at his wounded arm, then at Winter, still abandoned on the Helhest, and finally at the young stranger half-hidden among the brambles. "Vunjo didn't make it," he explained dryly, trying to keep his voice steady, but without success.

He was battered and muddy. He had risked a lot with that trick of the landslide, but now he was there with them again, and hope returned to dance in Nate's soul. "He's Cress and says he can help us hide from the Jötnar. Give us refuge."

Reidar looked at the boy closely, then pursed his lips and nodded.

"Thank you. It would be better to move then. I don't know how much the landslide will be able to stop them."

They moved away from the main street, entering the thick of the forest, on paths that only the red-haired teenager seemed able to identify.

"They could follow our tracks," observed Nathaniel after a while, leading Jera by the reins, trying not to think of the painful flashes that went up his arm, from time to time moving his gaze to Winter's lifeless body and his overly pale face, uselessly looking for signs of recovery.

Cress shook his head. "Nah ... I already told you that I'm a heks, haven't I? They'll not find anything. This is my territory, and it's protected."

Nate cast a puzzled glance at Reidar, who merely looked back, shrugging his shoulders. However, he seemed to trust the little guy leading them through the trees, and neither of them added anything else.

Eventually, the forest thinned out, giving way to a small valley set like an emerald of an intense green amidst the rocky hills where they had penetrated. A rushing stream full of waterfalls crossed it; they crossed it using a bridge of boards and trunks, solid enough to hold the weight of the two Helhestir. On the other side, Cress led them over a grassy slope and up a small path carved between rocks drawn by wind and weather to a flat ledge, wide enough to allow the horses to stop side by side. In the wall, there was the wide entrance of what appeared to be a rather deep cave, covered in part by a screen of branches tied together. Cress pushed it aside and disappeared inside.

A few moments later he leaned out again. The hood of his heavy cloth cloak had slid over his shoulders, revealing a short ruffled mop that seemed made of living flames. "So? Get your friend and come on in. You can leave the horses under that rock." He pointed up at the ledge that would protect the animals from the rain. "If you have fodder for them, it's time to hand it out. They deserve it," he added, returning to the cave.

Nathaniel and Reidar exchanged glances, then the Norseman nodded with his chin on the other's injured arm. "Do you think you can help me, Smukoj?"

Nate nodded. He gritted his teeth, forcing himself to ignore the turns of barbed wire that seemed to stick into his shoulder when Reidar pulled Winter down from the saddle, grabbing him from under the armpits, and letting him lift the boy's legs. They carried him together inside the cave. When they finally put him on a bed, Nathaniel realized that an unhealthy cold sweat had stuck his tunic to his back, and he was forced to sit down on the floor covered with woven mats. The dizziness that had caught him left him gasping and dazed for a moment.

Reidar looked at him, with concern. "Stay here. Rest. I'm going to fix Jera and Berkana, then we'll see if we can take care of that wound."

Nate nodded, swallowing hard to try to calm the sudden rebellion in his stomach. He narrowed his eyes to focus. A myriad of bright acid-green dots floated in front of him, while a sinister darkness barricaded itself at the corners of his field of vision. He leaned back, pressing his nape against the cave wall, taking slow, deep breaths, until he thought he was feeling better.

When he opened his eyes again, Cress was sitting on his heels looking at him very closely. He had not heard it coming.

"I really think it's time to take a look at that wound, you know?" he commented in his low, gentle voice that seemed to fascinate the horses.

Nathaniel smiled slightly, realising that he liked it too.

"How did your friend call you? Smukoj?"

Nate nodded. There was something in the little guy that instinctively made him feel good. "Yeah, because of my eyes. They are different."

Cress came even closer, curious. "It's true! One is green and the other blue." He smiled with contagious enthusiasm. "Never seen before, eyes like that. It's a powerful symbol, you know? Surely you were born for something big."

He said it with such conviction that Nathaniel found himself staring at him, surprised by the other's bizarre intuition and not knowing how to respond, or what to add. He could have told him that he was part of an ancient prophecy he had known by heart since he could remember, but something held him back. The bizarre moment seemed to pass as it had come.

"Well, Smukoj—I can call you that too, right? Of course I can." He had answered his own question. "Now I'd better deal with that ugly scratch, uhu?"

Nathaniel took a deep breath, exhaling the air in a sigh. Then he looked at Winter. "I don't think my injury is that bad. But I'm worried about him," he admitted, frowning. "The Jötnar ... one of them—the one who seemed to be their leader ... I think he was the one who did this to him."

Cress became more serious. "Likely. He must have got into his head to subdue him and he couldn't stop him. It's not strange if he didn't know how." He shrugged. "Were they after you, because of him?"

Nathaniel pursed his lips. "I think so. What about this mental attack, then? Can it have caused him damage? He's been unconscious for a long time now, with no sign of recovery." He couldn't say those words without anguish.

Cress reassured him. "Don't worry, the White Ones are cruel, but if there is one thing they would never do is cause permanent damage to their half-breeds: they are the only future they have."

"Why doesn't he recover, then?"

"Be patient. It's not a pleasant experience when one of them gets into your head, you know? His brain must have switched off to defend itself. Let him rest and he'll wake up soon enough," he said with conviction. Nathaniel felt soothed by that pleasant and confident voice.

"On the other hand, we'd better take care of your arm. You don't want it to swell and go black, do you? Sorry, but I'm not a laege, and if your friend isn't either, we'll have to work on it the traditional way. More unpleasant, but I assure you I can do it well."

*He talks so much*, Nathaniel thought, stunned. Then he sighed. "I am a laege. But I can't heal myself, right?"

Cress chuckled. "Of course not! You say you're a laege and you don't know? Funny that ... These are the basics."

"Yes, but I *am* at the basics," muttered Nate, annoyed. "Some things I discovered very recently. And in the world where we come from, Winter and I work differently."

The boy raised his palms up, as if in a cheerful gesture of surrender. "Alright, alright! One day you'll explain to me what world you are talking about. Come on, let's get you back on your feet."

At that moment Reidar returned to the cave, while Cress disappeared in the semidarkness at the back of the shelter. "How are you?" he asked, settling himself next to Nathaniel.

The boy raised his healthy shoulder. "I was better before I had a piece of glass in my arm."

"That's not glass. It's *ice*," explained the Norse as Cress returned, bringing a wooden bowl filled with water and several cloth bags tied with knotted coloured laces. "Many Jötnar have power over the elements; wind and ice are the most common for them. Those splinters also injured Jera. You were lucky to get away with it so cheaply."

"Big guy, how about giving me a hand?" Cress asked at that moment.

Reidar smiled a little, looking at the boy with the red hair with a certain curiosity, as he placed everything he had brought with him from the back of the cave onto the mats beside Nathaniel.

"As for you," Cress resumed, handing Nate a cup of terra cotta adorned with thin black geometric motifs, "drink this. It is for the pain, and it will help you heal."

The liquid in the cup was warm and had a full-bodied taste with a vaguely sweet and fermented aftertaste, almost alcoholic. Nathaniel swallowed everything without a word. Almost immediately, it seemed to him that he could no longer focus, and as his vision blurred his perceptions became more distant and distorted. "Dammit, have you drugged me?" he muttered, struggling to form the words that intertwined in his mouth, his tongue suddenly numb.

He heard Cress's low laughter, hoarse and a little altered. "Drugged! I know much more powerful substances than these. It's just a little help. Don't fight it, let yourself go and relax. Everything will be fine."

Nate could do nothing but give in. And it was good in the end, because when Cress said that dealing with that wound would be an unpleasant thing, he wasn't wrong. The splinter of elemental ice, solid and sharp as a diamond, had planted itself in his shoulder deeper than he had imagined and, after they had ripped off the sleeve of his coat to gain access to the laceration, Reidar was forced to keep him still to allow the boy to extract the foreign body.

After a while, Nathaniel realized that the strangled screams and the breathless and unrepeatable impulses he heard coming from abysmal distances were his. When Cress began to mend the wound after cleaning it as best he could, the darkness swallowed him completely, wrapping him in a thick velvet blanket. It was soft and warm, and he let himself sink into it.

# Chapter Sixteen

*The first thing he realises is that it's cold. An intense cold, burning, that bites the skin with thousands of tiny fangs. There is nothing around him, except for that milky dense fog that makes one blind. It seems that myriads of annoying black stars explode in it, expanding to infinity and then starting again, in an incessant kaleidoscope, which cancels the distances.*

*He stands still, his naked body pale as the fog, marked by the barbed and black intertwining of tattoos and the clearer play of scars, and continues to tremble uncontrollably. He wouldn't know where to go, even if he could move. And he's not sure he can do it.*

*In that chill that sinks its thin and sharp claws to his bones, he suddenly feels as if he sees something. Further up, right in front of him, stands an indistinct figure, imposing and white as himself, strung with tense muscles, promises of violence and tendons like steel cables, silvery and sparkling. The fog seems to dance around him as if caressing those powerful limbs, covered with plaques and weaves that send back dreamlike and lunar reflections.*

*He tightens his lips; he takes courage and moves forward. One step, two painful steps. Cold blades that sink into his feet, calves, up to his stiff thighs. "Who are you?" Even his voice pays tribute to the ice. It comes out from his lips, thin and tired, broken by the unchecked chatter of his teeth.*

*"Receive it. Don't fight it. Cold is your element, frost is your power. Make it yours. Become the ice that assails you ... and you will dominate it." The figure turns to show himself as the curtain of grey mist splits, fraying and recoiling at his command. When he speaks, it's like listening to the rumble of thunder, the low and threatening roar of a tiger. And he doesn't really know that language. For a moment he seemed to feel only a series of incomprehensible syllables intertwined together in a chant, but then he realises that he understands every word. He knows, somehow, that idiom. As if his mind recognises it instinctively. A concept crystallises in his brain,*

*direct, intense, almost to the point of harm:* mother tongue.

*He remains motionless, surprised and dismayed. He recognises the face when he sees him. He had stared at those eyes, transparent and fierce as his own, just before all hell had broken loose in his head. Before the blackout.*

*He tries to do what he's told. He stops fighting the pain of those glacial splinters embedded under the skin. He welcomes it, surrendering to himself. He stops fighting the violent chills, and lets them be. He breathes. And finally, it seems to him that the air does not hang halfway, somewhere inside the chest. Something changes. Something is in the making. Something works. The cold is no longer intense, or painful. It's not his enemy.*

*The face in front of him, sculpted in clear and feral lines, loses its austere air, hinting a smile. He nods, approving.*

*"Who are you?" he asks.*

*"Trygve Håkon of First Glacial, commander of the Third Shape-shifting Division. The real question, boy, is who are you?"*

*He looks at him, his eyes widening. The heart that begins to beat violently in the chest, up to the temples, echoing in his ears. A premonition closes his throat, insinuating its twisted roots down the oesophagus, planting itself in his bowels to become certainty.*

*"You were torn from your destiny eighteen years ago. You've always been looking for belonging, without ever finding it," continues the white giant. "But you've always had it engraved on your heart. And now you have it in front of you, Trygve Lars Håkonson," he concludes, after a moment of silence so total as to be deafening. "And now that I've found you, I won't let them take you away again."*

*The figure in front of him begins to become indistinct. The grey fog thickens, confusing lines blinding him again. The revelation enters his bones as he begins to understand its extent. His head is spinning, and the tears that run down his cheeks burn with a violent fire. He cannot help thinking for a moment that he will be scarred.*

*"Wait!" he manages to scream, raising his hands in an effortless way, trying to hold on to the white warrior. He is no longer able to distinguish his features, only the metallic sparkle of his eyes. "Don't go, wait!" But his frozen fingers only grasp the fog, which closes mockingly, still thicker. He tries to move, but his legs do not respond to the command, and his knees bend, causing him to fall. An endless fall, in that grey nothingness, as cold as the embrace of death.*

*

Winter woke up with a gasp, pulling himself upright. He instantly regretted it, when sharp and cruel nails responded to the sudden movement, digging insistently in his brain.

It was the feeling of waking up after a colossal hangover. His temples were hammering, his eyes seemed too big for their sockets and his mouth was dry. A violent thirst scarred his throat. "Shit," he rasped, taking his head in his hands. The after-effects of that dream still floated in his mind, quiet and full of implications that he had no idea how to deal with. He didn't know whether to hope that it had only been a convoluted projection of desires and insinuations of recent times, or that the Jötunn had truly sought him, in that foggy nowhere, to reveal a shocking truth to him and to offer him the belonging he always sought. The answer, whatever it was, was still distressing.

For a long time he remained motionless, trying only to breathe and repel the dense waves of a migraine. He took a few long breaths, feeling the smell of wood smoke around him, and something more intense and pleasant, like burnt incense. His eyes narrowed in the dim light. He was surprised to find himself in a large cave. High up, in a vaulted ceiling stained with soot, was a large hole dug into the rock that caused a blade of milky light to enter. It must have been almost dawn and outside the sky still seemed cloudy. The first light of day also entered from the mouth of the cave, but the interior was lit by the glowing embers of a large hearth arranged to spread its warmth into the surrounding environment, and from what appeared to be several lighted lamps. Winter realised he was sitting on a pallet composed of a straw mattress placed on a structure of intertwined branches, wrapped in blankets. As he became accustomed to the light, he noticed an overlapping display of woven mats on the floor, and on the wall coloured graffiti, mostly a jumble of incomprehensible symbols and writings.

By the mouth of the cave were the imposing shapes of the horses; there was someone, with them, a tiny little figure moving around; a peaceful monotonous dirge reached his ears. That someone out there was humming.

Not far from his cot was another bed. On it was a curled up figure over a bundle of blankets, and it didn't take him long to recognise Nathaniel's raven mop. "Nate?" His voice croaked, tired. He cleared his throat and tried again: "Nathaniel?"

There was no answer. He started to get up, but was seized by a violent dizziness and a wave of nausea; he gave up, lying back down with a grimace.

"He's resting now. He needed it, but he will recover."

Reidar's calm and deep voice took him by surprise. He reopened his eyes, searching for him. He was standing there, a few steps from the pallet.

With an effort, Winter sat up. He sighed, exasperated by the weakness he felt. "What happened?"

Reidar approached, sitting cross-legged on the mats, next to the cot where Winter was. He was holding a leather flask and handed it to him.

Winter grabbed it with a grateful look and brought it to his lips. He didn't think he'd ever felt so thirsty in his life. And that water, cold and with a ferrous flavor, seemed to him the best he had ever drunk. "Thank you," he murmured, refreshed, when he had finished drinking. "I needed it." He seemed to have overcome the last stumbling block of the language, and was able to speak it with a new confidence, now. He wondered if that dream he had had was not somehow the cause. *Mother tongue.* Even if the giant in his dream had spoken yet another language. But the idea made him shiver, and he decided not to think about it.

Reidar nodded. "You were unconscious for a long time," he said, watching him carefully with his penetrating green eyes. "How do you feel?"

"Like after a hangover," the other admitted, wrinkling his nose. "And I have no idea what happened. The last thing I remember is the valley we were crossing. Then ... the Jötnar?" He shifted his restless gaze to Nathaniel's sleeping figure at that point. "He didn't answer me when I called him. Is he alright?"

Reidar stared at him with wonder and perplexity, between the signs of fatigue and the subtle hint of an unshaven beard on his jaws. "You're talking my language," he pointed out, raising his eyebrows. "Like a native."

Winter smiled faintly. "That's my gift. I learn quickly. Nate told you, didn't he?"

"He told me. Only I couldn't imagine it was something so remarkable." Then he looked towards Nathaniel. "He was injured in the flight. Nothing too serious, but we had to mend the wound and Cress gave him something to sleep. Nothing to worry about."

Winter's lips tightened. "Cress?" He repeated, puzzled.

"Oh, right. You don't know him. This cave is his home. He's hosting us and has taken care of Nate."

He frowned, looking back at Nathaniel, who had not yet moved. Then he gestured to the surroundings with one hand. "Can you tell me what happened?"

Reidar shrugged. "Those Jötnar attacked us. They weren't from the same division that followed me after my escape. They didn't know that I'm a lynnewulf, not until I revealed myself. They wanted you." He stared at him, frowning. "One of them must have attacked you with his mind, but Nate didn't allow him to take you. It's thanks to him if you are here now."

Winter swallowed hard and peered at the sleeping boy. "He was injured because of me." It was not a question, but a grim realization.

"He succeeded in riding behind you and leading Jera to the passage between the hills. It was during the escape that the leader of that shapeshifter division wounded him. Elemental ice splinters. It could have been a lot worse than that." A slow sigh. "I caused a landslide at the mouth of the canyon to stop them, and then we met Cress who helped us. We lost Vunjo because of the landslide. I couldn't control it as I hoped. But we still have Jera and Berkana."He nodded toward the entrance to the cave, from where the low, pleasant chant could still be heard. "As for Cress, he lives alone, in a valley hidden among the rocky hills. He says he is a heks ..." He noticed Winter's perplexed look and hastened to explain. "A shaman, consecrated to the Mother Earth. Heksir, that's what we call them. And so far he has proved it without a shadow of a doubt. He's powerful too, for one so young. He speaks to animals, from what I understand, and is an excellent doctor. The Jötnar haven't found us, so his territory is really protected as he claimed. And if you think he's thirteen at most ..."

"I'm sixteen," someone said, from the mouth of the cave. A red and rebellious mop leaned out from behind the screen. A low and pleasant voice, reassuring, and a candid smile in the midst of a sea of freckles. "Oh! You woke up, finally!" Cress returned to the cave, moving the screen to let in the dawn light. Outside, the sky was still frowning and grey, but at least it had stopped raining. The boy moved towards the hearth, bringing with him a basket full of what looked like tubers and roots. He set it down by the fire, which he began to revive with a supply of wood kept safely in a niche in the nearby rock wall. "You will all be very hungry, I suppose. Even Nate Smukoj, when he wakes up. I'll take care of it; this soup will give you back strength. It's my specialty." Then he turned to Winter. "Feeling better? I guess your head is hurting after what you've been through. I can give you an infusion that will help you. It tastes horrible, I warn you, but it works wonders. If I were you, I would say yes." He nodded, convinced.

"Does he always talk so much?" Winter whispered, turning to Reidar.

The other grinned. "He's probably compensating for living alone ... if he takes a liking to you, even more. Pray he doesn't," he whispered, amused. Then he let out an amused laugh at Winter's dismay and at Cress's protest.

"I heard you!"

Nathaniel chose that moment to turn over in his bed, a low groan warning that he was returning to the world of the living.

The little boy's attention was instantly poured over him.

*Rise and shine*, thought Winter at the scene, with an ironic little smile. But the idea that Nathaniel had recovered filled his soul with profound relief.

# Chapter Seventeen

"So, are you the rejsend?" asked Cress, turning to Winter, the curiosity plain in his wide, glittering grey eyes.

They were gathered near the hearth, sharing the soup prepared by the shaman, three out of the four guests rather the worse for wear, but grateful for that moment of respite.

He shrugged. "Apparently. But now the trick no longer works, and we are stranded here—me and Nate." He grimaced in disgust after taking a sip of the infusion Cress had given him against the headache. "I hope this stuff works, because it's like rinsing your mouth with fucking penicillin."

The red-haired boy stared at him perplexed, while Nathaniel barely held back a laugh, risking choking on his soup. "He means that the infusion tastes bad," he explained, before peeking at Winter. "You're speaking the Norse language as if it were your own."

"So you all keep telling me," he replied, embarrassed. "It happened suddenly. As if I just unlocked a bonus ability."

"Perhaps this place has a strange effect on us," Nate murmured thoughtfully. After all, he had felt his abilities growing too, since arriving.

Reidar looked at them in silence, continuing to eat without speaking.

"Anyway," Cress resumed, his curiosity still demanding, "if I understand correctly, you have come from another reality, and now you can no longer go back because you don't know how to reopen the Nodal Point."

Winter nodded. "It had never happened to me before. Although ... I never had to open the portal from here. Always on the *other side*."

The Norse raised an eyebrow. "Hold on. How long have you been going back and forth from your world to ours?"

"I did it often, several years ago. I always came out in the same place—an uninhabited valley, a few miles from where we met," Winter replied, laying the empty earthenware bowl that contained the infusion on one side and starting to eat too. "I'd stay for a while, then go back and close the portal." He swallowed a couple of spoonfuls of soup, ravenous. "Really good," he said, licking the residue from his lips. He peeked at Reidar, who seemed to be waiting to hear the end of the story, and resumed. "Then I stopped doing it for many years. And when I opened it again, it was a few days ago, with Nathaniel." He looked at the other boy, becoming more serious, perhaps feeling responsible for what had happened. "It all seemed as usual. The place was the same, as if it had never changed despite the passing time. Only that the ... Nodal Point? Whatever you call it ... it closed without me wanting it to. On this side. And I haven't been able to open it since."

Cress had listened to the story in silence, without interrupting or intervening as he usually did. He scratched his beardless chin with a thoughtful look on his ephebic face. "In my opinion, the problem is that you don't have the *nux*," he declared finally, with a crystalline certainty. Reidar suddenly frowned, looking at the boy. He said nothing, but it was clear that he understood what he was referring to.

"I don't have the ... what?" Winter repeated, confused.

Cress sighed. "Ahhh, Morjord! Don't you know anything! The nux, I said. The striped stone of the giants. Nothing? You have no idea what I'm saying, do you?" He rolled his eyes and looked at Reidar sideways, taking the last spoonful from his wooden bowl and adding, with his mouth full, "I'm *coinc* to do it, or *fill* you? *Tat* is ..." he swallowed the morsel, "...don't tell me you don't know anything either? I wouldn't be surprised."

Reidar gave in. "Cress is talking about a Jötnar artifact. The nux is a reactive rock, of which we don't know the origin. For the Norsihir it is useless; its energy doesn't respond to our abilities. Instead, it reacts in contact with the Jötnar, who exploit it to strengthen themselves. Some believe that, without that material, they would lose their elemental abilities and everything that makes them so fearful. And since the energy that the nux contains is consumed with use, the White Ones need to find other deposits when they run out."

"It is so, indeed," interrupted Cress, nodding firmly and becoming more serious and attentive. "It's not a simple theory; they arrived in the lands of the Norsihir in search of new deposits. They conquered them together with our regions and our cities and, now that they are starting to run out, they have moved again. They crave another world to conquer, where nux is present, as they have always done since they left their world of origin."

Reidar frowned, watching the boy. "And how do you know these things? How can you be so certain?"

The young shaman snorted. "Don't tell me you're among the skeptics? You—a lynnewulf—one of those who has the most to lose in this business. My father, like several other heksir of the Circle of Rynne, had known this for years, since Hveit Wulfgar, a renegade half-breed, joined the Circle. It was thanks to him that we learned so much about the Jötnar and their plans."

Reidar seemed shocked by this news, especially as it was revealed by what looked like little more than a child.

"Even Koen Rurik from Wunderbaar knows this, and in fact, he entrenched himself in his own lands and keeps them out, waiting for them to run out of power or go elsewhere. A somewhat selfish policy, if you ask me, but a choice nonetheless. And not so wrong either, if you think about it: if the energy of the nux at their disposal ends, the Jötnar will stop being so dangerous, and he can organise a counteroffensive. If instead they find the way to migrate elsewhere with a Nodal Point, goodbye forever. In any case, the problem would be solved, from his point of view."

Reidar tightened his lips, his face darkening. "Sure. And in the meantime, the other clans are attacked, the people massacred and persecuted, the women kidnapped and raped to give them children ..."

Cress sighed. "It was always like this, even before the Jötnar showed their ugly white snouts around here. We are a divided people, and until there is someone who can really unite all the clans ..."

"Some, years ago, thought that Rurik was the right man to do it. But after what happened, I don't believe that anymore."

"It could still happen. I've heard that many have taken refuge in Wunderbaar. And didn't you say you would go there too?"

Winter cleared his throat, looking at the two with barely concealed annoyance. "Well, it's all very interesting, really, but maybe a thorough discussion of your clan policy isn't what we need now. We were talking of this damned nux, right?"

Nathaniel coughed, trying to hold back a laugh in the face of such frankness.

Cress pouted and glared at him. "The next time you say he's not one of their bastards, I swear I'll set a snake nest at you, Smukoj."

Winter rolled his eyes. "Hey! I am still here, if you hadn't noticed, little boy."

"All right, both of you, calm down." Nathaniel hastened to raise his hands in a conciliatory gesture, noting his friend's impatience and fearing that the more angular aspects of his character would return to prominence. "We'd just like to understand the situation a little better, Cress. You said that perhaps Winter is no longer able to activate the Nodal Point because he has no nux. What does this mean?"

"It's clear, no? The Jötnar use the striated stone to enhance their innate abilities, and this also applies to their half-breeds. They also grant the nux to their children, once they ensure their loyalty. And a half-breed will never be able to reach their full potential without using the striped stone of the giants." Then he looked at Winter. "Smukoj says you are not one of them, but I say that if you want to reactivate that Nodal Point and go home, what you need is a nux, and its energy."

The silence that fell on the group was heavy. Winter had become serious and thoughtful and was no longer looking at anyone. Reidar and Nathaniel seemed alarmed, perhaps for very different reasons.

It was Nate who spoke first, eventually. "If what you say is true, Cress, why was Winter able to open the portal on the other side, then?" He had an urgent tone in his voice, as if he were trying to cling to logic beyond all possible limits, so as not to have to admit a truth that was too disturbing to accept.

"In your world, it's obvious the rules are different. It could also be that the Jötnar are even more powerful there, and that they don't even need the nux. Maybe it's actually your world they want to reach, and not because there are deposits. Have you ever thought about it?"

Cress let the sinister possibility hang between them for a few seconds. Nathaniel wondered how the boy had come so easily not only to the right conclusions—the Jötnar had been trying for some time to reach his world—but also to give an explanation that no one had ever offered to the Waerne, even if they were meant to guard their unsuspecting world. At least, from what he knew. Never before like now did he want to talk to his Norse ancestor.

The boy didn't give him time to reply and ended his argument with a faint flourish of his hand. "From there, a rejsend could know how to activate a Nodal Point without effort. As it happened to Winter, in fact."

Nathaniel tormented his lower lip with his teeth, nervous. He glanced at his friend, who seemed equally troubled. He didn't dare to imagine how he could feel in the face of that revelation. "We would still have to understand how the hell a half-breed of the Jötnar could end up in our world," he tried again, frowning.

"There could be different explanations," Cress commented, not at all discouraged by Nathaniel's refutations. "You know as much as I do that the Nodal Points are rarely activated. After all, this is how the White Ones seem to have arrived in our world. Or maybe they had a rejsend able to open the portal on the other side, in your corner of the universe, Smukoj."

Nate watched the young shaman with a veil of gloom in his eyes. Everything he was saying could make sense, after all. And what did he know about Winter in the end? Very little. That he had never known his family, and that he had grown up in a foster home in New York. He turned his gaze on him. And he realized, with impressive clarity, that maybe they were thinking the same things at the time.

"All right, all of you," said Winter at that point. "We have no certainties, but this seems to me the closest thing to a solution since we've arrived here." He shifted his eyes to the others, while a resolute flash passed through his own. "Maybe this nux story won't work for me. But if it works, it would mean that I would be able to reopen the portal and bring Nate home. So at this point, there is only one thing I need to know." He stopped his gaze on Cress, and did not remove his eyes from him. "Where can I find it?"

# Chapter Eighteen

After Winter's resolution, the group had been talking for a long time about what to do. And while Cress seemed certain about where to find a core of nux to help the foreigners return to their world, Reidar had been much more cautious, even uncertain on whether to join the expedition or proceed to the Wunderbaar. In any case, they would have to wait both for Nathaniel to recover a little more and for the injured mare to travel without problems. Reidar had forbidden Nathaniel to try to use his healing abilities on Jera, at least for the moment, explaining that he had lost too much blood and that he would do nothing but slow down his own healing. And Cress had agreed. They had spent the day studying possible itineraries on the worn map that the young shaman had pulled out of the warehouse at the back of his cave, taking an inventory of the supplies to take with them, and deciding where to get a couple of new mounts—it would have been too inconvenient to proceed only with the two remaining Helhestir.

The storm clouds had shifted during the night, swept away by a warm wind coming from the southeast. The sun shone with silvery reflections on the water of the stream under the cave and on the mossy stones that rose from the clear surface; its light was warm, but didn't burn the skin, and Winter had taken advantage of it for a swim, though that the crystal-clear water was colder than he had expected.

When Nathaniel joined him, cautiously descending along the path carved into the rock of the cave wall, Winter was on the grassy bank, his back bent forward, showing the slight relief of the vertebrae under his skin of an opalescent whiteness and the tight and thorny weaves of black ink that moved in rhythm with his breath, as if they had a life of their own. It looked like he was trying to get the better of the shabby hint of a faded blond beard that had appeared on his jaws, using the thin and sharp blade of Reidar's razor over his stretched skin.

Nathaniel stood looking at him for a while, from the end of the path, a light smile touching the corners of his lips. It was good to see that he was serene now, after the restless night. He had heard him turning over and over in the bed, muttering disconnected phrases. And he had felt the impulse to reach him and hold him against his chest, as he had done those two nights at Nivak. But in the end, he had stayed where he was, just trying to go back to sleep.

He approached with quiet steps, without sudden movements; the last thing he wanted was for Winter to jerk or turn around, cutting himself with that razor. "Reidar and Cress took Berkana and went to the nearest village. They'll be back with two more horses and supplies for the journey," he explained, sitting on the tall, emerald green grass that grew on the bed of the small river.

"I wonder how they'll get them," Winter observed, setting the razor to one side and leaning forward to rinse his face. He had done a good job and, apart from his slightly reddened skin, there were no clumsy cuts along the taut lines of his jaw. "Unless the economy of this place is completely unconventional compared to the one we know," he added shortly thereafter, straightening up and running his hands through his still-damp hair.

Nathaniel smiled. "They'll do it the same way Reidar bought our supplies and weapons at Nivak. Apparently he is the heir of one of the most ancient noble families of these lands," he clarified, leaning back on the palms of his hands and raising his face to the warm and pleasant sun. "From what I understand, he recovered his wealth in the house in Nivak. So, at least from this point of view, we will have no problems."

"Not bad. We made friends with a daddy's boy," chuckled Winter. "Good for us he wants to help us, then."

"Somehow I feel that he took us to heart. Although he may not follow us to Kernesfell. But if you want my opinion ... I am not so sure that he is really convinced to go on to the Wunderbaar and leave us alone."

"What's that—one of your empathic insights?"

"Maybe ..." Nate smiled, enigmatic.

"In any case, I hope he changes his mind and comes with us," concluded Winter. "I don't think it will be as easy to cross the Jötnar territories as Cress thinks. And the idea of doing it just us two and that weird kid does not make me feel very relaxed."

"But he said he knew a safe road, so we shouldn't find ourselves in the middle of their platoons," the other objected.

"And you trust him? I mean, did you see him ... Doesn't it seem strange to you that he's so young and he knows so much?"

"Here we go again, Wint. You and your belief that there is no one to trust. Come on, I don't think he wants to get into trouble just to follow some kind of sudden impulse. And his idea is the only concrete hope we have of going home." He looked at him for a moment, just tilting his head towards his shoulder. "You were the one to approve of the idea first."

Winter sighed. "Yes, I know." He leaned back, stretching out in the grass that bent obediently under his weight. The arms extended and the transparent gaze turned to the sky that was reflected in it, colouring the irises with an intense blue that was not theirs. "It's just that ... looking back, I'm starting to have some doubts." He raised a hand to stop Nathaniel before he could object. "I didn't say I didn't want to do it. I just hope everything goes well. That boy gives me hives, I admit. But I can't deny that he has proved he knows his stuff."

"You saw it though, didn't you? He lives alone in this valley and knows how to take care of himself. The Jötnar haven't followed us, and his abilities are obvious. One who knows nature and knows how to survive like him is the best guide we could find. And he's also an experienced healer," he added, pointing to the bandaged arm, which was indeed healing without problems.

Winter rolled her eyes. "So much flattery..."

"Are you jealous?" Nathaniel laughed, shaking his head. But it died in his throat shortly after, obliterated by an embarrassed cough. The emotion that seemed to emanate from Winter was just that, he could tell now. He cleared his throat and stood up faster than he'd wanted to. "I came to get fresh grass for Jera," he changed the subject, starting to look around, as if there wasn't any where he stood. "Reidar's seeds have finished and Cress has no hay, other than that of the mattresses ... I don't want to make her move, but I hope to recover enough, maybe even from tomorrow, to be able to heal her." He began to tear off large tufts of dewy grass, near the bed of the stream, without looking at Winter anymore. He heard him sigh, behind him.

"Alright. You shouldn't move too much either with that suture on your arm," he commented, getting up again. "Come on, I'll give you a hand."

*

Reidar and Cress returned towards evening; the sun had already stretched its lazy reddish fingers over the valley, hidden below the rocky hills, warming the shelter in front of the cave with its last rays and giving the schists warm hues that sparkled with shards of mica. They rode two horses smaller than the Helhestir, a young chestnut with an almost blonde mane that opened the line and scrambled up the path, and a grey that made Nathaniel immediately think of his Gornil. Berkana followed them without visible ties, the saddle loaded with provisions.

Jera was the first to hear them, calling back with a neigh, to which the other Helhest responded enthusiastically. Nathaniel, coming out on the rocky open space in front of the cave, saw them and greeted them from afar, grateful that they had returned quickly and without problems. Reidar returned the nod, urging his horse to take the trot on the last piece of the steep path and rising on the stirrups to help him. Winter came out of the cave soon after, standing beside his friend; he must have also heard the clatter of the hoofs approaching, and Jera's whinny greeting. "They seem to have found what they were looking for in the end," he said.

"I told you that Reidar has his resources. Fortunately for us." A small sigh of relief left Nathaniel's lips.

"I guess we must hope that he comes with us all the way."

"Maybe I'm wrong, but I feel he will." Or at least, Nate hoped his intuition was right.

The three horses and the two horsemen reached the clearing in front of the cave. Berkana joined Jera, as if she were trying to make sure of her condition, and the two Helhestir began to brush against each other with their noses, satisfied to be reunited again. Reidar and Cress dismounted, arranging the two new horses on the other side of the rocky plateau and starting to unsaddle them.

"Everything went well," said Reidar, with a smile that lit his severe features. "Cress here is a born negotiator. You wouldn't say that he lives isolated in a cave from how he barters in the market." he chuckled, and the little boy's slightly hoarse and cheerful laugh echoed him.

"I'm not surprised. At the very least he's stunned them all with his talk, if I know him a little," commented Nathaniel, amused, beginning to free Berkana of bags and packages tied to her saddle.

Cress laughed and showed him his tongue cheekily.

Reidar shook his head, smiling. "You're not wrong." He seemed to have found a way to leave behind the grim seriousness that had weighed on him since they had reached Nivak. Maybe it was the idea of that journey, and of having a purpose again, that lifted it. Or maybe it was little Cress that had a positive influence on him.

In all this, Winter was the only one to remain silent, and soon he collected some bags of provisions and disappeared into the cave. He didn't look too cheerful. Nathaniel peered at him as he passed the screen made of branches that partially closed the entrance to the shelter, wondering if the emotions he had felt coming from him that morning were what they had seemed. He wondered if he was really jealous, somehow; that abrupt reaction now, that closing and moving away while he joked with the other two could confirm his hypothesis. And, after all, it wouldn't have been so strange. Winter had connected to him since they first spoke in the Maple Tree room. He had abandoned his natural distrust; somehow he had opened up, he had chosen to trust someone, perhaps for the first time in his life. And now, his reaction resembled that of a much younger boy as he had to share his best friend with other people. How could Nate blame him if he had never had a best friend? He sighed, caressing Berkana's neck thoughtfully. He loosened and unbuttoned the girth before removing the saddle, now free from the purchases. He placed it together with the others and returned to the cave. Cress and Reidar, intent on looking after the new horses, exchanging a few jokes, didn't even notice.

Winter had placed the sacks of provisions in a corner not far from the burning hearth, above which, hanging on a hook, bubbled the soup pot that the two of them had tried to prepare for dinner. The rich and intense scent of mushrooms and spices that they had found in the niche at the bottom of the cave, along with other provisions carefully preserved by Cress, indicated that they had not done a bad job. It looked like an inviting dinner.

Nathaniel smiled slightly, moving closer to him. "Hey."

"Hey." The answer was a little hesitant, cautious. As if Winter was asking him why he was there, not out having fun with his new friends. Typical.

"It smells good. We will amaze them with special effects, those two," Nate said, with a vague nod to the hearth and the cauldron, trying to temper the tension he felt, sudden and strange, between them.

The other merely nodded.

Silence fell again. Dense, broken only by the simmering of the soup over the hearth and by the voices of Reidar and Cress, coming from outside, interspersed with complicit laughter and some puff of horses.

"Winter, I ..." Nathaniel tried again, feeling suddenly uneasy, without even knowing why. Perhaps due to a reflection of the emotions of the other.

"There is nothing to say, Nate. You don't need to justify yourself. You feel comfortable with them, you are one who easily socialises. I don't. That's all."

"This doesn't mean I'm not your friend, or that anything has changed between us," he said, looking for the other's fleeting gaze, loaded with the warm, amber reflections of the embers burning in the hearth.

Winter just raised the corners of his lips in a small sarcastic smile. "Are you sure? That nothing has changed between us?"

Those words remained there, hanging in the air, floating like dancing confetti thrown from the uncertain hand of a child. Nathaniel found himself looking Winter in the eyes, in that glass of clear translucent blue that seemed able to reflect every colour, able to show the world and to stay out of it. And it seemed to him that there was among them the silvery ethereal flow of a connection. Destiny or attraction or chance, or all of these. A primordial pulsating mass that sparkled in tight cords. Indissoluble and sudden.

He pursed his lips as Winter raised the pale ghost of one hand to touch his face. He could not leave his eyes. And maybe that was right. He felt the gentle and warm mark of his fingers on his cheek, but before he could really touch him, the voices of the other two came closer and the screen in front of the cave entrance was completely removed.

Winter jerked away, turning his back on him and pretending to be busy with the bags of provisions.

"My stomach is stuck to my spine!" announced Cress. "What do we eat?"

"Well, we've taken your supplies from back there. Do we want to find out if it was worth it?" But he couldn't stop glancing at Winter, who had returned to his stubborn silence. He remained on his own for the whole evening, his eyes distant, thoughtful, full of the warm reflections of the embers. A closed book even for him.

*

*The window is too high and he's too small. He has been there for a long time, staring at it, and the light of day has given way to the shadows of the evening. He keeps wondering why Romilda has left him alone in that room, why she has left him behind once again. He too wants to see the white warriors gathering in the main square. Now he hears their passage, the people who acclaim them and the roar of their shapeshifters; all the older children are watching, but not him. He is there, alone, locked in that room. Sitting on his little bed staring at that window too high, from which the inviting noises come. Unreachable. He has heard that something important is going to happen. That if they are there, it's for a reason, even if he doesn't know why and he isn't big enough to understand it. Imagination is not enough, no; it's no longer enough. He stares at that opening with hatred, blanching his pale lips, his infantile face hardened in a protracted grimace. That's not good, like that. It's not right.*

*He slides off the bed, reaching for the closed door. The small pale hand grabs the handle; he barely manages to cling to it, standing on tiptoe. But even if he hangs on it with all his strength, the door doesn't open. He's locked inside. And he feels anger pounding, his eyes burning with tears. She left him alone. His mother abandoned him. Once again. Why?*

*He crosses the room, stopping under that window too high. Heavy steps of marching men, their powerful voices carried away by the warm summer wind, in the sunset light and in the glimmer of the first lit torches. The buzz of the crowd gathered on the sides of the main road. He clenches the small fists, hitting the wooden wall. Again and again, sobbing. He wants to get out of there. This is not his place. Every day he dreams that he, who they say is his father, will return to that gigantic and luminous house and take him away, as he did with some of the greatest. He doesn't know where they go, Yngvi says they train them to become warriors. To be like them, to become worthy of their trust and the power of the stone.*

Nux. It's called nux. And it will make him like them.

*And he wants to be like them.*

*But no. He's there alone in that room, wishing he wasn't there. Wishing to feel loved for once in his life.*

To belong to something, to someone, for once in his life.

*He envies Yngvi because he's older than he is, yet his mother still treats him as if he were small, and at night she holds him close to her in her bed. "Her white foal," she calls him. Romilda is not like that. She doesn't call herself "mother", she doesn't look for hugs. She never wanted him, and he understood that early on. Even before he heard her say to Yngvi's mother words he didn't fully understand, but enough to know that what he suspects is true.* "He's not my son, he never will be. He is a child of violence, a dirty half-breed, and in violence, he will grow and will become like them. How can I accept it?"

*Sometimes the tone of a sentence is enough to understand what it means. She doesn't want him, and in fact, it is often other women who take care of him.*

A dirty half-breed.

*When he's not alone, in this small room that looks like a prison.*

A dirty half-breed.

*But isn't Yngvi one too? And the others? And what does half-breed mean? Why does she say that word as if spitting out a bad mouthful?*

*He passes the small fists on his face, drying the tears. Sniffling, clenched teeth. Enough with the crying. That's enough. He will go away from here. One day, everything will change.*

He will become like them, yes.

And he will belong, finally.

*And it is while repeating these words, with force, that it happens. The earth shakes. Someone shouts outside, above the intense buzz of the crowd. Without warning, the window that was looking angrily disappears, as does the wall and the floor beneath his feet. It's like when Yngvi pushed him from the dock, and he ended up in the lake and risked drowning: a violent whirlpool that grabs him and overturns him without mercy. An opal vortex where nothing makes sense anymore.*

*It's a moment, just a moment. Then he opens his eyes and realises that the earth is under his feet again. But the earth shakes, and he falls on his knees, with a sharp, dismayed cry. Loaded with despair. Dark, apart from the violent glow of the fire. A pungent smell makes his eyes water, the dangerous smell of a lightning storm too close, while in front of him a wall splits and crumbles. Another cry escapes his lips, his throat broken by sobs. Where is he? What's going on? He has never felt so small, helpless and alone. Around him there is only dust and debris and smoke. He hears screams, somewhere, dry sentences, broken in half. But he doesn't understand them. Sobbing in terror, crawling on all fours to a dark niche, a sheet of metal that acts as a temporary roof, a shelter that seems safe, in the midst of all that chaos. He's curled up, confused, dazed. In front of him, a crack opens in the black stone floor, exhaling the ancient, putrid breath of the deep earth. More screams, and a vibrating twisted moan, which seems to contain in itself the indignation of a Titan awakened from its sleep. He brings his little hands to his ears, pressing hard to stop hearing that horrid bellow. Perhaps, if he closes his eyes long enough, all this will disappear.*

*

He woke up, stifling a cry. He was curled up on himself, his hands pressed against his ears, his coat stuck to his back with sweat that also flooded his face. It took him a few moments before his wide eyes became accustomed to the darkness. The reddish embers of the hearth allowed him to see familiar profiles and to remind him where he was. His heart pounded in his ears with a violent gallop. He inhaled deeply the air that smelled of wood smoke, forcing himself to take his hands away from his ears, to stop planting his nails in the sweat-damp hair on the back of his neck. He slowly stretched his legs on the couch, making a face as he heard the contracted muscles protest. How long had he been stuck in that extreme defensive position? Carefully he sat up, running the back of his hand over his eyes. From the hearth came the crack of an ember that broke, with a slight puff of ash. Outside, one of the horses gave a low neigh. No one seemed to have noticed his violent awakening. The others slept on their makeshift beds.

But then he realised to be wrong. In the semidarkness of the cave, someone had sat up. And was looking at him, eyes sparkling in the warm light of living coal. "Winter?"

Nathaniel's voice, a faint whisper, reached his ears. Despite being almost a whisper, he was able to feel the worry that was vibrating in that single word. "It was just a nightmare. It's all right," he hastened to whisper in response.

Nate continued to watch him, silent. He didn't seem convinced. A few moments passed. They stood looking at each other, their features carved into the darkness, barely visible, shadows against shadows, in shades of grey. Then Nathaniel slipped off the bed, making no noise. It didn't take him long to close the gap. He saw him hint a shy smile. He said nothing, but slipped under the blanket with him, inviting him to lie down again, and curled up beside him. Winter looked for something to say. He couldn't find it. He closed his eyes and put an arm around his shoulders, holding him close.

# CHAPTER NINETEEN

They had left a few days later, when Cress had removed the stitches from Nathaniel's wound, and he had insisted on completely healing Jera. And, as the boy had guessed, Reidar had finally decided to travel with them and help them in their undertaking. Perhaps he had found a purpose after what had happened to him. Perhaps it was the enthusiastic insistence of that crazy Cress that did it. Or perhaps, secretly, he hoped to find some information on the sister kidnapped by the Jötnar. In any case, riding the new horse with the blonde mane named Sol, he followed them westward. Cress had chosen the grey one that looked like Gornil, more suited to his size than the two Helhestir. And besides, Jera and Berkana had been very clear about their respective riders, and it seemed that the daring escape from that handful of Jötnar had linked them to the two foreign boys.

"It is the Helhest who chooses his knight when it's time," Reidar had commented, struck by that show of will. "I have the impression that they will not be happy to see you return home in the end."

Nathaniel felt a strange emotion at those words. As had happened between his father and his Helhest, Raido, that moment had arrived for him too. His familiar seemed to have chosen him. If someone, just a few weeks before, had told him how much things would have changed in such a short time, he certainly wouldn't have believed it. And he couldn't help but think back to his last meeting with Richard. To what he had told him. *"Every circumstance occurs just when it has to."* As always, his Norse ancestor had been right. *"These seventeen years of yours will never come back."* Finally, he seemed to begin to understand the intrinsic truth of those words. Never as in that moment, he had felt so alive, and that he was where he was supposed to be, despite the precariousness of his situation.

*

At the end of the first day of travel, they camped near a long lake, set in the middle of hills covered with dense vegetation and fed by a small river full of jumps and waterfalls that came out of a nearby wooded gorge. The last rays of the sun danced on the calm and clear waters, lighting them with warm reflections. Completely illusory, as Nathaniel discovered when he tried to dive to get rid of the dust of the journey.

"It's freezing, damn it!" he blurted out, laughing and shouting a little, and coming out immediately to go and warm up in front of the crackling flames of the bonfire.

Winter, on the other hand, did not seem to suffer so much from the cold. Nate turned to look at him as he plunged completely, a few yards from the shore, where the bottom came down abruptly, and then returned to the surface with a play of sprays lit by the gold of the dying sun. He looked at him as he stretched out safely on the water, cutting through the small rippling waves with a series of powerful strokes, moving away from the bank. And he felt seized by a pungent sensation, at chest height. He did not notice that he had sighed until he heard Cress's low, gentle voice at his side.

"Are you envying him because he's not cold? You shouldn't be surprised, I told you he is a half-breed of the White Ones."

Nathaniel turned towards the red-haired boy. "No, that's not it. I..." But he couldn't find the right words to say, and let the sentence remain suspended between them, without concluding it.

Cress pointed his clear grey eyes at him. Then he smiled. "How much time are you going to lose?" he asked him suddenly. That frank look seemed to stick right into his soul. "Some things happen, or they pass. And they never come back," he said, still smiling, with a sweetness that gave his little clean face an even more youthful and bizarre air.

Before Nathaniel could answer, he hurried away to the edge of the gorge, where they had arranged the horses, and where the two young stallions seemed to have some reason to squabble. "Ahh, Morjord! Calm, you two! Calm, I said!"

The boy watched while the little shaman placated them, using the natural grace of his innate abilities. Then he shrugged, reaching Reidar to help him with wood and supplies. But he just couldn't get Cress's words out of his head.

*

"We will stop in Riven tomorrow night," Reidar explained, pointing to a spot on the old map that they had brought with them with a stick pulled out of the pile of firewood. "It's a fortified village, the last Norse outpost before the no man's land and the regions in the hands of the Jötnar."

"From there on, we won't meet other towns, right?" Winter wanted to know, eyeing the dark and essential lines of the map.

"Exactly," Reidar confirmed. "We'll cut this way," the twig pointed westward, diagonally across the map, "to avoid encounters with groups of sentinels or roving militias."

They were sitting around the fire, on whose embers they had roasted the wild rabbit that the Norse boy had shot down with two quick shots of his sling. Cress had not eaten it, however, contenting himself with tubers, cereals and other provisions among those they had brought with them. "The heksir do not eat meat," he explained, for the benefit of the two foreigners.

Nathaniel watched the map silently, barely narrowing his gaze as he took a last bite of a round fruit that looked very much like a small wild apple in shape and taste. He chewed the sharp morsel, a thoughtful expression on his face. The nux field of which Cress knew the location—in his opinion, thanks to the information in the hands of the heksir of his Circle—was about ten days' journey away, in the middle of the Kernesfell mountains. They would take less travelled paths, staying away from any enemy strongholds or towns. Cress had explained that, if they could reach it, it wouldn't be too guarded, as it was one of the almost completely depleted deposits by now. But for what they needed, just a fragment, a residue of power, it would be enough. There were many uncertainties, but the only hope for him and Winter was that the information Cress had in his possession was accurate. And that the plan really worked. And that the striped stone of the giants gave Winter that extra push he needed to reopen the portal and bring them back home. Too many "ifs", too many variables at play, to pretend that everything would go smoothly. But he tried to banish that pessimistic thought, hinting a smile when Cress and Reidar started to hum a nostalgic Norse ballad about travel and return, in which he seemed to recognise, with some variation, something that Rachel sang to him at night when he was small and didn't want to fall asleep. The two voices seemed to complete each other, Reidar's darker and deeper, vibrant with bass tones, and Cress's, which instead rose oddly, becoming much more limpid and crystalline than it usually was. The way in which the two shades intertwined with each other was perfect, and it had something intense, something that enjoyed playing with some deep chord inside of him.

It was listening to those pleasant contrasting notes, which spoke now of the discovery of the journey, now of the inevitable homesickness—as if they had decided to give voice to his current feelings—that finally the boy, exhausted from the long day in the saddle, ended up curling up in his blanket and slipped into sleep.

*

He woke up, as often happened to him, without immediately understanding where he was. Disoriented and confused, he lifted his head from the padded saddle he was using as a pillow. Around him there was the smell of treated leather and that of grass and wood smoke. He narrowed his eyes, focusing on the still-hot embers in the centre of the small bivouac, and everything came back to him. Each time, the awareness of being so far from home and from his extended family caused him an acute stab right into his heart. He sighed, propping himself up on his elbows and sitting up. In the cold and pale light of the two moons that lit up the sky of that strange world, he saw the dark figures of the horses—Berkana and Jera, taller and more powerful than Sol and Grey—piled near the brook by the bed of thorns. Around him, the silhouettes were three, wrapped in their blankets. Winter's unmistakable mop, silvery in the reflection of the moons; the clear and powerful line of Reidar's shoulders and back; and then ... then he frowned, noticing that Cress's bed was empty. He looked around, trying to get his eyes used to the dim light that reverberated over the waters of the lake. There didn't seem to be any trace of him. Farther on, beyond a dark scrub of bushes, he heard, however, the sound of lapping water, though not that of the small waves sighing on the shore of the lake.

Intrigued, he stood up silently, walking barefoot through the grass towards the source of that liquid and barely audible sound. It took only a few steps before he reached the bushes which hid part of the shore. At the bottom of the grassy bank that sloped down to the water, a slim figure was immersed up to the waist.

Nathaniel stood there, motionless, surprised. He immediately recognized Cress's red hair, which took on a darker tone in the light of the moons, but was still unmistakable. What did not add up was the rest. He was staring, with undeniable surprise, at a silhouette made of feminine curves. He swallowed without knowing what to do, as he felt his heart speed up and a blast of heat crawling up to his neck and cheeks. Many of the small inconsistencies about Cress suddenly made sense. That low, raucous voice that turned out to be counterfeit when he sang. The beardless and delicate face, so ephebic and child-like, and the delicacy of his figure. Cress was a girl.

He started to back away, feeling uncomfortable spying on her like that, while she was about to stretch out on the water, unaware. But a twig snapped beneath his heel, and his aching jolt, as he felt the rough bark scratching the sole of his foot, followed the loud lapping of the water, while Cress turned abruptly, ready to flee or defend herself.

He saw her grey eyes exploring their surroundings until they opened wide as they found him. Then, with a small gasp of dismay, she put her arm across her chest, covering the small breasts before suddenly dropping into the water, causing a concentric motion of waves around her.

"Nate ...?"

She had recognized him.

"It's me. I'm sorry ... I..." he stammered, embarrassed, standing there, not knowing what else to say.

She looked at him again, still startled. Long seconds of silence passed before a resigned sigh escaped from her lips. She shrugged and stepped out of the water, as she was, without modesty. As if, now that he had discovered her, there was no longer any reason to hide.

Nathaniel blushed even more as he stared at the naked figure coming out of the lake with the nonchalance of a water sprite. She had a wild and delicate charm about her. It was like watching a doe, or a wild horse, in its natural environment. And she was beautiful. With her short and unruly hair, the delicate traits of her face, the slender shapes which in the light of the moons had the soft whiteness of milk, she sported a natural beauty, though oblivious of it.

When he realized that he was staring at the contrast between her white skin and the dark red stain in her lower abdomen, he turned his back to her, abruptly.

A few seconds passed, punctuated by the powerful beat of his heart pounding in his ears. A light rustling, and Cress's small hand landed on his arm, making him wince. When he turned, he saw that she had wrapped herself in a blanket. So bundled up, her femininity became much more ambiguous—and bearable for Nate—but he realized that he would no longer be able to mistake her for a boy.

"What's the matter?" she laughed softly, a crystalline sound, as natural as the flow of a stream. "No need to wallow. You caught me. You can't go back."

Nathaniel took a deep breath, filling his lungs with the fresh night air, which smelled of green needles and wet grass. Finally, when he was quite sure that his voice wouldn't tremble, he dared to reply. "No, it's just that ..." ...*That I saw you naked and I felt my blood stirring?*... Best not. He cleared his throat, running a hand through his hair. He looked towards the warm glow of the embers, in the small camp behind the bushes. "Why didn't you tell us you're a girl?" he finally tried, whispering.

Cress sighed, clutching her thin white shoulders, scattered with light freckles under the silver light of the two moons. Then she sat down in the grass, there in front of the lakeshore, and tapped the grass next to her with her small hand, inviting Nathaniel to do the same.

When he settled down beside her, gathering his long legs to his chest and hugging his knees, she looked at him furtively and began to talk. Perhaps out of habit, she continued to use that low, ambiguous voice. "See, I have to do it. I've always done it since it became clear that I was born with the skills of the heksir." She wrinkled her nose in a small grimace. "To you, a stranger, it may seem odd, I understand ... but the inheritance of a heks is inherited only through the male line. It has always been like this since the beginning of the world. There are no female shamans; there have never been any. Oddly, the Mother has always consecrated only her sons, not her daughters." She nodded and gave a bitter smile. "At least until I was born. Cressida, so my mother wanted to call me. She had barely time to choose my name, you know, before dying giving birth to me." A small pause, the girl's pale lips barely protruding, in a thoughtful but rather detached expression. Maybe deliberate, after all. "My father had no sons, so he thought his lineage would die with him. I was his last child, born when he was already older. I imagine it was a great disappointment for him to realize that Mother Earth had not fulfilled his wish."

Nathaniel listened to her in silence, struggling to keep up with her story. He was amazed, realizing how those features that on a male face had seemed ephebic and childish suddenly became attractive in a female face. *How beautiful you are*, his blood sang.

"And since my mother was gone, he had to raise me. I grew up in the woods and in the midst of nature, and it soon became clear to him that Morjord had answered him in the strangest and most incredible way. I had inherited his ability." She looked at him, frowning. "Are you listening to me, Smukoj?"

"Oh yes. Yes, of course, I'm listening," Nathaniel said quickly, praying that by the moons' light she couldn't see the fire burning in his cheeks and above his ears. She smiled. Indulgent. Was she aware? Was it female intuition? Damn!

"And so you see," resumed Cress, an amused smile on her lips, "no shaman would ever have accepted to educate a female and allowed her into a Circle. It wasn't possible, it had never happened. And believe me when I tell you that, for them, tradition is everything." She rolled her eyes, as if that story was annoying and absurd to her. "My father took a while to accept it. In the end, he decided to teach me, but also that no one should have known what anomaly I was. So ... Cressida became Cress. And I got so used to it that, by now ... I mean, it's okay." Nathaniel remained silent for a while. He looked at her sideways, smiling hesitantly. "Have you ever thought about changing things? To stop hiding and convince the other shamans that you are as powerful as them and there is nothing wrong with you?"

"It's not that simple, Nate. And I don't want them to send me away from the Circle, or to find a way to deprive me of my abilities. There are stories ... bad stories, about what happened to the shamans judged unworthy by their brothers. I don't want that to happen to me. I don't want to stop being what I am. In the end, it's all I have, and I don't want to give it up."

She pouted in a way that seemed delicious to Nathaniel. *Stop that!* "I see," he murmured. "So ... do you want me to keep your secret?"

She seemed uncertain. Then she nodded, biting her lower lip. "Yes please. I know that for you or Winter it wouldn't make any difference. You come from another place; you don't have to deal with our traditions. But Reidar ... he wouldn't accept it. And if he told someone ..."

"Are you sure he wouldn't accept it? He seemed to like you."

"He wouldn't if he knew I was female!" she objected.

*I don't think so*, Nathaniel thought, but he merely raised his hands in a gesture of surrender. "Alright. Your secret is safe with me, Cress." The girl's smile filled his chest with satisfying warmth, but he didn't expect what happened next. Cressida embraced him eagerly, laughing gently. A laugh that smelled of wild honey.

"Thanks ... I really mean it."

He felt her small breasts press against his chest and stiffened for a moment, before returning the embrace. He sighed, smelling her hair. Pine needles and something that resembled the scent of mulberries.

"Don't mention it," he muttered awkwardly.

He didn't see the dark shape watching the scene from behind the bushes. He didn't see him walking away with his head bowed, his fists clenched against his hips. He withdrew into the shadows without a word, shoulders curved, defeated.

## CHAPTER TWENTY

"If your father is a storm warrior, you should know something of how it works," Reidar said, looking at Nathaniel thoughtfully. They stood in a quiet clearing, surrounded by trees that looked centuries old. The Norse had agreed to help Nathaniel develop his potential as a lynnewulf, and they had decided to stop for a few hours for training, in the middle of the travel day, sure to reach Riven before sunset anyway. But perhaps Reidar had not expected to have to start with the basics with his impromptu pupil.

Nate made a small, contrite grimace. "I told you, the first time this thing happened was the night before me and Winter ended up here. Until that moment, no one knew I had inherited this ability from my father." He felt frustrated. "I saw him use it, but he didn't do what you did when those Jötnar chased us, or what I did during my first time. In short, you brought lightning down from the sky. The same thing I did. My Dad, instead, had this ... *energy*, in his hands."

Reidar smiled indulgently. "There are two ways to exploit the power of the storm, Smukoj," he explained after a moment. "And they're both useful. What you have seen me doing is most effective from afar, but it is difficult to control, less precise and more tiring. The other, what you saw your father doing, works well at short distance, or if you are in a melee. Basically, you would use the lightning energy that is *within* you, not the external one. And you can hurl it at your opponents or boost your bare hands' attacks." He paused, nibbling at the inside of a cheek. "My father was able to transfer his power on to his weapon, but it's a more complicated art. I've never mastered it. And we need special weapons anyway, which we don't have."

"So ... where do we start?"

The other didn't hesitate and patted him in the middle of his chest.

"We start with you. From here." He moved sideways, settling down beside the younger one. "Did they teach you to concentrate? Alignment with your kern—the centre—is always the first step, whatever power you are about to exploit."

A shadow of relief passed over Nathaniel's face, and the corners of his lips rose upward. He nodded vigorously. "Yup. I can do that. The alignment with the kern, I mean. I was taught it as a child."

Reidar chuckled, satisfied. "Finally, some good news. Alright then, centering and alignment. Find the kern and concentrate," he suggested, as he narrowed his eyes and inhaled the fresh, woodland air of the clearing. It was obvious that he was doing the same.

Nate followed suit, regulating his breathing and closing his eyes for a long moment. He didn't find it difficult; as he had already noticed, the world of the Norsihir seemed to recognize his intrinsic nature and favour it, enhancing his natural Norse heritage. In a handful of seconds, he had excluded the outside world, and focused, sharper and stronger than it had ever happened in seventeen years of life, on that core of warm energy that swirled around his chest, below the sternum. The same energy that he had begun to feel and exploit since that night that seemed to belong to another era, when he had saved Winter.

Reidar looked at him, a serious and focused expression on his face. "Can you feel it, Nate? Inside you, deep inside. The kern and its energy. Everything starts from there." His nostrils flared, like those of a wild colt, as he raised an arm in front of him, showing it to Nathaniel. "Let it flow. Like when you heal someone. The principle is the same, but in this case you have to focus on the offensive energy. You must feel the strength of the storm within you, and transfer it into your hands." Nathaniel shifted his eyes to him, trying to keep his concentration, and he opened them wide when he saw the outstretched hand of the Norse vibrating with energy and surrounded by a bright and crackling aura. The power of lightning was collected there, between his fingers, ready to be thrown against the enemy. He saw it fade away, a little later, as if it had never existed, and Reidar lowered his arm to his side.

"Now you try."

*

*Now-you-try* had proved, for Nathaniel, an invitation to plunge into a mixed chaos of frustration, stubbornness, effort and intuitive improvisation as he had never known before. If the kern had responded immediately, transferring that warm and pulsating inner energy had been a struggle. He had wished for it, thinking of a way to control it and manifest it without unleashing it in a random and dangerous way as he had done in the Ocala parking lot.

The most he managed to conjure, after an exhausting hour of trials, between Reidar's advice and several failed attempts, was a slight glimmer of sparks that seemed to follow each other along the main lines of his palms.

"Crap," he muttered at that point, chuckling between embarrassment and exasperation. "I'm beginning to think that that lightning fell from the sky without my help, and that I imagined everything."

Reidar, who was very patient, laughed back and shook his head. "Don't ask for too much," he reassured him, leaning against the flat rock on which he had settled, his long legs dangling and brushing the grass with his toes. "You're trying to tame the storm, and from what you've told me, you're not even a full Norse. You're doing well, considering that it's the first time."

"Really?" murmured Nathaniel, setting his thoughtful eyes on the other. "It seems to me that I've achieved almost nothing, no matter how much I tried. Apart from feeling like a Helhest rode over me." With a sigh, he dropped down into the grass, lying on his back and spreading his arms. He stared at the clear sky above them, which was beginning to darken in the east, the pale presence of the two moons in the blue of the air, barely visible in their daytime transit, halfway across the horizon. It was still several hours before sunset, but it was already cooler. Nate shivered, blinking. "Let me rest for a moment, and then go back to the others. I think I wasted enough of your time today," he concluded wearily.

The Norse was watching him with amusement. "Are you always this much in a hurry?" he asked, raising an eyebrow. "The first time you unleashed the lightning it happened because you were in an extreme condition. Winter was in danger and you didn't know how else to help him, right? Your negative emotions have shown your ability to be a lynnewulf, then. Without any control. And you realized by yourself how disastrous it could be. Harnessing this ability is not something you will accomplish in a day. This is not what happened to your father, nor to me, nor to my father before me."

"But if the Jötnar return, I can't take it easy and wait for the day, who knows when, the enlightenment will come for me too," objected Nate, sitting up again with a disappointed grimace on his adolescent face.

"Haste will get you nowhere, Smukoj. And in any case, the *enlightment*, as you called it, does not come like this, without warning and without reason. What you'll need to do, if you want to succeed, will be to practice every day. Without rest, without skipping a single day. Even when you feel like you haven't achieved any concrete results for weeks. It's the only way, believe me." He paused, chuckling at the exasperated expression of the younger one. "In any case, don't get too worked up on whether or not you are useful to the common effort. Remember that you are a laege, and a powerful one, from what I've seen. Having a healer like you in the group is a blessing. Never forget that."

Nathaniel sighed and nodded, rising to his feet and gesturing to the other to return to the camp, beyond the clearing and the shrubbery. He promised himself to try again, from that day forward. And then again and again, until he got it. For his father it must have been like this, at the time of that last crisis that finally resolved thanks to him. His son would not be any less.

Perhaps that flash of decision was evident in his eyes, because Reidar smiled, and gave him a friendly pat on the shoulder. "You'll make it, Smukoj. But try to enjoy the trip, too, from time to time, instead of just thinking about the destination. The days that pass ... those won't come back," he concluded, with a sudden melancholy in his tone. He started toward the path that wound through the undergrowth, leaving behind the clearing and a perplexed and struck Nathaniel.

Those words, and the way he had spoken them, had reminded him of his chat, a few weeks earlier, with another Norse, older and more closely connected to him. He tried to say something, but stayed silent and hurried behind him.

# CHAPTER TWENTY-ONE

When they reached the small hilltop of houses of wood and stone, surrounded by walls dark as obsidian, it seemed to Nathaniel that Riven was a smaller version of Nivak. Perhaps that kind of fortification was a typical Norse construction. Or at least it was in the historical period in which they had been catapulted. They rode the winding path that led to the top of the hill and beyond the village gates and found themselves proceeding along the main road.

"Welcome to Riven, the last outpost of civilization," commented Reidar, ironically, barely restraining Sol, unnerved by the comings and goings of people wandering among alleys and shops.

Although the sun was setting, the village was still bustling. The paved road widened as they advanced, finally opening into a square, likely to be the main one. It was crowded, lit by a series of torches burning cheerfully, chasing away the long shadows of the evening with their scorching dance. The buzz of conversations, coming from the stalls of merchants and peddlers of spicy food, could not stifle the notes of string and wind instruments set in the centre of the clearing.

"It looks like they're about to have a festival of sorts," said Nathaniel, curious.

"They *are*, in fact," Cress explained enthusiastically. "On this night the Norsihir celebrate the Midsummer Sun, and Riven is no exception."

Nate's smile widened. "We are lucky to be here, then!"

"Real lucky ..." Winter echoed, rolling his light eyes sarcastically.

Nathaniel gave him a sorry look. Winter had been distant and in a bad mood all day; he had hardly spoken to him, closed up in his silence, and Nate had not been able to explain it. Between the need to travel fast and the hours he had spent with Reidar working on his lynnewulf skills, he hadn't found the time to talk to Winter. He realized, now, that he should have done so. Perhaps his mood was a pre-emptive response to the attitude that the people of Riven would show him, as a half-breed Jötunn. Or maybe there was something else that Nathaniel didn't know. In any case, his attitude was beginning to worry him. Winter was moving away. Even from him. He could feel it clearly and it wasn't good. *He* didn't like it.

He promised himself he would talk to him that same evening and clear things up between them. He looked away from Winter, distracted by a group of kids swarming around him to take a closer look at Berkana, while Reidar led them to an inn to spend the night.

When they had settled down, darkness had almost completely fallen. From the centre of Riven came cheerful shouting, verses of songs accompanied by the pinching of stringed instruments, the tribal rhythm of percussions and the intense fragrance of meat roasted on large braziers.

"Come on, come on! It's starting," Cress urged, enthusiastically. She took Nathaniel by the hand, in a spontaneous gesture, dragging him behind.

"Hold on, Cress," he tried to object, giggling at her haste. "I should…"

"I've never missed a Midsummer Sun in my life and I'm not going to start now," she cut in, with a big blunt smile and that warm, low, pleasant voice that hid her secret well. "And you two rejsendir can't miss it! You can't go home without having attended at least one of our most important parties."

Nate felt infected by her cheerfulness and allowed her to drag him out. The other two followed them a short distance away, Winter closing the line, doing nothing to hide a sullen and gloomy air. He pulled the hood of his cloak up to his forehead and followed Reidar in silence.

Outside, the celebrations had already begun. The music was the background to the buzz of conversations, the laughter and the shrieks of the little ones chasing each other around the square. At the center, an imposing resinous wood pyre had been erected, waiting to be burned.

"What's that?" Nathaniel asked, pointing to the cone-shaped pile whose top reached the height of the roof of the lower houses.

"That's the Solbrand," Cress explained. "It will be lit at the height of the party, when we dance the Ballad of the Sun, symbolizing the union of Sol and Morjord, the Sun and Mother Earth, thanks to which the Norsihir have enough to live."

Nathaniel nodded. There was something intriguing about the festival, in the atmosphere he could breathe in that square. A crackling background of emotions and expectation that made it difficult for him not to get involved. As he looked around, Cress went with Reidar to one of the wooden stalls around the square, where the fragrant smell of food and fermented drinks came from. He couldn't believe that being in the middle of the emotional peak of a celebration would affect him so much, on an empathic level. To the point of making him forget that he should have talked to ...

"... Winter?" He turned around, looking for him, but couldn't see him. He was not with Reidar and Cress, and he was not on the square. He pursed his lips, edging slowly toward the inn on the other side of the crowded yard. Perhaps, after all, Winter had decided that the evening wasn't for him and had turned back. But he needed to be sure and, above all, he wanted to be sure that he wouldn't get into some trouble. Gloomy and ill-tempered as he had seen him, Nate wouldn't be surprised if he ended up in a fight, even for no reason. He started to walk through the crowd, but the other two returned at that moment, loaded with wooden plates and mugs.

"Give us a hand, Smukoj. Don't just stand there," Reidar said with a laugh.

"And you've *got* to try the mead, it's the best I've ever tasted," Cress added, pushing a dented pewter jug into his hand.

"No, wait ... Have you seen Winter? He disappeared," he replied, frowning.

Cress shrugged. "Maybe he went for a walk. With all these people, it's easy to lose sight of someone. Don't worry, he'll join us later."

Nate looked at her doubtfully, then turned his eyes to Reidar. "Maybe he went back to the inn. I don't think he likes crowds."

"I can't blame him. Eat and go look for him after. You could bring him something to eat," he suggested.

Nathaniel sighed, looking around again. He wondered if it was appropriate to explain to the other two that Winter might have decided to go looking for trouble, to vent how he felt. But in the end he decided against it; it didn't seem right. It would have felt like a betrayal to talk about him like that.

Thoughtful, he brought the mug that Cress had given him to his lips and took a sip. His eyes widened, surprised, when a torrent of liquid fire invaded his mouth, then the oesophagus, expanding in his chest like a flame that left him gasping like a fish caught in the hook while the sweet aftertaste of the drink tickled the tongue. "Shit ..." he gasped as he found his voice.

The others were laughing loudly.

"Don't you tell me you've never tried it before?" Asked Reidar.

Nathaniel shook his head, echoing their laughter and trying again, this time more cautiously. It went down better, although it was probably the most aggressive and raging alcoholic beverage he had ever tasted. And the most delicious, he decided after the third mouthful.

"So, is it or is it not the best mead that has ever been fermented in the lands of the Norsihir?" urged Cress, who had already finished her first tankard.

"It's delicious, even if it's only my first one, so my judgment is not worth much, I'm afraid," granted Nate, laughing. And while he was there, he brought the mug back to his lips, beginning to understand why, even in his world, that stuff had often been called "the drink of the gods".

*

At the third tankard of mead, Nathaniel had not only forgotten that he had promised himself to go and look for Winter, but perhaps also where he was and his full name. He found himself in the middle of a group of people, on one side of the square, trying to sing the traditional ballads very loudly. Reidar and Cress were not far away; he could see, even through the mead-fog, the red mop of the young heks, and it seemed to him that the two acted in perfect harmony, bursting out from time to time in loud laughter.

"See?" he said to one of the boys stretched out on the dark steps under the porch where they had taken refuge. "Those two are obviously into each other. But..." He frowned and thought about it. It would have been natural for him to talk about Cress in the feminine, but he had the good sense to check himself at the last minute, despite the alcohol that ran through his veins, making everything more complicated. "...but Cress doesn't want to tell him."

The young Norse next to him, his matted hair blond like the grain and a shaggy young beard barely darker on the square jaws, laughed at that and filled his mug with the flask held in his fist. "My friend, some things aren't easy to say, but give them enough mead and a Ballad of the Sun, as I say, and you will see the courage come fast." He clinked his mug with Nathaniel's, and brought it to his mouth, knocking his head back and emptying it into a few convinced sips. "Trust Jorgen. By morning they will have rolled into some barn until they no longer know their names. It's always like this during the Midsummer Sun."

Nathaniel chuckled and sipped his mead, letting himself be grasped even more by all those sparkling emotions, almost visible before his eyes: floating translucent ribbons, lysergic-coloured auras that danced around the people and intertwined in streams fluids, merging into each other. He sighed with pleasure, feeling good. Although a part of him somehow envied Reidar and Cress, their smiles and laughter that said more than a thousand words, suggested to him that there was something he was supposed to do. Something about words, talking ... clarifying, before it was too late. But he couldn't bring it into focus, that feeling of veiled anxiety that crept beneath the deep empathic well-being he felt.

He didn't have much time to dwell on it. In that moment, the rhythm of the percussions changed decisively, becoming a powerful and clean staccato. Emotions peaked, turning on warmer and restless tones. Someone in the centre of the square set fire to the Solbrand, which in a few moments began to burn with violent enthusiasm, raising a tumult of flames towards the starry sky.

It was like a signal. Nathaniel saw the others around him get up and head towards the centre of the square, which had emptied, leaving a large circular space around the lit and crackling bonfire. Stunned and intoxicated in equal measure, he staggered to his feet, following them. They stopped at one end of that circle, called there by the unspoken demand of the light and heat of the Solbrand. At the other end of the clearing a second large group of men had formed, and a row of young women came forward in their midst, gathering in a circle around the fire, hands clasped. While the rhythmic cadence of the drums filled the air, Nathaniel noticed that Reidar and Cress were in the group in front of him. Cress caught his eye and smiled with an intensity that infected him, forcing his heart to a cheerful somersault. He smiled back and understood. That was the Ballad of the Sun, and it was about to begin. The rhythm of the percussion was soon joined by the equally weighted one of the feet of those around him. He followed them, imitating their pace, the sure swaying of the body that allowed itself to be conquered by the music and the glowing emotions, spectres of light that filled the air and touched it like the breath of a lover. Then the singing began. Low, masculine: hot and rounded words that rose in slow waves, intertwining over the wild dance of the flames. He couldn't understand exactly what they were saying, but it seemed to him that it was an invocation to light.

His lungs filled with air that smelled of fragrant wood smoke, sweat and emotions, and he threw his head back, closing his eyes and letting go of the sensations. He moved together with the others, approaching the centre of the circle. The clearest voice of the girls rose into a countermelody that crept into the low vibrato of the masculine tones. The words mixed in a fluid and primordial dance that instinctively found its reason for being, and it seemed to Nathaniel's eyes that those words took shape and pulsed at the same rate as the fire. The night was illuminated by that beacon of light, and of voices, and of passions.

> *"Vei ehr at med*
> *Den gaendre Sol*
> *Eyven, eyven, eyven."*

The clearest tunes chased each other, slipping on the chorus of bass.

And there was the certainty of being at one with that warm and rising sun, and with the dark earth, in an eternity that went beyond the single existence. A union with everything, mimed one movement at a time.

The steps that had brought them to the centre of the clearing led the dancers to intertwine with each other. In a sure choreography, repeated so many times as to be engraved in the memory and in the instinct of those people, their bodies touched, between the white flashes of smiles, sure like eternal promises. Nathaniel didn't know that choreography, but perhaps it was the emotions of the others that guided him. Or maybe he was so drunk he didn't care. And he, who had always avoided school parties, graceful and safe in the saddle or in the violent dance of a melee, but rough and clumsy on a dance floor, now seemed to be born to merge into that celebration in a sensorial synaesthesia that intoxicated. He allowed himself a liberating laugh, letting those agile, hot and sweaty bodies move around him, touching him, looking for him, intertwining his fingers, arms, glances from time to time, glistening with the reflections of the fire, which covered the skin of a shiny veil of sweat.

He realized how hot it was, and how excited he felt. In a fluid movement, which seemed to be part of the choreography, he took off his sweat-soaked jacket and dropped it carelessly to the ground, smiling intoxicated with the immediate relief that the gesture gave him.

Someone, on his right, looked at him and smiled. The eyes so transparent to reflect every single shade of the Solbrand. He had no colours of his own, and he let the world brush them on his body; like a pale moon in the dark, it shone with warm reflected light. Of a silent, secret beauty; but those secrets he would have given to him without delay, if only he had asked. And he looked at him, and in that look Nate read the melancholy and poignant certainty of a broken destiny. A life spent pursuing the mirage of belonging. "Winter ..." he gasped, his eyes widening. And he knew he wanted to join him. He wanted to intertwine his steps with those of his friend, to hold him still like on those nights when he had chased away his nightmares. He wanted to change the fate he had read in his eyes, grabbing it and bending it to his will, as Ashur had told him the berserkers did. No wyrd was marked. And that was his choice. He was tossed about by a sideways movement of the group, the voices rising higher, the excitement growing like the intensity of the fire. He looked up, searching for him. But he was no longer there. He looked around. A sense of dismay gripped his heart. "Winter." But his voice couldn't overcome the choir.

> *"Vei ehr at med*
> *Den gaendre Sol*
> *Eyven, eyven, eyven."*

He felt his head spinning suddenly. The intense harmony he had felt was broken. Staggering, he slipped through the sweaty bodies, the rustle of the fabrics, the feet that beat a sure time. The light of the fire became less powerful, its heat no longer intense. The square was packed with people, and now everyone seemed to have joined the invocation of the dance. He struggled to extricate himself, pointing to the outside of the circle, the burning chaos of alcohol in his veins and all those emotions that pulsed in his temples. It was too much now that he had lost that wavelength, now that he could no longer let himself be carried naturally by the flow. But he didn't even have the strength to move away.

Nathaniel stopped at the edge of the square, leaning against the wall of a low building. No one seemed to mind him there in the shadow of the low arcade, and he tried to catch his breath. Thoughts escaped, liquid inside his head, and nothing seemed stable anymore. His stomach stirred, undecided about what to do, sending waves of nausea back up to his throat.

*I'm going to vomit*, he thought, the sad awareness of being drunk and alone in that alley hitting home. Instead he wanted only to find Winter and dance with him, in the synesthetic harmony of the time just passed. He didn't think he could find him now. Someone touched his shoulder. He looked up, clouded, and for a moment his heart leapt. But it wasn't him.

"You drank too much, didn't you?" Cress was standing there, hair ruffled and head bent. The touch of her thin hand was gentle on his bare shoulder. "I feel like throwing up," he moaned, wrapping his arms around his body. "And Winter is gone again," he added, his voice scraped with frustration, at the back of his throat.

"Come on ... let's go for a walk. I'm sorry I have nothing to give you for how you feel now. But a breath of fresh air ... well, it will do you good."

"And ... Reidar? Where is he?"

"As drunk as us, panting by a wall. He knows I came to get you back."

She must have had drunk too, because her cheeks were red as ripe apples, and she had an almost feverish sparkle in her eyes. She took him by the arm, and they walked together along the little alley lit by some runic lamp. They both stumbled a little, he more than she.

It seemed that all Riven had gathered around the Solbrand, leaving the streets of the fortified village deserted.

"Let's go back to the inn," murmured Nathaniel after a while. "Maybe Winter is there."

Cress nodded and dragged him behind, trying to get her bearings. It didn't take long for them to reach the small building. They climbed the stairs to the top, but the room under the roof was empty. Nate dropped onto one of the beds with a frustrated sigh. He looked out of the open window, where the warm reflections of Solbrand and the column of smoke rising toward the sky managed to blur the stars. And he felt that way. Clouded and confused. As if there were a misty screen, or thick drops of rain, between him and the world. He remained there, abandoned, feeling a melancholic sense of defeat.

Cress sat down next to him. For a while, she watched him with those grey eyes made uncertain by alcohol, yet more sparkling than ever. The runic light gave them warm reflections, revealing golden specks that Nathaniel had not noticed before.

"Does he know that you care so much?" she asked suddenly.

Nathaniel frowned. "Why shouldn't he? We are friends, I have always shown him ..."

Cress chuckled, interrupting him. "You do know that it's not with the eyes of a friend that he looks at you, right?"

The boy stared at her. He pursed his lips, caught by a sudden sense of unease. And yet, a little earlier, when he thought he saw him dancing around the Solbrand, a few steps away from him, he could not deny that he had felt a flash of need, of desire as hot as the flames rising in the centre of the circle. For a moment, eternal and perfect, *he* had been his Solbrand. The kern around which everything else gravitated.

His eyes narrowed. "I ... I don't know what to do," he stammered, the voice stumbling in the bumps of his hangover, too pathetic to please him.

"You should do what you feel is right, that's what," suggested Cress, with a smile of disarming simplicity. She bent over him, bending her head slightly to the side. "What you feel is right. You have only one life, and you have your instinct to guide you. Do you really want to live on regrets?" She placed a small hand on Nathaniel's bare chest, on his heart. "The answers are here. They will ... always ... be here."

He looked at her. At those words, he felt overwhelmed by a feeling so poignant he had to swallow twice to loosen the knot that closed his throat. The memory of her coming out of the lake, with the graceful naturalness of a wild animal, her slender body wrapped in the cold light of the moons, filled him suddenly. He raised a hand to her face. Those delicate features that, knowing his secret, could never have belonged to a boy. He smiled a little. "You, too, you shouldn't live on regrets," he whispered. "But anyway ... thank you, Cressida," he whispered hoarsely. And in calling her by name, the name her mother had given her before leaving, he felt seized by a tenderness that had no name. With a simplicity that he could not even understand, in the rush of gratitude he felt for her, he leaned towards that face and kissed her on the mouth.

Her lips tasted of sweet mead, and something that recalled the first strawberries he had tasted in that world. He felt her bend over him, responding to that kiss, in such a safe and natural way as to make one think that everything in the world should be so simple. So obvious. The crackling desire that lit up in his blood left him breathless. He pulled her to him, without thinking of anything else, his big clumsy hands holding her back. And she let him do it, gently, as if she understood instinctively that his was his first time, and that it was what he needed.

He felt her fingers brush against his cheeks, up against his jawline and slipping into his matted black hair. He smiled against her lips, letting himself be guided by her body, in the fluid naturalness with which it moved. Cressida's lips didn't leave him even for a second and he found himself looking for her, opening his own in a kiss that became deeper, more intense, feeding the liquid fire that flowed in his veins.

He forgot everything, and let her guide him, without haste, in the slow and languid dance of caresses and warm breaths. Rationality tried for a moment to recover ground, fragments of untidy thoughts that danced in his mind, judging the opportunity of that gesture, asking him if it was what he really wanted. But his thoughts caught fire like moths in the light of a lantern when a small hand crept under the fabric of his trousers, taking possession of his overbearing and youthful erection. He groaned hoarsely against her lips, trying to get rid of too many layers of clothing. Cress laughed softly, helping him gently, and in turn slipping off the loose, masculine clothes that hid her form. When she freed herself of the bandage that compressed her breasts, she brought the boy's hands there, letting him caress her with a satisfied sigh, going back astride him, bending to kiss him and indulging the urgency of his physical and burning desire. There was a tenderness in her gestures that made her seem older than any girl of his age that Nathaniel had ever met.

He felt her guide him against herself, in a delicate caress, and welcome him naturally into the warmth of her body. He stifled a hoarse cry of pleasure and surprise together, sinking into her, a liquid flash that ran through his nerves like an electric shock. It was so intense that it hurt, and he thought he would be finished right away, but he also wanted it to never end. Cress moved over him in a slow, sensual dance of the hips, mixing her breath with his in a succession of voluptuous sighs. And Nathaniel could do nothing but go along with her, finding a rhythm with her, holding her against him with a tormenting need, his trembling hands running along the slight curve of her back, pursuing her movements with his own, in perfect harmony, in the soft and wet sticking of skin against the skin. And that tremor he felt in his loins became an earthquake, as he moaned against her mouth in a further, liquid search, and his mind filled with light, and the body with a wave of pulsating, warm, raw energy. Energy that left him immediately after, rapid, intense, leaving him gasping breathlessly, squeezing Cress against him as if he feared she would be torn from that storm.

He felt her crumble against him, her breathing short and gasping as his own. Then the girl slipped sideways, rolling onto her back, close to him. They stayed there, staring at the ceiling and catching their breath. Nathaniel tried to rearrange his thoughts, which floated like wrecks in the restless sea of his head, amidst the earthquake-settling shakes of a little earlier, the one with the epicentre somewhere deep in his loins. But when he looked for a reason, he couldn't find it. And at that point, he didn't even ask himself anymore. He curled up against Cress's side, without a word, sighing for a warm satisfaction never felt before. And sank into sleep.

# Chapter Twenty-three

Winter leaned over the thatched roof of the building he had climbed on, perhaps a warehouse, at the end of a dirt road adjacent to the walls of Riven, and looked at the stars that were beginning to pale. To the east a reddish line began to spread, announcing the first light of dawn. He wondered if he would have done better to get drunk like the majority of the village's population, then vent the frustration and impatience he felt in a fight, as he had always done. The deliberate provocation, the adrenaline pumping in the veins and then the hot and violent impact of the fists, the burning sweat in the eyes, the salty taste of the blood, its heat on the skinned knuckles. A twisted pleasure even in the pain that reverberated in the bones. The sensual satisfaction of the struggle.

But not this time.

He had remained sober, aside, his hood pulled down over his face to hide his half-breed features—because he knew, by now, who he was—to watch Nathaniel get drunk. To think back to that evening in the parking lot, to the beers and laughter. *Don't tell me you're drunk already ...*

And then there had been that moment when he had let go of the doubts and had stepped forward. In Nate's eyes he had read a reflection of his own feeling, and he had the illusion that they had finally found each other. The time to lose sight of him, just for a few moments, tossed about by the chaos of that tribal dance in the centre of the square, and he had seen him walk away with Cress. And then every illusion had fallen. What he had only seen the night before, the secret of that little girl who pretended to be a boy and the way Nathaniel had looked at her and clung to her, had turned out for what it was. His umpteenth broken search for a sense of belonging that had never existed.

He spread his arms on the sloping straw, pursing his lips. The last trick had ended. And he should have expected it, from the beginning.

He exhaled slowly from his nose, closing his eyes. Now, more than ever, he would have liked to be drunk, away from his feelings. But it was not that which tore him from his thoughts. It began with a flash of pain that extended from the centre of his forehead to the temples. His eyelids shot up as he brought his hands to his face. It was the same pain he had felt that morning, in the saddle, when the Jötnar had attacked them. He kicked out, convulsing, trying to sit up or at least regain control of his body. Aware of being on a roof, a good six meters from the ground. But he was not able to. He fell back with a groan, pressing his fingers hard against his temples. And it seemed to him that the crackling straw sank, as the abyss that opened beneath him embraced him in an endless fall.

*

*The cold. Intense and enveloping. Still that white and indistinct non-place. But this time he didn't oppose it. He welcomed it, without asking for explanations. And the cold entered him, became part of him. And he was winter, and he was snow. And he was ice.*

*"You are my son," he heard him say, his cavernous voice like the speech of a glacial crevasse. It came from every direction. "And now that I've found you, I won't give you up, Lars."*

*He sighed and closed his eyes. There was nothing to see. But the icy white of the frost followed him. It was part of him. "Why did you bring me back here?" he asked, though his lips did not move.*

*"To find you. So you could find me." He paused. "Because I know a part of you is looking for me, and that's why I can reach you, and meet you."*

*"I have something to do first. A promise to keep. And then I'll be yours."*

*"Are you sure? Your loyalty is one. And it is not to the Norsihir."*

*Winter fell silent for a while. Wrought between his feelings. Disconnected thoughts and images, in his mind. A cheerful smile, open on the irregular incisors, and his eyes. You too have a place to go back to now. He had it, yes. But it wasn't what Nate had believed when he spoke in Niels Newth's barn.*

*"Keep looking for me, Trygve Lars Håkonson. Because when you find me, your destiny will be fulfilled, and you will be what you were meant to be," the soft voice whispered.*

*"I don't know where to find you," he objected, the frustration reverberating inside him, making him want to punch even the place that existed only in his head, until he no longer heard anything. Neither cold, nor remorse, nor that desperate desire to belong.*

*"But I can find you. It's enough for me to want it."*

*A long silence fell in that white and cold place. And it seemed to last an eternity, before he spoke. Before he chose his path. "I want it. I want to be like you ..." A pause, the deafening silence in all that white. "Father."*

# CHAPTER TWENTY-FOUR

"You really don't care?" Cressida was looking at Reidar with the confused and somewhat pathetic look of someone caught in the act. She was clutching the sheet of the unmade bed she had shared with Nathaniel the night before. Her short hair shot out in every direction, bright and vivid, like seeds of Solbrand's flames. The freckles stood out clearly against her pale face.

And Nathaniel? He had disappeared. Grumbling an apology—perhaps partly truthful—about his bladder threatening to burst, he hastily put on his trousers and evaporated from the room, leaving her and Reidar to face each other.

But the young Norse burst out laughing, with a strange sweetness that almost didn't suit him. "Do you want to know the truth, Cress? I already knew."

Those words left her speechless. She stared at him, blinking, her lips opening and closing a couple of times like those of a tench. "You ... you knew?"

Reidar nodded, sitting beside her on the edge of the bed. "Call it intuition. Or ... attraction, if you prefer," he admitted, simply.

She looked at him, her eyes widening. Her cheeks grew pink. Finally she smiled, almost shyly. An unusual reaction for her. "And you don't care ... anyway ... that me and Smukoj ..."

The young man ruffled her red hair. "Should I feel sorry because you did Smukoj a favour? It was about time he became a man," he said, chuckling. "You're a heks, right? Although no one would believe that there are any female ones, it doesn't mean that you are not. And if you celebrated the first rites of Morjord with him, tonight, it was your right to do it, and it was right that he had them."

Cressida looked at him. And it was her turn to laugh. "I admit I didn't think of it that way. I was drunk like a skunk and ... he's so sweet ..." she sighed. "But in the end, yes, it's how you say. I hope he'll understand ... the context, the situation, I mean."

"Can I hope that this doesn't exclude me from your choice, then?" Reidar murmured, becoming more serious.

She smiled. A large one, her dimpled cheeks even rosier.

Then he nodded decisively. "Then it would be better for you to go and clarify with him," concluded the young Norse, pointing to the door behind which Nate had fled. "I think he really needs it."

Winter hadn't come back all night. They found him with the horses when they came out, intent on saddling Jera. He looked at them with a detached expression that froze Nathaniel's relief at finding him again, like the sweat after a run: the same damp and cold feeling, which filled his empathic sense of unease. They exchanged a fleeting glance and he seemed to read disappointment and disillusionment together in the transparent irises of his friend. He felt a deep discomfort, even more embarrassing than what he had felt when Cress had tried to try to talk about what had happened between them the night before. And that embarrassment closed his throat in a vice.

"You've finished partying, yes? Can we leave now?" they heard him comment, sarcastically, taking the Helhest out of the inn's stable.

Cress and Reidar, talking about the best way to go while saddling their horses, didn't pay much attention to it, but Nathaniel felt called into question. He wanted to say something, but he couldn't.

When they set off again, leaving Riven and the still smouldering embers of the Solbrand behind, it was daylight. They entered a sparse area of narrow hills and valleys, crossed by rapid streams fed by the perennial glaciers of the mountains to the west, their final destination. The dense forest of that region did not allow anyone to go very fast. The fact of having to proceed often in single file on narrow and barely marked paths, with due caution, made them go on mostly in silence.

Cress led the queue and Reidar joined her whenever she could. Those two seemed to have found their alchemy, and Nathaniel found himself experiencing the harsh bite of envy, noticing their harmonious emotions, complementing each other, just like when they had sung together before the campfire. It wasn't jealousy though. What had happened with Cress had been beautiful, and part of a moment in time. But they both knew it hadn't changed their relationship. He was also aware that it wouldn't happen again. Instinct had guided them, along with the excitement of the Sun Dance, and the mead. He loved her, and was grateful for the bond that had been created between them, but rationality spoke of something else to him. And his emotions too. Where was, he wondered, the naturalness with which until recently he had related to Winter; the obvious brotherhood of those who were peers and with a profound affinity? When had this loosened up to the point of breaking; that feeling born and nurtured in the days spent at Maple Tree, the friendship between them, so different; an unlikely bridge, yet an intense and powerful friendship typical of their age?

And then he realized how far apart they had grown, in so little time, when instead, given the circumstances, they would have to be even more united. And he realized how much it hurt.

He missed him.

He turned in his saddle to look at him. He closed the line, on Jera's back. Silent, thoughtful. He seemed far from there, with his mind, who knows where. An impenetrable expression. An ivory casket whose key had been lost. Nathaniel tried to say something. Once again, he failed. He stared at the chiselled, pale face of the moon boy, and the details he had come to know, which belonged to those features, contributing to their alien beauty. The irregularity of the nasal septum broken who knows how many times, the hard fold of the lips. The delicate jaw, even in its clear line, veiled with a bristly hint of a too-light beard. He had looked at him like that, without him noticing it, once before. The memory hit him like a hammer, along with a renewed awareness, as he turned back, looking ahead.

*

*The evening air was warm, the windows of the old Mustang completely lowered, capturing that feeling, those perfumes that mixed together on the quiet streets of Ocala. In the halogen light of the street lamps, the heat of the early summer smelled of humidity and fertile land, of Spanish moss and of the old stone of the buildings warmed by the sun, now disappeared under the horizon. The radio crackled a Huey Lewis and the News classic, syrupy notes pouring out of the speakers at the risk of getting stuck in it.*

*Nathaniel drove unhurriedly, one arm out of the window. "I'm hungry, let's go get something to eat," he said, peering at Winter. "What do you want?"*

*"Conch fritters," he chuckled, aware of the reaction he would have provoked.*

*"Again?" laughed Nate, stopping at the intersection, the red spot of the traffic light calling the shots. "But it's three nights in a row ..."*

*"Your fault for making me try them. I like them and now I want them," Winter cut short, a warm thrill of amusement in his voice.*

*"Alright then. Conch fritters it is," Nathaniel surrendered, venturing another look at him.*

*Winter was leaning against the open window, giving him a clear view of his profile, pale, as if he had been chiselled in marble. The immaculate white one that came from the land where his mother was born and raised, and that when sculpted looked like soft wax. He brought a cigarette to his pale lips and took a drag that hollowed his cheeks, making the glowing end shine in the shadows. Sharp shadows like those that defined his face.*

*The traffic light changed. The green light seemed to hurt the dark, acidic and artificial.*

*They moved on. The road was empty, and Nathaniel risked a little more gas. The warm wind slipped through Winter's light hair as if caressing it. And it was then that Nate wondered, for the first time since he had known him, what it would be like to run his fingers through it. A vague thought lost in the thrill of that race on the wide tree-lined avenue. He felt life singing inside him and he wanted to be out all night with that weird and crazy boy he had beside him, savouring every moment of their silent sharing. With the certainty that the summer ahead would have been unforgettable.*

*Only at that moment he didn't know just* how much *it would be.*

# CHAPTER TWENTY-FIVE

"They weren't supposed to be here," Cress murmured, staring worriedly at the Jötnar encampment stationed near the narrow path, lower down, where the pass opened into a clearing. "This area should have been free."

Next to her, Reidar looked at the improvised camp with the fire of hatred in his green eyes, a hand held tightly on the hilt of the short sword he wore on his belt. He said nothing though, merely studying the situation.

Behind them, crouched in the undergrowth that hid them from the sight of the Whites, Nathaniel and Winter remained motionless, in silence, waiting to figure out what to do. A few days of travel had passed, and the wooded hills had been left behind to climb along winding paths that were much steeper and narrower, which proceeded, rising in altitude, between patches of conifers, tracts of lawn and shrubs, rocks and bare screes. Their destination was beyond a small pass, advancing even more in that region that must have been among the richest areas of extraction for the Jötnar. Now it was dotted with abandoned quarries, like open wounds on the sides of the mountains, and dark caverns of disused mines, which sometimes they had used as a night shelter, after making sure that some ferocious animal had not had the same idea.

They had not encountered traces of civilization, and the only crumbling mining village they had seen in the distance had seemed uninhabited anyway. It had been an unpleasant surprise, therefore, to find the enemy guarding the pass they would have to cross, in the middle of the thick woods that clung tenaciously to the sides of the mountain.

Nathaniel risked a closer look at the Jötnar. There were five of them, or at least so many were visible around the fire of their bivouac, reduced to burning embers. They spoke in a low voice among themselves in what must have been their language. The one closest to the path was stripping the bone of a *firfugl*, certainly hunted in the area.

By now it was not difficult to recognize them: they were large, heavy birds, with a livery suitable to camouflage in the undergrowth in which they hid, made more to stay crouched on the ground than to fly. Reidar had shot down more than one of them in the past few days, to swell the provisions they brought with them. One was enough to feed three of them; enough, given that Cress didn't eat meat.

"They're not like those who attacked us after Nivak," he whispered, touching Reidar's shoulder to get his attention. "They look younger."

And, Nate realized by looking at them, it was not just a matter of age. They were less imposing than the giants who had chased them, although they sported the same light colours, the same type of protections that seemed to be made of silver scales, and the long intertwined hairstyles. And somehow, in features and expressions, they seemed less alien.

Reidar nodded, pursing his lips. "Those are half-breeds. Perhaps a group sent to train in an abandoned place like this. No particular threats; a pass that in any case leads to their inhabited lands is ideal to wean them."

Cress grimaced. "Damn those bastards, couldn't they find another point for their damn drills?" She watched them closer too. "Look, they're so novice that only one has earned the nux."

Those words also seemed to awaken Winter's interest, who dared to lean over the bushes to look in the direction indicated by the redhead. It took him a while to understand what she was referring to, but then he saw it: only one of the five visible individuals sported a wristband of engraved metal around his right wrist, where he could see the silvery shimmer of an oval stone, set inside it so that it was in contact with the skin below. It was about the size of a child's fist, had the metallic colour and reflections of mercury, and was crossed by thin, irregular black streaks.

He could not look away, fascinated by what he saw. Not only that stone which was in fact the purpose of their journey, but also the young man who wore it. He looked only a few years older than him, and the more he looked at him, the more it seemed to him that he had a familiar air. He shook his head, confused. Maybe it was just the unsettling awareness that he could have been there, in his place. If those dreams he had made were not only dreams, if the Jötunn who called himself his father was right, shouldn't he have been in his place now? Whatever had taken him away from his world, eighteen years earlier, had deprived him of his belonging.

"What do we do now?"

Nathaniel's hesitant voice took Winter away from that loop of dangerous thoughts. He closed his eyes for a moment, trying to remind himself that although Nathaniel had somehow betrayed him, he had promised to bring him home. And there was only one way to do it.

"I say we attack them when they least expect it and we eliminate the problem," Reidar replied, his voice cold and full of gall. For him it was just another chance for revenge, that much was clear.

And it was also understandable, but Cress put his hand on his arm, calmly answering him. "It's too risky, Reidar. Even if they are not trained Jötnar and only one of them has the nux, they still have numerical superiority. And we don't know if there are others around on patrol. Besides, they are all armed and able to use those weapons."

He didn't argue any further, but it was clear what she was saying. That little group of warriors had spent their life preparing for such eventualities and knowing that dying for the cause was the right thing to do. But them? Their situation was quite different, from every angle they wanted to look at it.

"So what do you propose we do? They are camping on the path," the Norse objected, with the annoyance of having been contradicted vibrating in his voice.

"We can try to get around them," she replied. "Keep in the thick and walk around the camp. It will be more difficult, since we have horses, but we can stay away from the pass and take advantage of rocks and trees to get past them without being seen. And even if they suspected our presence and came looking for us, it would be easier to take them by surprise, in the thick of the woods, instead of having to face them all together in an open battle."

Reidar seemed to think about it, perhaps trying to put the rationality and security of the group before his own revenge.

"Hold on," said Nathaniel. "That's a nux. I mean, we didn't expect to find one, but if we could get it ... I mean, our problems would be solved, right?" He looked at the others hopefully.

"It's not that simple, Nate," Cress whispered.

"Not even worth trying?"

"I think we're disadvantaged. And you know it too. We have no idea what they are capable of." She looked him in the eye, seriously. "I say we stick to the initial plan and avoid them."

Reidar sighed. "Cress is right, the direct approach is too risky." He pointed to a slightly outlined path, among the trees, which led away towards the rocks, turning left. "If we leave the path at that point and try to make our way up to the rocks above the passage, we could do it."

Nathaniel slumped his shoulders and peered at Winter. The boy stared at them, impassive. Yet somehow he seemed troubled by the presence of that small group of individuals so similar to him.

It was that feeling, finally, to convince him his idea was too risky.

"Agreed," he concluded. "Let's get around them."

They moved cautiously, leading the horses by the bridles and moving so as to stay away from the main road, climbing along that side path and hoping that it would not lead them too deep into the bush, or into places too steep to proceed. The carpet of dry needles and grass softened the sound of their footsteps and of the horses' hooves. They were forced to deviate several times in front of spurs of rock or steep gorges on the mountainside. It was a long and tiring crossing. They gritted their teeth and moved forward.

*

Nathaniel looked back, beyond Berkana's dark mass. The animal followed him with unimaginable grace for her size, as if she understood how important it was not to make a noise. "We can't go through here," he whispered, pointing to the rocky ledge that opened on a steep slope.

Behind him, Reidar cursed in exasperation and started to turn the horse in search of an alternative route. "If we continue like this, the darkness will find us here, still trying to go through the pass, damn it."

"Or we get lost," Winter mumbled in a low voice, casting a look of accusation at Cress.

The girl felt called into question. "You have me. You won't get lost, I assure you."

She had said it with such certainty that Winter didn't reply, realizing that he was dealing with some particular ability of the young heks.

They made to retreat, returning to the last fork in the path carved by the deers, in the hope that the other choice would lead them further, or to a gap for the highest ridge, so as to go down along the opposite side.

It happened suddenly. Nathaniel moved a few steps beyond the roots of a tree, and found himself in front of one of the Jötnar seen in the clearing of the pass. He was taller and more imposing than him, his long white hair entwined in twisted patterns, similar to what would have been spectacular dreadlocks in his world. In that moment of clarity brought by the rush of adrenaline, he saw the bared, glassy blade he held in his right hand. It wasn't the warrior with the nux, but that didn't make him any less dangerous. He let out a cry and jumped back, hitting Berkana who neighed and backed away, lifting her front hooves and looking for space. The half-breed gave a hoarse call as he threw himself forward towards Nathaniel, a flash of ice in his transparent eyes, the raised dagger seeming to glow with blue and liquid energy. Nate backed away, fumbling with the hilt of his short blade at his belt, as he realized he was cut off from the rest of the group, Berkana blocking his way behind him, the rocky gorge to his left. He stumbled over a root and sank down on his back, landing on the bed of coniferous needles with a painful thud that snatched his breath for a moment. That fall perhaps saved him. The Jötunn had calculated the momentum and the dagger cut the air, hissing a good span from his face.

At that point, Nate stopped trying to free the dagger from its sheath, rolling to the side to get out of the opponent's reach, preventing him from pinning him to the ground. He jumped up again, panting, the taste of the soil and the metallic one of fear and adrenaline in his mouth. The other faced him, a few steps away, his lips drawn back into a snarl. Perhaps he had expected to finish him immediately and saw him bend his knees to shoot forward again. He felt his heart pounding in his temples. All of Ashur's teachings about melee flooded his mind. He knew how to fight, he just had to remember how. And avoid thinking that, this time, a mistake wouldn't have cost him only a few bruises and sore joints.

He heard excited cries all around him, the voices of his friends and those of the other half-bloods who must have heard the call of their companion and joined the fight. The horses neighed and dispersed, Sol and Gray taking the gallop and moving away, the two Helhestir trampling on the edge of the improvised battlefield, perhaps looking for the right moment to intervene to defend the humans they had chosen. He seemed to see, out of the corner of his eye, Winter already clinging to one of his adversaries in a violent melee, and he felt the striking screech of two blades crossing each other with impressive clarity, while Reidar too jumped into the fray.

The Jötunn in front of him snapped, covering the distance between them with an unnatural speed that reminded him of Winter's. It was at that moment that the fear that blocked his limbs dissipated. His mind cleared and instinct took over. His body knew what to do, choosing movements repeated for years without the brain having to think about it. He sidestepped the opponent's lunge with graceful footwork like a dance step and, grabbing his outstretched arm, he exploited the inertia and the weight of the other against him, using his own strength to make him continue with his forward movement; at that point, it was enough for him to quickly stretch a leg between his feet to finish the move and send the enemy rolling against the trunk of the big tree behind, taking advantage of this to put more distance between them.

The half-breed stood up with a growl, shaking his head, stunned. But he had no intention of stopping, and Nathaniel knew it very well. He gritted his teeth and braced himself for the new assault.

*The storm, Nate! You must use the storm!*

His eyes widened, because that sudden thought was not his own. He realized, a moment later, that it was Cress' voice he had heard it inside his head. He had no time to think of anything else, however, because his opponent had come forward again, this time more cautiously, after realizing that he had in front someone capable of defending himself. He faked a couple of times, and they found themselves walking in a circle, a tense dance made of attempts at attack and dodging, until Nathaniel, who had remained defensive all the time, didn't see what the half-giant had done. They were now on the rocky ledge, with only the abyss behind them. There was no escape for him. He gritted his teeth, seeing him move forward, ready for what could have been the decisive assault.

*The storm, Nate! You will not be able to win without …*

Still the voice of Cress in his head. Insistent, almost desperate, as if everything depended on it.

From the position in which he was now, he could see, beyond the enemy, the clash amid the trees on the slope. And, in the throbbing of his blood and in the rush of the adrenaline that poured into his veins, time slowed down almost to a halt, and everything seemed to take place in slow motion. He saw Reidar get up abruptly, tearing a bloody sword from the body of a White with a violent jerk and launching himself with a berserker scream against the nearest opponent, grabbing him by the throat with his left hand surrounded by a crackling aura and spilling him onto the ground with a brutality that left him appalled. The inarticulate and high-pitched cry of the young Jötunn broke into a gurgle and fell silent. He couldn't see Winter, but Cressida's red mop stood out like a bloodstain against the dark background of the forest. She was set back, compared to the centre of the fray, dominated by Reidar and his combative fury. Berkana and Jera seemed to have decided to defend her, settling themselves in front of the heks. He thought he saw her raise her arms and throw her head back, emitting a wolf howl that was lost echoing through the trees.

The scene was becoming more and more surreal. He didn't have time to wonder where Winter had gone or if he was okay because at that moment his opponent stopped lingering and attacked. In those few seconds between the momentum and the impact, he realized that those could be his last breaths. That maybe he wouldn't go home and his journey would end here. He tried to avoid the violent and rapid arc with which the opponent's weapon cut the air, glistening with icy reflections that made it blind in the sun, clear and strong in the bare rock point where they were. And he realized that he had been too slow. He closed the distance with a hoarse sob that broke in his throat, clinging to that heavy body in an impact that took his breath away. He felt the bite of the blade, deviated at the last moment by his desperate attempt, to draw him a lacerating and hot flash against his back. He screamed as they both fell on the rock, his side slamming on the uneven stone.

The young half-giant was uttering an endless string of what appeared to be furious curses. With a brutal stroke of his back, he tipped Nathaniel back, pinning him to the ground, straddling him. He raised the blade for a final decisive thrust. The weapon stopped at the height of its ascent, capturing the sparkle of a ray of light on its smooth and lethal surface. But before it could drop, Nathaniel freed his left hand and pushed it with all the force he had against the attacker's face. He felt the recoil of the energy that was vibrating inside him, even before he felt it discharge along his arm in a violent impulse. He flexed his fingers in a furious gesture, shouting, feeling his nails sinking into the pale skin of his opponent, and a moist yielding when he planted them in his eyes. The sizzle of sparks was so powerful that they were visible in full daylight. The half-breed uttered a scream of agony that no longer resembled that of a human and that mingled with the angry neighs of the Helhestir and with what sounded like wolf barks, all too close for comfort.

Nathaniel was suddenly aware of the revolting smell of burnt flesh that came from the contact between his hand and the face of his enemy. His crushing weight disappeared as he rolled to the side, still screaming. He had a quick, nightmarish vision of the face he had disfigured. The, a pale, haggard hand entered his field of vision, grabbing him by the coat. A tug, as he struggled to free himself from the grip, and suddenly the edge of the rock ended, and the embrace of the void beneath closed in on him. Before the impact against the ground could plunge him into darkness, he heard several dry crashes. If they were branches and shrubs, or his bones, he couldn't tell.

*

*Winter is facing one of the enemy, the only one to sport the nux. They look into each other's eyes recognising who the other is. The blood flowing over Winter's cheek stands out on his evanescent skin, an angry accusation, a nameless tribute. In his eyes, there is a tormenting need that frightens him.*

*"Yngvi ..." he hears him murmur.*

*The half Jötunn's pale irises widened as if someone had slapped him. A twisted and incredulous flash of recognition touches his expression.*

*"Lars ...? It's not possible..."*

*Nathaniel would like to call him. Call it by the name he has always used.* "Winter! WINTER!"

*He knows he's losing him, from wherever he is now, from wherever he's observing, unseen, that surreal scene. Suddenly, everything seems clear. In an impossible and absurd, instinctive and obvious way. But he hurt so badly that he can't even find the strength to groan in pain.*

*The young half-giant shakes his head, then turns and runs away.*

*"Yngvi, no!" Winter tries to stop him, leans toward him with a trembling*

*hand. One plea that remains unheard, the other doesn't stop.*

*He has no time to feel relief, nor to elaborate that dream scene.*

"Nate! Come back ... please come back to us ..."

*Once again, Cressida's voice breaks into his head, setting his synapses on fire. But where should he return to, if he doesn't even know where he is?*

*Winter. He must prevent the Jötnar from taking him away, claiming him as one of their children. Perhaps he's wrong, and perhaps it's only his selfishness to speak, but he cannot allow it. He doesn't want that to happen. But it's happening. If he stays where he is, it will happen for sure.*

"Nate ... listen to my voice. Follow it and come back to us."

*He tries to find his way. To follow Cressida's voice in his head and get out of that unknown labyrinth.*

*As bad as it is, there are no other choices that seem acceptable.*

# CHAPTER TWENTY-SIX

"Where are the boys?" Ashur asked with some impatience, looking at the other Waerne gathered around him in the rustic living room.

He had returned from New York, where he had remained for several days, shortly after dawn, and had been rather peremptory in wanting to see them immediately.

"They're not at home right now," Lea explained, frowning at the urgency she felt coming from the imposing figure of the berserker. "They came back at some point in the night; I don't know when. Nate's Mustang is in the garage, but they must have gone out before dawn. And Nate left his cell phone on his desk *again*," she concluded, exasperated.

"Anyway, Gornil is in the stable and no other horses are missing," Charlene said quietly. "So they have to be around, on foot. They'll return for breakfast, as always."

Ashur nodded. "Maybe it's better if they're not here right now, given what I have to say," he commented, attracting the group's puzzled looks.

"What did you find out about him?" Sven asked quietly, giving voice to the question that was on everyone's mind.

The berserker became even more serious. "He really grew up in a New York family home, as he told us, and the name he has on the documents is his own. Not the age, as we imagined. According to the official records, he is almost twenty years old, although when he was found nobody had a clear idea of when he was born, and the age was established with medical checks, so it could be inaccurate. He was never adopted permanently, and at eighteen he chose to leave social services and went his own way."

"I guess that's not why you got us all gathered here at this time of morning, Ash, right?" Rachel said, wrinkling her nose.

"Let me get there. The story becomes interesting for two reasons. On the one hand, the fact that he has always been considered a special needs child. In Winter's case, we have a child and then an adolescent with above-average intelligence and learning skills, paired with what seem to be serious emotional traumas and extreme socialization difficulties, with numerous episodes of aggressiveness towards of other boys and educators. In practice, he has not forged bonds of any kind in the almost fifteen years he has spent in foster care."

"His friendship with Nate seems like a miracle, seen in this light," commented Kenneth, until then intent on listening to Ashur's report.

The berserker nodded. His low and deep voice, which resembled the rumbling of distant thunder or the sound of a loose scree on a mountain, continued the tale. "The second reason is his finding, a most noteworthy affair. The fact dates back to about eighteen years ago, coinciding with a violent summer earthquake that shook New York and caused several injuries and missing people. He had to be more or less a couple of years old, or so they established, and no living relatives were found to care for him. He didn't speak and didn't seem to understand any of the languages in which they tried to talk to him. Then, suddenly, after about six months of absolute silence, he began to speak with a control of language that surprisingly exceeded that of his presumed age." He didn't say anything else; he didn't need it. He had five sets of eyes on him now, displaying a range of emotions ranging from disbelief to dismay.

"Are you saying that Winter was found, alone, after the event that threatened to open the Alpha Nodal Point in New York?" murmured Lea, blinking.

Ashur stared at her and nodded slowly. "And I'll tell you more. He was miraculously pulled out by a dog unit from the depths of the old collapsed station. Right where the Node should have been activated, or rather where you two prevented its activation, triggering the earthquake," he concluded, looking at Lea and Sven.

The silence fell over the room for several seconds, while everyone elaborated the implications of that information, reaching a single, inevitable conclusion.

It was Sven who finally spoke. An uncertain note, worried, in the voice usually kind and calm. "We are considering the hypothesis that when I unleashed the storm, down there ... when I faced and defeated Laine ... that I *opened* that portal?" He swallowed, looking at them one by one and finally resting his deep blue eyes in Ashur's cooler ones. "Are you saying that boy is a Jötunn?"

Still a moment of silence, the tension that ran between them like a crackling electric flow.

"I believe so," Ashur finally replied. "There is no other explanation."

"If so, he's not aware of it," said Lea quickly, standing up. "I felt enough of his emotions and his thoughts to be able to say it with certainty."

"This doesn't change his nature; however, if he really entered this plane of existence that day, and through a portal..." the berserker objected. "We have to make sure and understand how dangerous his potential can be."

Lea looked at him for a moment, dumbstruck. In Ashur's voice, in his emotions that she felt with empathic clarity, she saw both disillusionment and restlessness; a subtle anguish that seemed to come from the awareness that Winter, in whom in recent weeks Ashur seemed to have placed great hopes and a fatherly form of affection, could prove to be a danger, and an enemy. And, considering what he had suffered after the betrayal of Niklas Laine, their most dangerous adversary at the time of the last crisis, she couldn't blame him. "Don't worry, we'll find a way to help him, if he really is one. No wyrd is marked, remember?" she reassured him, placing a hand on his tense arm.

"I think we should go looking for them," Sven said. "I don't know about you, but the idea that my son has spent the last few weeks in close contact with a probable Jötunn is giving new meaning to the definition of *bad company*." He hinted an uncertain smirk, all too similar to Nathaniel's, and the others giggled at his attempt to lighten the atmosphere.

"Yes, let's," agreed Ashur, making for the door. "They can't be far away."

# CHAPTER TWENTY-SEVEN

The quiet was almost absolute, apart from the placid crackle coming from a lit hearth, and what seemed to be the low whine of a dog. Nathaniel opened his eyes carefully, trying to focus. When he tried to move, the pain in his back advised him not to try again.

"Nate! You gave us such a fright!"

He shifted his blurry gaze to Cress's face nearby and blinked until it was clear. She looked worried, but there was a deep relief in her large grey eyes.

"I'm here ..." he swallowed, confused. "You called me from I don't know where ... I heard your voice inside my head, telling me to come back."

She smiled at that. "It was instinctive. What happened between us, during the Midsummer Sun, created a bond, I think. And now I can reach you like this," she explained.

Nathaniel tried to smile, embarrassed. "You remained inside me," he joked, before trying to sit up, despite the protests from his back. "You spoke into my head even during the fight," he added, "and had it not been for you, I wouldn't have tried to use the power of the storm."

"Slowly now," she admonished him. "You have a wound on your shoulder, thanks to that bastard, and a serious bruise right in the middle of your back. Sheer luck saved you!"

He propped himself up on his hands and looked around, realizing he was sitting on a real bed, in a small room with stone walls. A lighted lantern chased away the darkness of the night, and a small fire crackled in the corner. There was a grey dog with a sharp snout lying in front of the hearth. No, not a dog, he realized: a wolf. Then he remembered Cress throwing her head back in the middle of their fight, and howling. A call?

"Where are we?" he asked. "And why is there a wolf in the room with us?"

"After crossing the pass, we found a small abandoned village and decided to camp here for the night. It didn't seem that you would recover so soon," Cress explained. Then she smiled. "The wolf and the rest of his pack came to our aid when I called them. It was also thanks to them we managed to survive against those Jötnar. In the end, there were well over five and they all came. We couldn't have done without them." She grimaced. "We are all more or less unharmed, apart from you. It's absurd if you think about it: you are our laege and it's already twice that you are hurt worse than others," she joked.

Nathaniel remained silent for a moment, trying to gather his thoughts. "What happened in the end? The last thing I remember is that half-breed dragging me down." And his disfigured face. By his hand. And then that strange oneiric scene, in which Winter faced one of them and seemed to recognize him. Concern gripped his stomach, but he tried to tame it, and waited for Cressida's reply.

"You made a nice dive over the ledge. That's why I said you've been lucky not to break your neck, or any other bone. The Jötunn you were fighting with was not so lucky."

"And the others?" Nate almost held his breath waiting for that answer.

"They are fine. Some bruises and scratches. Your skills won't be needed." Cress paused for a moment, looking down. Then she continued. "Reidar is furious at how things went. But it will pass, I guess. I'll try to talk to him. He's standing guard at the entrance to the village, and I think it would be better if we let him cool down for a while."

Nate frowned. "Furious ... why?"

"Winter let one escape. The one with the nux," Cress explained, grimacing. "Not only do we not have a nux to try to send you home, but we risk that all the Jötnar in the surrounding area will soon know of our presence here and come looking for us."

Nathaniel thought about his strange dream. He must have seen, somehow, what really happened between Winter and ... how did he call him? *Yngvi*? It was a disturbing prospect. He tried to get up, with cautious and slow movements. His back hurt, between the burning of the wound and the blow he had taken in the fall, but he realized that it was still bearable. He sat on the edge of the bed, bending down to put on his leather boots, bought days earlier under Nivak's arcades. Watching him move, the wolf near the hearth raised its sharp snout and stared at him curiously, with eyes as pale as Winter's.

"Reidar makes it sound too easy," he said, darkening. "I saw him, how he faced them. He looked like a berserker and killed them without remorse, one after the other. How many did he off, three? More? And I can also understand it, with what they did to his family. But he can't pretend that we're all like him."

"Nate ..."

"No, you must understand. I feel disgusted by what I did to that boy, and I know full well that I'll have nightmares for who knows how long. The way he screamed when I burned his face... I will not stop feeling remorse, even if he wouldn't hesitate to take my life. I don't know about you, but Winter and I are not trained warriors like Reidar. I had never faced anyone with the knowledge that I had to kill him so as not to be killed. And yes, Winter is a shitty brawler who fights with anyone, but that doesn't make him a murderer, damn it."

Cress sighed. "It was as if he recognized him. And even that half-breed ... for a moment he seemed to remember Winter. Even if he called him by another name."

Nathaniel froze at those words. "Did he call him Lars?"

It was Cress's turn to gasp. "How do you know?"

He seemed to feel a vibration of suspicion in the girl's voice, and hastened to reply. "I saw that scene in a dream. I saw that they faced each other and seemed to recognize each other. And he called him Lars."

"Yes, it went more or less like that. They confronted each other and eventually Winter allowed him to escape. And it seemed that they knew each other." She sighed. "Why didn't you tell us he came from here, that he's one of them?"

"Because it's not like that!" Nathaniel protested forcefully. "I don't know why he recognized that half-breed, but he grew up in my world and knew nothing about the Jötnar until a few weeks ago. I was the one who told him the whole story."

Cress wrinkled her freckled nose. "But he has always known how to open portals to *our* world. Towards *this* space and *this* time, Smukoj," she pointed out, in a low, calm tone. Gently. "The Whites recognized him as one of their children, and now ... now this too."

"All right, he may really be one of their half-bloods, but he wasn't aware of it. Not until what happened today."

"Or he did know but didn't say anything?" she suggested.

Nate's clear eyes widened, as if, instead of answering him, Cress had slapped him. But then he thought back to everything he had lived in the last few weeks and shook his head, in a denial that had something indignant, impetuous. "Impossible."

She stared him straight in the eye, with a serious and involved expression that Nathaniel had never seen on her sharp little face. Finally, she nodded. "I believe you. But it will not be easy to convince Reidar. He thinks that Winter has lied to us from the start. And maybe you too.

And you can imagine how it feels."

He stood up. He gritted his teeth for a moment, getting used to the dull pain of the bruises and the way the wound was pulling on his back, then he started for the door. "Where is he now?" he asked dryly.

"Who, Winter? I don't know. Around here, I think. He wanted to be alone. Wait, I'm coming with you. The last time I saw him he was in the barn where we put the horses and—"

Nathaniel turned to her and held up a hand. "No," he said.

"No what?"

"Don't come with me. I want to talk to him alone."

She thought about it for a few moments. "All right. Let's see if we can make them both reason. I'm going to look for Reidar," she concluded, leaving the room after him.

*

Nathaniel pushed open the wooden door of the old abandoned barn, on the edge of the small ghost village, and lifted the lantern to illuminate its interior. The light projected warm dancing reflections on the walls with peeling plaster, without being able to reach the corners full of cobwebs.

Winter wasn't there.

Berkana lifted her great muzzle and shifted, looking at him and beating a hoof on the ground a couple of times. She seemed agitated. And suddenly, Nathaniel understood why: there were only three horses in the barn. Jera was missing.

For a few moments that seemed to stretch forever, the boy silently contemplated the scene and its implications. The incredulity within him gave way to the violent pounding of his heart, a suffocating knot in the throat, finally reaching an overwhelming awareness.

Winter was gone.

"Oh no," he groaned hoarsely. His free hand closed into a fist until his short nails dug into his palm. "No, no, no ... Come on, this cannot be ..."

But that denial couldn't change things. A thousand thoughts passed through his head. A thousand whirling, anguishing, unanswered questions. Had he gone to look for his tribe? Had he abandoned him there, with no chance of going home? Or maybe he just needed some time alone after what happened? But that just seemed like a pitiful lie. Inside, he knew that if Winter had gone, just after what had happened ... it was for good.

He ran out of the barn, holding the lantern in front of him, on the dusty path that led away from the village. He thought he saw the prints of the big hoofs of the Helhest, and those of someone walking beside her, heading towards the woods that clung to the side of the mountain, on the other side of the pass.

He no longer thought of anything; he didn't think of taking Berkana with him, he didn't think of warning Reidar or Cress. This thing was between him and Winter. He began to follow those tracks, almost running, his heart in his throat and a new rush of adrenaline and anxiety sharpening his senses, making the night around him vivid, the details showing between clear and sharp shadows, under the pale and spectral light of the two moons.

He went through the trees, leaving behind the few empty houses of the abandoned village, leaning against each other as if to defend themselves from an imminent attack.

# Chapter Twenty-Eight

"How did you find me?"

Speaking that language—his *mother tongue*, like a splinter in his mind—had come naturally to him as he stood in front of the white giant he had already met in his dreams. But this time it wasn't a dream. And, perhaps, it would have been more correct to say *paternal language*. Trygve Håkon, that was his name.

His father. The real one, the one he had never known and whose face he had always tried to imagine. The belonging he had always looked for in the wrong places, in the wrong people. Now he was there, in front of him, in all his imposing safety. Winter sought in his glacial look, in his leonine features, some resemblance that he couldn't find. They were so different, apart from the pale skin and alien eyes, that he doubted himself for a moment.

"I've been looking for you for a long time, Lars. Since you were taken from me, many years ago. And you know it." He paused. "After all, you were the one who looked for me this time and allowed the wyrd to run its course. Is it not so?"

The voice of the white giant was low and deep. At times it touched almost subsonic tones, recalling the vibration of an earthquake, the crash of a glacier.

Winter thought back to the confused dream in which he had seen himself as a child, captured in a world that wasn't his own. The memories were vague, uncertain, but by now he was pretty sure of what must have happened. And why he was able to speak a language that should have been unknown to him. Or the fact that he had, all his life, opened portals that brought him back to that world. Only there. He nodded. "Yes. I've looked for you. And I know you are my father."

Håkon nodded, and for a moment it seemed to him that the corners of the thin upper lip, split in the middle, like a cat, rose in a hint of a smile. "Then come with me, Trygve Lars. And be what you were born to be."

Winter took a step forward. Behind him Jera, already nervous and agitated, stamped and tugged on the reins, intent on standing her ground. The boy turned to her, saddened. "You won't come, will you?" he murmured, turning to the language of another world, one he had believed, for over eighteen years, to be his own. He laid his hand on the wide muzzle of Helhest, while the animal snorted, unsure over what to do. "No, you won't come. You belong to the Norsemen, and this is not your place." He sighed. "Then go. Go back, Jera. And thank you for travelling with me."

He tied the reins to the withers and left her. He heard her launch a whinny that sounded like an invocation, a warning. *Don't do it. Don't leave!* He didn't listen.

Soon after, it was not Jera's neighing that reached him. He hadn't moved more than three steps when he heard his name. That ridiculous name invented by a former hippy who had believed in him and his potential more than he had ever believed himself.

"Winter!"

He turned abruptly, dismayed, his eyes wide in the darkness. Pale as a ghost, against the reflection of the two moons, as if he emitted a light of his own. And he saw him. Silhouetted against the black of the undergrowth, the warm reflections of the lantern that danced uneasily on his young face, filling them with painful shadows. "Nate ..."

He bowed his head, lowering his shoulders in a gesture of defeat. He shouldn't have followed him. No one should have. But among all of them, Nathaniel was the last one he wanted to see there, at that moment.

"What the hell are you doing? Who is that?" the other boy growled, moving his gaze quickly from him to the Jötunn behind him, and back to Winter.

Håkon remained silent, motionless as a statue of snow and ice. He said nothing. He just observed, an unattainable expression on his face that resembled that of a strange human cat. Unreadable as the prohibitive wall of a mountain never climbed, or tamed.

"Nate ... you shouldn't have come," replied Winter, coldly. "You shouldn't have followed me."

"And what should I have done, then, let you hand yourself over to our enemies? Have you gone insane? Have you forgotten that you and I have a home to go back to? That we are going on this damn trip in the hope of going back home?" He didn't bother hiding anything, knowing that the Jötunn behind Winter couldn't understand a single word of the language of a world that didn't belong to him. Not yet, at least, regardless of his future plans.

Winter listened to him, every word digging into him, every accusing syllable a blade planted in his chest. For a few moments, he could only shake his head, the knot in his throat too big for speaking, the weight that oppressed his chest so stifling that he felt as though he was no longer able to fill his lungs with air. "No. You have a home to go back to. Not me," he said finally, his voice low and husky, as if he had screamed to the point of scraping his vocal cords in those few moments of silence. "But I said I would bring you back, and I intend to honour my promise," he finally said, with deliberate slowness.

Nathaniel stared at his face, carved with lines that made it look older than his age. All of a sudden, a man. When did it happen? He didn't know. "And how are you going to do it? Delivering yourself to *him*?" he hissed, incredulous, the tone of his voice like a wounded animal.

And Winter knew he had hurt him. He understood it with extraordinary clarity. Nate may have never returned that something he had always felt stirring inside since he met him, but he was still his friend. He had given him the warm and sincere trust of friendship with a disarming simplicity, to the point of forcing him, almost, to return it. To do something he had never done before in his life: to grant affection. Trust someone. And then? Then he had broken his heart. And he felt entitled to do the same. "*He* is my father, Nate," he said, with an eerie calm. "My house is here."

Where had his anger gone? Where was the red river of fire that he had always felt in his veins, since he remembered, ready to explode? He no longer felt it. In its place only ashes remained, filling his throat with a bitter, suffocating taste.

He watched Nathaniel open his mouth as if to say something, and then closed it again, dismayed. That revelation must have reached his brain with the violence of lightning capable of burning everything he touched in his path. Or maybe it was just a confirmation. He saw those odd eyes become shining. The awareness that there was nothing left to do, that the bond was somehow severed, made its way onto the face of the seventeen-year-old. And it was the thing that hurt him the most.

"Nathaniel ... now you must go," he declared, with that cold calm. It seemed the frost of his dreams had entered his body, somehow. He had conquered it and made it his own. And he couldn't go back. "Take Jera with you, go back to Reidar and Cress, and get out of here. There is nothing left for you in this place. Go back to safety. Reach the Wunderbaar, as the Norse wanted to do." He shrugged. "I don't want to go back on my promise. I will earn a nux one day. Very soon. And then I'll come looking for you, and I'll do what I have to do."

"Winter, I don't ..." the other tried to object.

Tears were trapped in the midst of his dark lashes, sparkling like flares in the light of the lantern. It was such a beautiful vision that Winter felt his heart tighten in a vice. He had never wanted to know how difficult it would be to face that farewell. "Go away, Nate. Go away and don't look for me. I'll find you when the time comes."

He forced himself to turn his back on him.

He heard him take a step, the dry needles of the conifers scrunching under his feet. But then he stopped, and said nothing more. Winter turned to Håkon. "We can go," he murmured, returning to his father's tongue.

The giant raised an eyebrow, questioningly. "You don't think I can let that Norse go free?"

The young man's expression hardened suddenly. He stared into his eyes, a thrill of that familiar rage burning under all that frost. "If you want your son back, yes. You will let him go," he declared, stopping where he was and looking at him with transparent eyes full of challenge.

For a moment, the gargantuan Jötunn and his bastard son, lost and then found, stared at each other in silence. Neither of them looked down. Finally, Håkon smiled almost kindly. The smile of a feline, curled lips to uncover white and pointed teeth, eyes that were thinning.

"So be it. But pray he doesn't follow us, or I won't listen to you again." He set off, with steps as long as his powerful legs, but with a grace that transcended his bulk. It looked like a lion advancing in its territory. Same pride, same composed harmony. "Consider it a welcome back gift."

∗

Nathaniel watched them go, out of the waving circle of the lantern light and out of his existence. It didn't take long for the darkness in the trees to swallow them up completely, and a few more moments were enough to conceal the rustling of their footsteps in the night.

Inside him, that incredulous denial that blocked him where he stood with rocklike roots became a rage that let hot tears flow down his cheeks, and then a sort of stunned resignation to the evidence. He felt as if he had been punched until he stopped thinking clearly.

But then that concept became obvious. A sharp splinter stuck between the throat and the stomach. Winter was gone. And he wouldn't come back. Though a part of him wanted to cling to his promise, he didn't believe that he would really keep it. He would become one of them instead, one of their enemies, and he would forget everything else. That was what the most disillusioned and desperate part of himself told him now. And it overruled everything else.

He couldn't say how long he had stayed there, staring into the darkness where the albino had disappeared following his Jötunn father. The Ragnarök of prophecies had never seemed so close or concrete to him. But that legendary end of the world had materialized just for him. For his world, which now lay around him reduced to twisted and meaningless rubble. He had failed; that was the alarming conclusion to which his every thought seemed to have come. It was he who had made the wrong and careless choices that led to it. And that outcome was his fault. His and his uncertainties' fault, his inability to recognize the strength of a bond that, in an unconscious way, he had helped to cut.

He raised a hand to his face, rubbing its back over his eyes. He didn't know how he could turn back to camp, having to confirm what Reidar and Cress had always suspected, the failure of their journey and of all that it meant. He didn't know what he would do from that point on, but he had no choice.

He was about to take Jera's reins when suddenly the Helhest retreated with a whinny of alarm, rising on the hindquarters.

Nathaniel barely had time to turn around when he glimpsed imposing figures in the trees, dark and indistinct shapes against a background of darkness. He saw them move. And it was the last thing he saw before a violent blow against his temple created a white and stabbing flash of pain in his head. His knees seemed to turn into jelly, unable to support his weight, as the lantern rolled to the ground, escaping from his forceless fingers, throwing restless, uneven reflections around it. He saw the ground covered with pine needles coming towards him at a disturbing speed. But he never felt the impact.

# CHAPTER TWENTY-NINE

The notion of time proved to be a very relative concept when Nathaniel regained consciousness. It could have been minutes, hours, or days, and it would have been the same. The darkness clung to him tenaciously, enveloping his synapses and preventing him from thinking clearly; it was there to stay. He could tell that he was lying on damp stones and that there must have been a faint source of light, somewhere up high, but he couldn't force his sight to focus on his surroundings. He tried to narrow his eyes, but the skin stretched over his left temple filled up with sharp hooks that pulled from the opposite side, as if someone had enjoyed planting fish hooks in his face.

With a grunt, he raised a hand to the sore spot. He felt under his fingers the unmistakable swelling of a bruise and the uneven edges of a wound. When he brought his hand to his eyes, he found himself staring at his fingertips, slippery with blood.

"Shit ..." he croaked in a low voice. And then he realized he had an atrocious thirst, which stuck his tongue to the palate and filled his throat with sandpaper.

He remained motionless for a while longer, stretched as he was on his side, the iliac crest pressing against the stone floor and his cheek in contact with that wet and cold material. Then he braced himself, gritted his teeth and struggled to sit up again. He succeeded, with an effort that filled his eyes with swirling sparks. He let them disperse and finally tried to look around.

It was immediately clear to him that he must have been in an underground cell, carved out of some unknown stone structure. The only two sources of light were a slit in the ceiling, from which a thin blade of daylight passed, and the corridor visible through the bars that marked the entrance to the small space in which he was confined. There was nothing there, only the dripping, damp rock.

He noticed, however, a wooden bowl left on the uneven floor near the bars. He tried to get up to approach it, but the violent dizziness that seized him forced him to change tactics. He waited for it to pass and then crawled with caution, praying that he had guessed right about that object. A sigh of relief escaped from his chapped lips when he saw that it was full of water. He grabbed it, his hands shaking, and brought it to his mouth. He took a few long sips, without wasting even a drop. It was warm and tasted metallic, but he didn't care. Even if he didn't know when or if they would give him more, he emptied the bowl. Only then, when he put it on the floor and leaned against the bars with his shoulder, did he begin to feel better.

Now that his mind seemed willing to cooperate, he thought back to the last memories he had. The discovery of Winter's escape, the clearing in the woods near the pass, the choice of the boy to follow the Jötunn who said he was his father. That memory was enough to grip his heart in a vice, but that was not the point now: the last memory was that of those menacing figures in the darkness, then Jera's warning and the violent blow that had knocked him unconscious. It wasn't difficult to imagine the rest; it seemed obvious to him that the Jötunn who had taken Winter away was not alone, and that he had decided not to let him go back to his friends. The most worrying fact was that he wanted to capture him alive. The implications of that choice were enough to freeze Nate's blood in his veins.

He tried not to think about it and, turning properly, he wrapped both hands around the cold metal that smelled of rust and pressed a cheek against it, trying to take a look at the corridor. Excavated also into the living rock, it was illuminated by a series of lanterns hung on metal rings along the ceiling vault. Several cells, seemingly empty, opened on both sides. To the left, the corridor hit a dead end, and to the right it continued onto a flight of stone steps lost in darkness. There was no one in sight. The silence was broken only by his breathing and by the dripping of water from the vault, near enough that he could hear it echoing in that eerie quiet.

"Shit, shit, *shit!*" he growled, pressing his forehead against the metal of the bars. "Now what?"

"*Now, Smukoj, can you tell me where you and Winter ended up?*" Nathaniel flinched and cried out, feeling shame for it immediately afterwards. He blinked and looked around incredulously. Then he understood, and an intense feeling of relief threatened to overwhelm him, making him feel lightheaded.

"Cress ...?"

"*Perceptive as usual, eh?*"

He felt his heart speed up. "Can you really hear me? I didn't think you could, from a distance."

"*What do you think? Anyway, they caught you, didn't they? Jera came back to us, wounded and terrified. And then she insisted until we followed her to the place of the ambush. Why did you do such a stupid thing? Leaving alone when we knew there could be White Ones around...*"

"Cress ... please. Wait," Nathaniel pleaded, leaning his back against the cell wall and massaging his temple. If he closed his eyes, he realized, he could almost see Cressida, her thin and delicate face framed by the incandescent copper-coloured mop. Her expression worried and frowned together. He kept his eyes closed and focused on her. "Winter is gone." There was no other way to say it, though that awareness continued to hurt. "And I ... yes, they caught me."

The silence that followed those words was so long that Nate began to think the connection had somehow been severed. But just as he was about to call out to her, with a hint of anguish in his heart at the idea of being alone, he heard her again.

"*Do you know where they brought you?*"

Just this. No reference to Winter, to his betrayal or to what it meant. He didn't know whether to be relieved or disappointed. "It looks like a kind of fortress carved out of the rock. I don't know anything else. I just woke up here," he told her, maintaining his focus on the bond between them. He seemed able to visualize it, too, as an ethereal silver cord that unravelled from his navel beyond the wall of the cell, disappearing far, and coming up to her.

Another silence. Nathaniel forced himself to maintain a slow and deep breathing, and not to panic.

"*I think I know where you are. And Jera also seems to know. Hang on in there, Nate, OK? I swear we'll come and get you. We'll find a way to free you.*"

He gritted his teeth and couldn't help but wonder if those words were just an attempt at comfort without any real hope. Or worse, the promise of a suicide mission. What could Cress and Reidar do against a Jötnar garrison? And how long could they have before the inevitable they were aware of, and refused to talk about, happened?

"Cress ...." He swallowed. It was not easy to speak his mind, but it was the right thing to do. "Don't take unnecessary risks for me. Do you hear me? If three of us die, instead of just one, it will accomplish nothing."

"*If you need me again, call me. All you have to do is think about it. Reidar says that you can focus on the kern and that you will be able to do it.*"

"Cress, did you hear me? I told you that..."

"*Yes, I heard you. And now stop wasting breath and energy. Call if you need. I'll do the same."*

It was such a surreal situation that he almost burst into hysterical laughter. "Over and out, Fox One," he muttered, pressing the back of his head against the rock wall behind him. As much as he was comforted by the idea of not being entirely alone in that desperate situation, the thought that Cressida and Reidar could get into trouble for him was much less acceptable than his most selfish and frightened part wanted to grant. He looked at the damp cell around him. He listened to the silence and let time go by, crumbling in minutes that perhaps were already hours. He didn't even realize the moment when the lanterns in the stone corridor became the only source of light, when he finally gave in to the weariness pounding in his bones, and let the dull pain in his head wrap his blood spirals around him, turning the irregular drumbeat of his thoughts into a dark sleep.

# Chapter Thirty

"You said you would let him go!"

When Winter stepped forward into the fortress' courtyard, in the shadow of those cyclopean walls that surrounded them, his father raised his glacial gaze to stare at him, unperturbed. All the fury and indignation of the young man seemed to bounce against an impassive and hard wall like that formed by the dark and polished stones around them.

Håkon watched him, observing with bland curiosity the angry expression of his rediscovered son, the restless flash that reverberated in the transparent irises, the furious nervousness of the steps with which he was pacing the ground. He lowered the large opal sword he held in his right hand and gave a curt nod to the young soldier in front of him, whom he was training. The recruit immediately understood the situation and slipped away without a word, sheathing his own weapon and disappearing in the shadow of the arcades that surrounded the courtyard.

"Have you got nothing to say?" Winter snapped, stopping in front of the giant, facing him with tight fists, a nervous shudder in his clenched jaw. "You assured me you wouldn't hurt him. And instead, he is a prisoner!"

Håkon's voice did not depart from the usual coldness when he answered. He didn't seem impressed by the boy's reaction. "I would have done it, after all, if Yngvi had not revealed to us that he is a Child of the Storm, Lars," he declared, the unnatural calm of his words making his tones resemble the low and dangerous ones of an avalanche. "And knowing that, I could not let him go." He took an eloquent pause. "Do you know what it means to us or not?"

The boy stared at him with growing dismay as his awareness made its way into him. "You want to use him to open the portal." He knew enough to feel his stomach close in pain at the thought. "You've been looking for ways to awaken one of the Nodal Points to reach the next world, and you think Nathaniel is your chance."

Håkon raised an eyebrow questioningly. "You speak as if he wasn't," he inquired cautiously.

Winter shook his head. "You don't need a lynnewulf, Trygve Håkon. Not when you have a rejsend in front of you."

He had done it. Perhaps Nate would have hated him forever for that. He had given the Jötnar the key to his world, the one that his ancestors had always fought to protect from the night of time. But what could that change at this point? He was sure Nate already hated him. And besides, it seemed that by now that portal was destined to be opened anyway.

The giant looked at him in silence for long moments. Then, much to the younger man's surprise, his feral features spread out in what looked like a bland smile, veiled with bitterness. "You are aware of it, then," he sighed, shaking his head. "But it's obvious that you don't know everything." He sheathed the long opaline blade he still held in his fist, and a large, nervous hand fell on the shoulder of the young half-breed, clenching it with rough kindness. "Come with me," he merely said, leading him to the stairs that led to the fortress ramparts.

Winter frowned, perplexed, but didn't resist and followed him until they found themselves on the narrow walkway of the walls. It was sunset, and the slanting rays of the sun dying behind the mountains flooded the narrow valley at the foot of the rock with warm reflections. A breath of cold wind reached them, ruffling the boy's smooth and pale hair and his father's long and braided, even lighter mane.

"I always knew of your ability to awaken the Nodal Points, Lars," the giant began, without looking at him. His glacial and transparent eyes were fixed on the wooded and wild landscape before them. "Since you were born, your destiny has been to lead us towards our future."

The boy frowned, staring at his strange foreign father with tight lips, not knowing what to say. He just looked at him, waiting for him to continue.

"If you hadn't disappeared in unexplained circumstances when you were still a child, you would have been raised and trained just for that. To receive the nux and get the power needed to open the portal through your energy."

"How did you know that? How could you be sure from my birth that I would be able to do it?" he asked finally, wishing Håkon would stop escaping his gaze.

As if in response to his desire, the giant turned to him. "You were born with the mark of Thurs on your heart. This has distinguished you from the beginning, from the other children of the Norse women. You have always been our only certain future."

He nodded calmly towards his chest, and Winter's eyes widened, suddenly remembering the interest of Nathaniel's family in that triangular mark that he had always carried on his skin, believing it to be a simple scar he could not remember the origins of. Now those circumstances took on a new meaning, and everything seemed to make sense. They, the Waerne, knew it. Somehow, they must have known it from the beginning, what that sign could mean. Still, they decided to trust him anyway. He shivered, and swallowed hard, trying not to think of all those implications. The remorse that gripped his guts, twisting them unbearably. He focused on his father's calm composure.

"If I am the only certain future of our people, and if I am now here, why don't you let Nathaniel go? You have your key, you have your way of activating the Nodal Point. What do you need him for?" he asked, and suddenly he was afraid of the answer. Instinct told him he was about to understand the final junction of the story. And he wouldn't like it.

"Because, against all odds, I found you, Lars, and I don't want to lose you again. That is why. Because you are my son, and if I have a Norse lynnewulf in my dungeons, I will not sacrifice my son to spare his life."

For a moment, Winter was overwhelmed by an emotion that he didn't think he had ever felt before, warm and comforting, which filled his chest with pleasant certainty. Belonging. That belonging he had always sought without finding. His father was there, in front of him. To tell him that he would no longer allow anyone to take him away or hurt him. But then, a far colder awareness overtook him. "Sacrifice?" he repeated, more appalled than he had intended to sound. "What are you saying? I opened a portal to come here, and nothing happened to me."

Håkon just narrowed his eyes, growing darker. "The laws of this world are different from those you grew up with. I know where you come from. Now, everything is clear to me." He paused. "Answer my question. Did you try to do in this world what you did in the other?"

Winter blinked, confused. Finally, he was forced to nod. "I tried. And I didn't succeed. But the nux ..."

"The nux will make your skills more powerful," Håkon finished, in his place. "And the portal will also open on this side, yes. But your body is not made to withstand the energy you will unleash. And that energy will consume you and claim your life."

They looked at each other in silence, after that final revelation. It was only the wind that spoke, among them, in its hissing and unknown tongue, as night fell over the fortress.

"Do you understand why I don't want your destiny to be fulfilled?" resumed Håkon, the tone lower and slower. "From your birth, I knew that one day I would lose you. That I would watch you grow in the awareness of a necessary sacrifice, that you would be raised to welcome it and accept it as an honour." He shook his head. "What I didn't know, Lars, is that instead of losing you, I would find you again."

Winter closed his eyes, tightening his eyelids to hold back the sudden tears, whose saltiness he could taste in his throat.

They said nothing more. What else was there to say? It would have been nice, Winter thought, to accept this belonging. Indulge in the abandonment that it brought, in the thrill of understanding his origins, of having found his people. That future of war and domination sang inside him, tempting him. It was part of him, of his origins, of the very fabric of his being. He would finally be granted a respite to all his inexplicable anger, to all his violent need to exist, and to the will to impose himself that had characterized his entire life.

It would have been nice, and it would have been easy, but only if it hadn't needed Nathaniel's blood. He stared at the red and jagged line of the sunset on the horizon.

He had never felt so desperate.

He had never felt so safe.

# CHAPTER THIRTY-ONE

The two young men walked side by side along a corridor of the fortress, whose tall stone walls were lost in the vaulted ceiling, illuminated by a row of lanterns.

Yngvi was slightly taller than Winter, but sported a more defined body and traits akin to those of the Jötnar, harder and more intense. His long hair was gathered in an elaborate and silvery cascade of intertwined strands. Winter remembered him somehow. Even as a child he was more like the wild side of his paternal ancestry than that of the Norsihir.

"I didn't think I'd ever see you again," Yngvi commented, snatching him from his thoughts. "And certainly not with a bunch of Norse strays."

Winter threw him a sideways glance. "It was much stranger recognizing one another more than anything else, after all these years." And yet, it had happened. The memories had taken over, invading his mind, as soon as he had seen his childhood friend.

Yngvi led him past a common room where some women conversed with each other, mending clothes and leather protections, while boys of different ages, half-breeds, were fighting in the middle of the room like wolf cubs. All albinos. All males. Winter watched them for a moment, thoughtful. By now, the process was clear to him: the Jötnar were always born males, and their only way of securing descendants was to take women from other peoples, whose children took on mixed characteristics while maintaining the albinism and potential of their fathers. It was the same for him too. Now he knew he was the son of a Jötunn and a Norse woman, whose name he also remembered: Romilda. But he hadn't had the courage to ask his father about her. Moreover, along with the memories, the awareness of never having been loved or wanted by that woman had returned.

Near a window, a very young girl cradled a newborn, holding him tightly. She sang softly in the Norse language, and Winter found himself listening to those words, with an aching heart that he didn't understand, but which reminded him suddenly of his resolution.

> *"The white birch falls,*
> *it falls offering itself in sacrifice.*
> *Without noise, it gently falls.*
> *The leaves rustle, in the final breath."*

"Are you listening to me, Lars?"

Winter's head snapped towards Yngvi, who looked at him with a puzzled expression. He had been talking to him for a while, without his realizing it. "No," he replied only, with a disarming bluntness.

The other half-breed laughed. "Alright. I had forgotten how weird you can be. Come on, I'll take you to meet others."

They entered a narrower corridor, with a low ceiling, on which several wooden doors opened on both sides. At the end of it there was a stairwell leading up to a tower.

"Our quarters are upstairs," explained Yngvi, pointing to the dark stone steps. "Actually, only those of us who have already taken the oath. But soon you too will gain the nux, from what they say ..."

"When are they going to awaken the Nodal Point?" Winter changed the subject abruptly.

Yngvi shrugged. "I have no idea. But it won't be too soon. This is a border fortress; it won't happen here. I believe they will bring the Child of the Storm into one of the central fortresses, after gathering the raid platoons. I heard that the First Division was mobilized to come and get him. As for the rest, it will still take time." He looked amused. "Are you so eager to start a war, Lars?"

"They keep him in the dungeons, right?"

"Of course, where else?" The other young man's eyes narrowed at that point. "Lars, they say he was your friend, that Norse bastard." He didn't say anything else, but the implications of those words were clear to both of them.

"I'm sorry," Winter muttered, coming to a halt.

"About what?" Yngvi turned to look at him.

"This." Winter struck without hesitating. A blow to the throat with the side of the hand.

Yngvi gasped, his eyes widening, becoming round and bulging as if to jump out of their sockets. He had been taken by surprise, and before he could recover and react, the other moved sideways with a fluid movement, sank his hand between the white and twisted dreadlocks at the base of the other's neck and pushed forward, banging his face against the wall of the narrow corridor. Yngvi didn't even utter a moan. He sagged in his grip, collapsing on the floor, losing consciousness before even touching it. Winter let him go, staring for a moment at his face, the blood running from his broken nose and the jagged wound on his forehead. A twisted remorse and a dark and familiar satisfaction chased after him at that sight, making his temples beat at the pounding rhythm of his heart. He looked around. Nobody.

He had to act fast. Carefully, he opened one of the side doors. With relief, he saw that it was a warehouse full of boxes, trunks and dusty old armour. He grabbed the half-breed under his arms and dragged him inside the small room, leaving him in a corner, hidden by two large wooden crates. He closed the door behind him, panting.

He tied Yngvi's wrists and ankles with a length of rope he found poking through the shelves of the warehouse, making sure to gain more time for what he had to do. And at that point, he bent down to carefully remove the cuff from his right wrist. The one in which the nux was set.

He swallowed, feeling his hands not completely still, as he held it between his fingers. He didn't know if it was only suggestion, but he thought he heard a sudden energy quiver coming from the wristband. He felt his skin crawl into a powerful shiver, his hair stood up on his neck and his eyes burned, as if a bolt of lightning had fallen too close. What he was feeling forced him to hesitate for a moment. He looked at Yngvi lying on the ground, his face broken and bloody. His own past. A promise that was about to fail.

And then he looked at the bracelet. He remembered a tear trapped between the lashes of eyes of different colour.

His future, tormented and scary. A promise he was about to fulfil.

He gritted his teeth and put on the bracelet. He felt the strange cold stone come into contact with his skin. The energy he had felt before was nothing compared to the violent but familiar one he felt now. It crept into his veins, rising from his arm to his shoulder, pouring into his chest, spreading into his lungs and heart into a dimension he had never felt before, in which everything was more vivid and intense.

More *powerful*.

And he realized that he hadn't really lived, that he hadn't been what he was meant to be, up to that point. But now, yes, now everything became possible.

Now he felt complete.

*

It was a cautious sound of steps to wake Nathaniel. He flinched, his breath caught in his throat with a hoarse gasp. Instinctively he curled up in the corner, the image of the imposing figures that came to take him printed like a negative on the retinas, between lysergic colours and twisted memories.

He clenched his fists, preparing to fight until his last breath. The gaze fixed on the bars that faced the corridor. He saw a single shadow stretch out on the floor, projected by the trembling light of those lanterns hanging from the ceiling, and then a figure stood on the threshold of the cell, on the other side of the bars.

Nate's eyes widened, opening his mouth for a moment in an expression of complete amazement.

In front of him stood a young woman of maybe twenty, the blondish-brown hair collected in a severe braid, her green eyes pointed at him, hopeful. The accentuated roundness of her belly betrayed a pregnancy that was not yet very advanced, but already evident. Yet it was another detail that led Nathaniel to fix her as a ghostly apparition. She was unmistakably similar to Reidar.

They looked at each other for long moments, saying nothing. He tried to make sense of that feeling of recognition. Instead, she seemed to have lost that faint hope that had animated her; the light in her eyes had gone out.

"They said they caught a lynnewulf," she murmured, hugging herself. "But you ... you're not him."

Nathaniel, at those words, stood up abruptly, oblivious to the dizziness that made him stagger, uncertain on his legs. "Wait ... you're talking about Reidar," he gasped, starting to wonder if he was in the middle of some dreamlike delirium, with all the strange and incredible things that were happening.

It was the turn of the young woman to widen her eyes, shocked.

Her hands snapped up, clinging to the prison bars. "You ... you know my brother?"

And suddenly, everything was clear. "Reika ..." the boy murmured softly. "You must be Reika, that's why you look like him."

More and more surprised, she nodded, her silence beckoning an explanation.

"My name is Nathaniel. And I know him, yes. We travelled together to the Kernesfell pass."

"He came to find me ..." interrupted Reika. Her eyes, as green as her brother's, had lit up again, becoming shiny. "I was starting to lose hope."

"I don't think he's far from here," he said urgently. "I have been in mental contact with the heks in our group. They want to find a way to free me." He paused, clutching the cell's bars. "He couldn't have imagined that you were here, but I can let him know," he added, searching for the girl's gaze.

She nodded again.

"Do you have any way to get me out of this cell? I don't know how long we have before they come for me. They know I'm a lynnewulf, so they will try to open the portal." And he didn't want to wait to find out what they would do to him.

Reika pursed her lips in a line that spoke of determination. "I heard them say that tomorrow a platoon will come from the west to take you away. But I'll get the key to this cell."

She made it sound like a certainty, to the point that Nathaniel felt invaded by relief. There was a charisma in that look, and in the young woman's tone of voice, which left no room for doubt. He couldn't help but believe her.

"There are passages that lead out of the fortress, and I studied them all," she continued. "Since they brought me here I've tried to plan my escape, but it's not easy by myself. And this damn pregnancy got in the way too. Months have now passed." She looked at Nathaniel. The strength in her eyes reminded him of Reidar's. And it reminded him of another Norse he knew, very far from there. "Now it's time to act. With the help of Reidar from outside, we'll make it, I promise you."

Nate nodded, and hope began to resurface. "I'll contact your brother. You need to tell me on which side of the fortress they'll have to go, to help us when we are out." He stopped, looking at the small window behind him. "How long since nightfall?" he asked.

"The sun has just set. We don't have much time before I have to leave. I know the watchers' rounds—when they come to bring you food and drink. If I want to get the key to your cell, I'll have to take advantage of that moment."

"And by then I hope Reidar and Cress will have reached the fortress, because we must do it tonight."

Reika nodded firmly. "Tell them to go to the north wall; it's less steep and there is a forest there to hide. A sewage tunnel comes out on that side," she explained, gesturing agitatedly. "But there are bars at the end. They will need to remove them. Do you think they can do it?"

"I don't think they'll have much choice—there's only one way to find out," he concluded, placing his forehead against the bars. A part of him couldn't help doubting the plan as he tried to rule out any other thoughts or feelings that were not the burning core of kern in the centre of his solar plexus. The success depended on too many unresolved possibilities, on too much luck. And once already, relying on the "ifs" had turned out to be a failure. But there was no time for doubts, and in any case, there was no point in letting doubts overwhelm him now.

He focused, trying to visualise every detail of Cressida's face. It was strange remembering the intense sweetness of her expression, and the liquid fire she had had in her eyes on the night they had made love.

Perhaps it was the strength of those emotions that led him to her. It seemed to him, shortly thereafter, he felt again the silvery, shining cord that bound them together. And, in the darkness behind his eyelids, he finally saw her.

"*Cress?*"

"*Nate ... I hear you ...*"

"*Something has happened. In the fortress where they brought me, I found Reidar's sister. Now she's here, in front of me, and says she will find a way to free me. But there is not much time—tomorrow they will take me away.*"

He saw an appalled expression appear on her face as she pressed her fingers against her lips. He wondered if it was her way of interpreting that mental dialogue, or if he was really observing her physical reactions as if they were happening in front of him.

A few moments passed before the young heks spoke again. "*We can do it. We are in sight of the fortress, hidden in the shelter of a gorge, on the east ridge, and we have hidden the horses. Perhaps it would be easier to wait and let you escape during the transfer, but the girl ...*"

"*Reidar won't leave her here, you know. We have to try tonight,*" said Nathaniel.

"*Tonight it is. What else can you tell me?*"

"*Reika says there is a sewage tunnel on the north side. And that there the forest is thick enough to guarantee a hiding place,*" he hastened to explain. "*But you will have to remove the bars at the end of it.*"

There was a longer pause. Then Cress's voice reached him again. "*All clear. I will be in touch as soon as we are in position. You do the same, including if there are any problems, agree?*"

"*Agree. Be careful, Cress.*"

"*You too, Smukoj.*"

He saw her smile with the same intensity as that night. And whether or not it was a suggestion, that vision filled his heart with hope. He wanted to tell her something more, but Reika's sudden call broke mental contact, forcing him to open his eyes again. He clenched his fingers on the bars, stunned by the abrupt passage, struggling to focus and prevent his trembling knees from giving way under his weight. He didn't imagine that their mental contact could require so much energy, and his fatigued body was pointing that out.

The first thing he saw was the pale and severe figure of a Jötunn. He felt his heart tighten in despair: it was over.

But then his eyes widened, and the indistinct shape became sharper. For long moments, he could do nothing but stare in disbelief. Finally, the voice came out choked in a single, uncertain word. "Winter?"

He was there. There, in front of him, on the other side of the bars.

More concrete than he had felt the last time they spoke, in the darkness of the woods, in what must have been a farewell. And it seemed somehow stronger, more impressive than last time. His arms and shoulders were strung with tense and twisted muscles. Fragments of the need to take action. In his eyes of a spectral transparency, there was a chill that he had never seen before. It was then that he saw the bracelet on his right wrist and the opal glow of the nux, evident even in the dim reverberation of the lanterns on the ceiling.

"You have..." He couldn't continue. His voice broke in his throat. He shifted his gaze to Reika, standing stunned a few steps away from them with a desperate expression on his face. She must have thought that everything was lost. And the question remained, suspended in the tension-laden silence between them. Was it? Was it all lost? Why was Winter there now? In what role?

Winter sought his gaze. And suddenly, that violent chill in his irises melted into a nameless melancholy. So poignant that Nathaniel felt as if someone had planted a sliver of glass in his heart.

The doubts melted within him, turning into the damp salty awareness of the tears that rose to fill his eyes. He saw him come forward, without ceasing to look at him. He put his right hand on the lock of the door and tightened his fingers in a convinced, conscious grasp.

The metal squeaked while thin filaments of ice and whitish frost extended to branch out on its surface. The lock groaned, and that icy element crept inexorably between the connections. And then, with a cracking snap, it crumbled. The cell door jerked, creaking open.

He was free.

Nathaniel thought no more about anything. He crossed that threshold in a flash of instinct and violent energy. A moment later, he closed his arms around Winter's quivering body, hugging him with all the strength he had. His familiar smell filled his nostrils, along with a thousand memories, a thousand emotions. Another moment passed, and he felt him respond to the embrace, bowing his head and placing his gaunt cheek in his hair. He heard him inhale hard. He heard a poorly suppressed sob start in his chest.

They remained like this, for long seconds that seemed to last for an eternity. Tied tight like twins in the mother's womb. Too incredulous to shake. Too shaken to talk.

# Chapter Thirty-Two

The tunnel where Reika had sent them was even lower than the dungeons where Nathaniel had been locked up. The young woman had led them to a trapdoor at the bottom of several flights of stairs, in an abandoned wing of the fortress, and had been careful to avoid common areas and rounds of patrols. She seemed to know by heart every movement of the sentinels, every change of the guard. It was obvious that she had been planning this escape for a long time. And finally, the time had come for her to put into practice the knowledge accumulated over the months of imprisonment. "This way," she whispered confidently, guiding the two boys behind her as they crossed yet another fork in the intricate sewer system. "We are almost there."

On the floor of the low-vaulted tunnel ran the fetid stream of the sewage. Streaks of a strange luminescent moss glimpsed on the walls of the cloaca and illuminated the surroundings with a greenish and disquieting opalescence.

The three proceeded in silence with quick but cautious steps, keeping to the edge of the tunnel, bordering on the muddy and faecal water that flowed in the centre.

"Reidar and Cress have found the mouth of the tunnel," said Nathaniel, breathing through his mouth to avoid the stifling stench. "For now they've not had much success in removing the bars. They couldn't even try. Cress says there are sentries above the walls and they could discover them."

"Let her know that it won't be a problem when we get there," said Winter, the voice charged with a certainty that didn't allow for second thoughts. "I'll take care of the bars. They must not let themselves be seen, or they'll ruin everything."

After seeing him open the door of his cell with the new ability that the nux had given him, Nathaniel had no more doubts. He focused on bringing the message back, trying not to stop.

As Reika had assured them, it didn't take long to finally reach the mouth of the tunnel. The fresh, clean night air blew into their faces, erasing the stench of the sewer and fueling their hopes.

Outside the tunnel, the darkness was lit by the silvery glow of the two moons, which had just risen behind the mountains. Nathaniel seemed to see the vertical and black line of the bars that closed the passage and, beyond them, two silhouettes crouched in the shadow. His heart began to beat fast in his chest, a tense expectation singing inside him. He saw Reika move forward faster, as if she too had noticed those waiting presences.

"Reidar?" he heard her whisper, and even in that almost aural tone he managed to feel the emotion that was vibrating in her voice.

"Reika! I'm here." It was Reidar, and he did nothing to hide the relief and gratitude he felt.

He and Cress were out there. Only those bars separated them. An instinctive smile lifted the corners of his lips. He looked up at Winter, left behind a few steps, and saw him smile back at him. He experienced a feeling so acute and poignant from him that it hurt. It was like watching him shine with too much light, which erased every other emotion.

Winter stepped forward, flanking Reika at the end of the passage, and Nathaniel followed him. He noticed the obvious reaction of the Norse, who for a moment stared at Winter with obvious hostility. But then that hard expression softened. And it was obvious to imagine what he was thinking: if it hadn't been for the decision of the half-breed to abandon them, and for all that followed, he would never know that his sister was a prisoner in that border fortress. Nathaniel found himself for a moment considering the paths of the wyrd: only now he began to understand the extent of it, and to understand why his parents and the other Waerne spoke of it with so reverent respect.

It was the mournful screech of metal that distracted him from those thoughts, and saw that Winter had set to work to break the bars that separated them from freedom. That twisted moan echoed along the vault of the stone gallery, amplifying itself to a deafening level. Nathaniel put his head between his shoulders, with a worried grimace, and looked back, towards the darkness where the tunnel was lost. He strained his ears, trying to figure out if anyone could have heard the noise. He noticed that even Reidar and Cress looked around, fearing that someone could hear them and give the alarm.

"Be quick, Winter," he whispered, seeing that one of the bars had been broken by the force of the ice between his fingers, and shifted to one side.

"I'm trying, damn it," he replied through clenched teeth. He was working on the second bar. A third would be needed to open a fairly wide passage.

His hands were surrounded by the blue and cold glow that spread the frost to the metal, weakening it to break it. The reverberation danced on his face, tense and full of dark shadows, on the twisted lines created by the effort. On his right wrist, the opaline core of nux seemed to pulse. The black streaks on the surface had widened. Full of dismay, Nathaniel wondered what would happen if the energy needed to break the bars had consumed the stone to the point of not allowing Winter to bring them home, but he forced himself to shake that thought off: escaping from the fortress was the only priority.

He remained, therefore, as silent and tense as the others, while Winter's glacial energy devoured the metal, loosening and breaking the second bar. *One more*, he thought, biting his lips. The tension was becoming unbearable, and the unease of the others came at him, torturing his nerves. He struggled to remain calm, digging his nails into his palms to control the slight trembling of his hands, caused by the powerful thrust of the blood in his veins. He took a deep breath to calm the crazed gallop of his heart, but it didn't help much.

Suddenly, something changed. From the top, someone barked incomprehensible words in the dry and guttural language of the Jötnar, and the two boys outside crushed against the wall of the fortress. "Damn!" Reidar snarled, while the screams grew wild. "The sentries must have heard something and have given the alarm. Quick, Winter!"

"I'm ... I'm ... trying!" he snapped back, desperation in his voice.

Nathaniel saw Reidar draw the short sword from his side. For a moment, he froze. Then something seemed to explode inside him, crashing the chains of terror that had forced him into immobility. He stepped forward decisively, grabbing the bar that Winter was trying to break. It was cold. So cold that it made him wince in pain. But the adrenaline that flowed in his blood carried him beyond that pain. He forced himself to close his fingers on the metal and tugged it with all his strength, to accelerate the consequences of Winter's action. Then he saw his friend stand aside as if he had suffered a backlash and, with a last strident moan, the bar yielded.

Nathaniel cried when the cold that had stuck his hands to the metal tore the skin from his palms. He clenched his fists, with a tight-lipped curse, seeing the blood dripping between his fingers and flowing through his knuckles. But when Winter looked at him, worried, he shook his head to try to reassure him and hurried to slip into the passage, immediately after Reika. Winter followed him in silence.

They found themselves on a narrow rocky ledge, over which bushes and brambles climbed up the steep ridge where the fortress stood. Its enormous and black bulk loomed over them, standing out against the darkness of the night, lit only by the pale rays of the moons and the lanterns that burned high on the walls. The screams of alarm kept coming.

"Come on, let's move! The horses are not far away," Reidar urged them after hugging his sister, briefly.

The rocky ledge sloped down towards a path between the rocks. As Reika had said, that side of the hill on which the fortress stood was less steep and, keeping low, the five started cautiously towards the thick. A series of angry whistles followed them, immediately after. "Stay down!" Cress warned, sensing the impending attack.

Reidar moved behind his sister, protecting her, at the exact moment when a flock of ice darts with an unnatural blue glow crashed around them, exploding in splinters that bounced everywhere.

Cress lurched forward, uttering a shrill scream, but then straightened up panting. "Morjord ..." she groaned, and Nathaniel, turning to look at her, saw that she was holding a hand to her cheek, while a stream of dark blood filtered through her fingers.

"Cress!" he yelled, taking her by her free hand, uncaring of his flayed palm, burning as if on fire.

"Just a scratch. One of those damn splinters," she hastened to explain as they went into the thick of the woods, following the downhill path that led to the base of the hill. "Run, Smukoj! We'll think about it later."

The sinister light emanating from the splinters scattered around like the remains of a fragmentation grenade began to illuminate the area, revealing their position to the Jötnar above, but at the same time providing them with extra light to orient themselves.

Shortly after, another round of darts exploded around them, this time rendered less effective by the thick brambles and trees that now surrounded them. Nathaniel was stung by some of the fragments and heard Reidar curse through his teeth with pain. But they continued to move, with the Norse at the head of the small column, to guide them towards safety.

The ground became less steep, and the silver light of the two moons began to leak through the branches. The forest opened up in a small clearing dotted with the almost stagnant bend of a stream, which poured down in a series of small waterfalls a few meters below. The horses were there, waiting.

Nathaniel saw Berkana lift her powerful muzzle and throw a whinny of recognition. It was the most beautiful greeting he felt he had ever received in his life.

"Let's go!" Reidar urged, passing an arm around his sister's waist—

she was panting audibly now, tired by the flight and by her condition. He led her to Sol, who was pawing nervously at the edge of the clearing. Before they could reach him, a group of imposing figures rushed out of the shadows of the trees, standing between the fugitives and their mounts.

Reidar stopped where he was, immediately pushing Reika behind him and raising his short sword in a threatening guard pose. A belligerent flash flew into his eyes as the crackling energy of lightning began to dance around him. Cressida joined him, with the same decision. She was unarmed but, from the thick of the woods, they heard dry barks and short howls. Rapid movements through the trees made it clear that she was once again calling Mother Earth and her creatures to help. Winter and Nathaniel remained on the second line, out of breath for the escape. And at that point, the two groups faced each other in silence, while the tension made the air dense and unbreathable.

Nathaniel felt himself overcome for a moment by all those violent and contrasting emotions, and he gritted his teeth to tame a dizziness and to keep at bay what he was feeling. At the head of the Jötnar group that blocked their way was the white giant who had chased them since the beginning of the journey. At that sight, he felt himself seized by an inescapable sense of foreboding. Next to him Winter stiffened, and Nate realized that father and son were staring straight into each other's eyes, as if there was no one else in that clearing.

It was Håkon who finally spoke. The rumble of his voice was low and vibrant, stronger than the chorus of wolves that danced around them. He spoke in the Norse language, with a harsh accent that carved words out of hard stones. "This confrontation is not necessary." He shifted his gaze from Winter to Reidar for a moment, whom he seemed to recognize as the leader of the small group of fugitives. "Give us my son and the lynnewulf, and we will let you go."

"Forget it," Reidar barked in response. "We will fight. Till death."

A displeased expression hardened the leonine features of the giant. He returned his glacial gaze to his son.

Nathaniel felt a sudden and violent shock and turned to look at Winter. He saw him widen his eyes and stagger, and he realized that what had happened the first time the Jötunn had sighted them in the valley outside Nivak was happening again.

"Winter ..." he called to ease the mental pressure he was facing. "Wint, hold on," he whispered, and stretched his flayed hand to grab his.

There was a moment's hesitation, then his friend squeezed it. So hard it made him grimace in pain. Through the veil of tears that had blurred his vision, he saw him draw his short sword on his belt with his left hand.

Winter continued to stare straight into his father's eyes, in a silent confrontation of wills. Every trace of colour had left even his lips, and soon a thread of blood came out of a nostril, tracing a scarlet line down to his chin, in violent contrast with the pallor of his skin. He raised the blade, his hand trembling. Håkon, on the other side of the clearing, seemed to understand the intentions of the boy and his eyes widened. The menacing mask on the feral face crumbled into an expression that spoke of disbelief and grief.

"*Lars! Nej!*"

His voice was the explosion of an underground charge capable of causing the collapse of the entire mountainside. In that violent denial was concentrated a desperation that went beyond any language.

Winter lowered the blade against the inside of his right forearm. A red line opened in the midst of the old scars, above the nux bracelet. A narrow, jagged crimson mouth that created a slow river of dark blood.

Nathaniel could not look away from the dense rivulets that ran down his forearm, down to his wrist, and to their united palms. He felt the heat, while the wristband and the striated stone were covered in the red liquid.

Håkon rushed forward, and the Jötnar's group behind him followed, a roar that broke the tension in a violent backlash. At that moment, time stopped. A flash of light cut through the air around Winter's figure, breaking reality in two, the jagged split opening like a crack in an invisible wall.

Then Nathaniel understood: his friend had exploited the energy of the nux and the strength of his blood to open the portal between the worlds. And this time he had succeeded. But it was not the placid and reassuring demonstration he had seen when they had crossed the Nodal Point that had led them into the world of the Norsihir. That portal was now unstable and loaded with uncontrollable and dangerous power.

He felt the earth tremble beneath his feet and the horses neighing in terror, fleeing, while a crack that looked like the mirrored and dark projection of the first one now opened onto the ground with a deep and chilling roar. The river overflowed, pouring over the short in a rapid, foaming spray as the rocks groaned and a tree collapsed, exposing roots covered in brown soil. The light of the wide-open portal threw cold and alien reflections onto the scene, while the Jötnar charge came to a halt in front of that violent manifestation of nature that rebelled against the laceration of the fabric of spacetime.

Instinctively Nathaniel clung to Winter. He felt his friend's body stiffen and bow in a violent spasm while the light of the portal enveloped them both, becoming unbearable. He heard his scream rise above that of the tortured earth. He had time to see Reidar wrap his arms around Reika and Cressida in a desperate and protective gesture.

Then the light became blinding, and a vibrant impact swept them away.

# CHAPTER THIRTY-THREE

Soft green leaves rustled delicately a few inches from Nathaniel's face. They sighed, trembling, under the cool breeze of the dawn. He felt the grass tickle his cheek, prick him a little. He blinked. What had happened? He tried an uncertain breath, realizing he was lying face down under the large weeping willow near the stream where he and Winter had taken refuge that morning, too many days before, when he had revealed his secrets to him. Yet time did not seem to have passed in that part of the universe. What he had around him was the same placid and unsuspecting dawn of when it all started.

He was so aware of it that, for a moment, he thought he had dreamed everything. That he had lived a crazy, incredible suggestion. But when he tried to sit up at least, the fire that awakened in his skinned and bleeding palms and the sudden pain in his head told him that this journey to another world had not been a dream, nor a suggestion. And that Winter must have brought them back to the starting point, in space and time.

As his heartbeat increased, he looked around. There was no trace of Reidar, Reika or Cress. He had no idea what had happened to the three Norsihir when the portal had opened wide. But one thing was certain, he was not alone.

"Winter!"

He was there, lying in the grass, sprawled with his right arm extended in front of him. The self-inflicted wound he had used to open the portal—the tribute, he recalled with unease—had stopped bleeding. The nux on the blood-encrusted bracelet was black as a piece of obsidian, its energy completely depleted.

Winter didn't move. He didn't answer his call. Nathaniel hurried to join him, turning him on his back with an effort, on his knees beside him, supporting his head and shoulders in his arms. "Wint ... come on, answer me…"

His face had a ghostly pallor, stained with the dark rust of blood on his lips and chin. Still, Nathaniel's healing nature did not respond to that body's obvious request for help. That awareness suddenly reached him, threatening to engulf his thoughts in a wave of panic. Then he saw the clear eyelashes tremble. He saw him frown in an effort to focus, and then the corners of his pale lips rose up, hinting a smile of relief.

"Hey …" he whispered.

Nathaniel felt his throat closing in anguish. "Hey …" he answered, unable to hide the tremor that broke his voice.

"See …? I've done it. I brought you home."

"You did." Nate swallowed, but the lump in his throat didn't melt, choking the words. "Don't strain yourself, okay? I'll take care of you now. Everything will be fine."

He gritted his teeth, struggling to regain contact with the warm core of his Norse heritage. But now everything seemed tiring and difficult. The instinctive simplicity with which he had drawn that power in the world of the Norsihir seemed to have vanished. He felt a tremor of energy and a hint of the reaction he was looking for. And he hugged Winter, praying he could give him the strength he needed.

"Nate." With an effort, the boy raised his hand and placed it on Nate's. "Stop that. It won't work."

"What are you talking about?" The panic rose from the heart and into his voice. "I can heal you. You know I can. I'm doing it," he said, in an increasingly frantic tone.

The other let out a slow sigh. "That's not how it works, Nate. My father told me." He paused, his eyelids fluttering as if he was about to lose consciousness again. "The portal … has consumed everything … everything I had to give. And you can't do anything about it, you understand?"

Nathaniel looked at him for a moment with wide eyes, green and blue, equally full of dismay. "Don't talk bullshit, Wint … Don't try. Don't even think about it," he protested, squeezing him even harder.

He felt the warmth of his healing energy abandoning him in waves, but Winter's cold skin didn't seem to react. It was as if his body absorbed that heat in a vacuum, dispersing it, discharging it into the ground beneath them. It was like trying to heat a glacier.

He saw him smile, opening his eyes in a last generous effort. That very clear look that sought his with a tormenting need. "How strange …" he whispered softly. "You're the one I saw … when I thought I was dead. It was this warmth of yours, the first thing I felt … in my new life." He swallowed. "I'm glad it's also the last."

Nathaniel felt the blade of remorse sink rusty teeth into his stomach.

"You knew it ... and you did it anyway," he murmured, shaking his head. He blinked to prevent the tears from taking his eyes off Winter's face. "You shouldn't have done that."

"Why? So I could die in the fight? Let them take you back alive, only to sacrifice you and invade your world?" Winter's voice surged suddenly, as if he had decided to use his last energies to pronounce those words so definitive. "No. It was my choice. And that's fine with me."

The young Norse half shook his head, unable to say more. He had never felt so wrong, so useless.

Winter squeezed his hand. "There are other worlds, and we both know it," he said, a barely audible whisper, but with a stronger smile. "This I'm about to cross ... it's just another door, after all. And if you're there, to accompany me to the threshold ... I think it will be easier." He left his hand to lift his own, inserting his fingers in the tangled and raven hair on Nathaniel's neck with a delicacy that had something timid and poignant, in total contrast with his normal behaviour. But it was with a flash of aggression that had characterized his entire existence that he attracted him to himself, pressing his lips against Nate's.

It was a moment, and it was an eternity. And it was intense and burning and desperate and necessary. And it was love. That troubled and powerful feeling that Nathaniel had felt without recognizing, all the time, and who came to claim its tribute at the worst of times. He felt his heart hammering as if he wanted to get out of his chest, and his tears flow free.

In the distance, someone started calling them by name. Familiar voices. He realized he really was back home. And he didn't care. He felt Winter's grip tighten against his neck for a moment, leaving a mark with his fingers. Then it loosened, gently. His hand fell into the grass, without weight, without noise. That was the moment when he felt the bond between them really weaken, that bond that began with the first contact, when he had saved him on the road to Ocala. He felt it become fragile until it melted completely. It was not the devastating jolt he had expected. It seemed rather a gentle sigh, the comforting shadow of a last caress. Not the sudden chill of an announced void, but a mild, timid and melancholic warmth.

Still, he knew that even that warmth would fade, as well as the memories and the pain he felt, like the taste of Winter's lips. But he didn't want to forget. He didn't want time to heal him, or that pain becoming bearable. He didn't want everything to be all right. He didn't want to stop feeling that desperate love. Nor did he want that deep wound inside him to stop bleeding. Because he had been the cause, and that knowledge would be with him forever.

The branches of the willow rustled. He held the still body of Winter in his arms, looking at that face that had not lost his sharp and wild beauty but had gained a serenity he had never known, even in his sleep. It seemed to him that the little leaves, dancing in the wind, carried with them the notes of a slow, monotonous dirge, with the light tones of a lullaby. And he seemed to hear words whispered in the cool breeze of the dawn. As if the tree, guardian of the secret they had shared and their last, fragile refuge, sang for them.

> *"The white birch falls,*
> *it falls offering itself in sacrifice.*
> *Without noise, it gently falls.*
> *The leaves rustle, in the final breath."*

The voices and footsteps got closer. There was not much time before that last greeting would end. Nathaniel listened to the gentle song with which that quiet corner of the world seemed to want to thank Winter for what he had done, accompanying him in the first steps of his new journey and wishing him good fortune. Then he bowed his head and let himself fall into a low cry. He suddenly understood it. That was the last time. The last tears of his adolescence. His silent farewell to the light-heartedness of his years, to what immature, innocent and uncertain feelings he had guarded until then. Only then did he fully understand the words Richard had spoken a few days earlier, in his New York apartment: *"These seventeen years of yours will never come back, Nathaniel. Don't waste them."* No, they wouldn't come back. Nothing would be the same again.

# EPILOGUE

Nathaniel was leaning against the railing of the terrace. From below came the muffled sound of the Manhattan traffic as the warm September sun descended more and more, hiding beyond the irregular skyline. From up there, everything seemed farther away, more acceptable, somehow.

It had been three months, but sometimes it seemed to him like a lifetime, so much had changed in every aspect of his existence. Other times, however, it didn't feel like a single day, and he wondered how he could return to his student life, to lessons, to going out with his friends. That last year he had left to finish high school seemed to be a bigger obstacle than the one he had faced to get home from another world.

"Your mother told me I would find you here." A low and deep voice, full of instinctive charisma, reached him. Richard.

Nathaniel didn't turn around and didn't answer. He just peeked to the right as the Norse came up beside him, leaning back against the railing.

"I didn't think it would take you this long to show up. You might as well have stayed where you were," the boy commented.

The accusatory tone wasn't veiled. He saw him hint at a smile, melancholic and intense at once. "It wasn't me you needed, these past months, Nate. But the comfort of your family, of your coven."

The boy frowned, indignation drawn on the sharp features, bending the corners of his lips downwards. "You always think you know everything, don't you? How do you know that I didn't need you instead? It's been three months, Dick. *Three months*," he said, doing nothing to hide the disappointment in his voice.

Richard turned to him. That smile didn't want to yield, despite the youth's hostility, softening the hard features of that ancient face and reverberating in his eyes. "You wouldn't have accepted what I have to tell you. Perhaps you won't accept it even now," he explained, with unusual kindness.

Nathaniel looked at him, puzzled. The straight wrinkle that had formed between his dark eyebrows spoke of ill-concealed curiosity. Somehow, the Norse had caught his attention, and now he wanted to know.

Richard sighed. "It's a long, long time since I've lived in your world, Nate. And your world has given me a very long existence, even by the standards of my people. I was one of the first Norsihir to reach this corner of the infinite possible universes, so special and so disputed. There were three of us when we first arrived here."

Nathaniel continued to stare at him, without understanding. Why was he telling him that story now?

"It was not a spontaneous Nodal Point that led us here," continued the Norse, "although it had not been thrown open for us, and the rejsend who had opened it was not willing to send us into this world. He had only awakened it to bring the person he loved back home."

This time, Nate's wide eyes widened as a sudden awareness seized him, and every trace of colour left his face. Long seconds passed before he could find his voice, which came out choked and crackling from his throat. "Are you … saying that …" He swallowed, trying to find the strength to state the impossible assumption. "Are you *Reidar*?"

The Norse nodded, letting the news sink deeper. "Much later, when I left the Old Continent behind me, I changed my name to Richard Gordon, and I became a rich American in the eyes of the world. I have played that part since then, making sure that the traces of my ancestry and my descent were lost forever."

"So … you ended up in the past when Winter unleashed the Nodal Point …" It was a head-spinning concept. That, and all the implications it entailed. "And Cress? Reika?"

Reidar looked at him with a flash of melancholy in his eyes. "We all found ourselves in that new world, the one the Jötnar wanted to conquer. And that's when it all started. Cressida and I have had several children, who have joined the sons and daughters of men. And also Reika gave birth to her child …"

"A half-breed of the Jötnar? So … there is also their descent, between us?"

The Norse nodded gravely. "It was their descendants who gave rise to the first of those whom you today call Fjandar."

Nathaniel clung to the balustrade with both hands, stunned by the revelations. "And what happened to them? Where are they now?"

"After a long time we managed to get back in touch with our world, and things were moving forward. Other Norsihir had come here through the Nodal Points, and we were allowed to go back. Reika chose to do so. She had never really tied herself to this world and the inevitable conflict with her son had marked her. But we stayed in touch until the end of her days." He paused as the melancholy continued to dance in his eyes.

That same look that Nathaniel had met in a much younger man, who in a shocking synchronicity had almost been his age and had been his first mentor, a Child of the Storm as he was, without knowing he was his ancestor. Three months before. A thousand years before.

"As for Cress," Reidar resumed after a while, "she remained at my side for many centuries, guiding our descendants, teaching them communion with Mother Earth, which is the same in all possible universes. She died to save one of the predestined of the Waerne, during one of the great crisis spells of the last century, the one that for you has gone down in history as the Second World War." He shrugged. "That was when I decided to leave the Old Continent and start all over again here. Unaware that the last descendant of my lineage would have come looking for me, and he would have become the storm warrior of the last nodal crisis. And unaware of the fact that his son, you, would have been the one who, a thousand years before, brought me to this world."

Nathaniel was silent for a long time, pondering the mind-boggling consequences of that incredible time loop. When he spoke, he did it cautiously, and in the most strangled voice than he wanted. "You knew it. You already knew everything. Is the wyrd so immutable?"

Reidar looked at him, an expression of understanding on his face. He placed a hand on his shoulder gently, almost fearing a refusal. "No. All choices are our own. The wyrd indicates a way, one of the possible futures. A prophecy is not immutable, Nate. But it was your choices that led you where you are today. And you did much more than being able to go home."

The boy looked back, unable to hide the pain he felt. Inside him, the wound was open and bleeding. "Then I didn't make the right choices. Because if I had made them, Winter would have been saved." It was there, the core of the whole matter. The burning core on which he had racked his brains without finding an answer throughout that interminable summer.

But Reidar squeezed his fingers firmly on his shoulder. The certainty there startled him.

"Your choices have prevented the Jötnar from conquering this world. Valoisa and Valkea's son has *really* been the ruin of the Ancient One, as the prophecy that everyone has always repeated to you, told us. And through you, for your sake, the Norsemen have reached your world, and have been able to defend it over the centuries. They, and their descendants." He smiled a little. "I know that thinking about it makes your head spin, but without all this, your parents would never have been born either. And you would never have existed."

Nathaniel pondered those conclusions.

"As for Winter," said Reidar, in a lower and quieter tone, "he also made his choices. He knew what he was doing. He knew it when he thought he wanted to choose his father's people, and then when he chose you, and he gave you the greatest gift of all."

The other felt his heart tighten. Although his ancestor's words were truthful, he could not get over it. As much as he had tried to process that mourning and find some peace, a part of him kept shouting that there had not been enough time for them. That it was all over before they had only one chance to start. And that everything remained unfinished, broken. A part of him kept telling him that this wasn't the way it should have gone.

Almost sensing the course of his thoughts, Reidar sighed softly. "There are other worlds, a synchronicity of infinite existences that we cannot understand," he declared, his low voice vibrating with a sure and powerful intensity. "And he knows. Believe me, wherever he is now, whatever his current path ... if he really wants it, and I think he does, he will find a way back."

It was strange, all things considered, and he hadn't expect it. But those words managed to do something that nothing else, in the last three months, had managed to do: he felt the seed of hope trying to plant timid roots in the tired and arid substratum of his soul. And finally, he let gentle tears wash over him, and allowed them to nourish him.

# "Without whom", said Stuart

My first story, *The Sign of the Storm*, was a long time in the making: almost casually built—even if nothing in this world is by chance, as Nate would say—quietly, over the course of ten years. It was a slow and peaceful journey, and it came into existence in a similar way. Without any expectations, but still leaving a seed in my heart.

This second story, on the other hand, was fraught with tension. Much like the adolescent troubles experienced by the two protagonists, it was a vibration that I began to feel under my skin as I wrote the book, which hasn't left me yet. The story of Nathaniel and Winter bears the lights and shadows of late nights and dawns, the smell of Chinese food devoured in front of a computer screen, the bitter desire to dare and the doubt of not having done so enough. It is a weightier story, perhaps more mature, even in the light of the immaturity of its protagonists. More focused, difficult: a year and a half of work that could be reduced to a few months, if I could distill the time it took to write. And I love the second book even more than the first.

There are so many people I should thank, whom I didn't at the end of my first novel. I was embarrassed to do so: the great authors are those with the words "Acknowledgments" at the beginning or end of their book, right? However, since we are here, I would like to borrow an expression from one of my favourite writers (yes, him, a great one), Stuart MacBride, as I list my *"without whom"*. Those "without whom" this story would never have seen the light of day.

Thanks to my Italian publisher, Francesca Costantino, who believed in my stories even before I began to believe in them myself, and to all the staff of Astro Edizioni; and to Francesca T Barbini and Luna Press Publishing for their trust in this new international adventure.

Thanks to my husband, Marco Accordi Rickards, in good times and bad, in joy and in pain, until death unites us even more ("There are other worlds, and we both know it," Winter would say); thanks also to our daughters, Mila and Giorgia, always ready to cheer for their crazy Mom; to my parents, Silvana and Enzo, without whom I wouldn't even have begun to cultivate a passion for reading or a dream of writing.

To Diego and Giorgia, companions on special adventures: I hope we continue to grow together. To Rosaria Trivisonne, for her wonderful cover illustration. Thanks to Nat Zang and Arcangelo, for having inspired me, in one way or another, in the creation of the characters of Nate and

Winter. To Poppy Z. Brite, her lyrical prose and powerful stories have been an undeniable source of inspiration seeping through some of these pages, and to Alessandro Manzetti, who gave me the opportunity to translate her works.

Last but not least, a heartfelt thanks to you, who have read this far and have chosen to be led into my world, accompanying my two boys on their difficult journey. I just want to give you one last, small tip before leaving: *turn the page ...*

## SOMEWHERE...

When he opened his eyes, he felt exhausted. It was difficult even to focus, and all he saw was a swirling chaos of snowflakes. The cold formed a powerful cape, crushing him. But, despite that and his weakness, he forced himself to his knees, levering on his palms. He seemed to know that place. To have seen it before.

*"Receive it. Don't fight it. Cold is your element, frost is your power. Make it yours."*

Those words reverberated inside him from who knows where. And he knew how to do it. He didn't know where those suggestions came from. He didn't remember. He didn't even know where he was, or why. But he knew he could control the cold and not fear it.

He wrapped his arms around his chest, narrowing his gaze and losing it in the greyness of the storm in front of him. He saw jagged rocks covered in ice and frost. The snow rounded each corner, erasing the reference points, but it seemed to him that a slightly outlined path wound downhill, losing itself in the fog.

With an effort that made him moan, he rose to his feet. He staggered and was forced to cling to one of those rocks. When the dizziness passed, he ventured to move a few steps towards the valley. He sank into the snow up to mid-calf, stopping after a few meters to catch his breath. After all, he could only hope that what seemed to be a path really was, and that it would lead him somewhere.

He continued to advance, pushed forward by sheer will more than by his exhausted body. There was something inside that forced him to react. He couldn't give up. He couldn't afford to give in, not yet.

There was something he had to do first. A promise he felt he needed to keep. But what?

He raised a hand to his lips, confused, feeling an odd heat. He felt himself gripped by a sense of melancholic nostalgia he could not explain. He sighed, shaking his head: he could do nothing else for the moment. Just move on, and hope to survive long enough to remember.

He could not tell how much time passed before something changed in that desolate and inhospitable landscape. He narrowed his eyes, looking ahead; at first he thought it was a joke of his fatigued sight, but then he was sure of it: something was moving, perhaps ten paces away, further downhill.

He stopped cautiously. He didn't know what to expect, and he looked for a hiding place. But the indistinct form approached, taking shape, turning into a human figure, wrapped in thick fur against the cold of the storm. When he got close enough to face it, he realized that he was a tall, imposing middle-aged man, wrapped in what looked like a heavy cloak of silvery grey—the fur of a wolf, he thought. Only his eyes could be seen of his face. Clear, intense. Almost hypnotic.

They looked at each other for a few moments, the only noise the moaning of the wind whistling between the rocks, bringing with it icy snow gusts.

Then the man spoke. "They said you would come, riding the storm. I didn't think, however, that you'd be so young." His voice was low and husky, but full of incomprehensible power.

The boy could not help thinking that it somehow belonged to a leader. "Who are you?" he managed to ask, despite the knot in his throat.

"My name is Niklas. And we should have met a long time ago."

The boy looked perplexed.

"I'm Winter." It was only when he uttered that he realized he had remembered his name. Or what he thought his name was. He paused. He tried to give voice to that primordial necessity that sang within him. "I have to find someone," he said forcefully. "Will you help me?"

He watched a cautious smile dance in those restless eyes. "I too must find someone. Someone I haven't even had time to say goodbye to." He nodded, and held out a hand to him. "I will help you."

Winter hesitated for a moment. Then he sighed, and there was relief in that sigh. As he had done with someone else—he didn't remember where and when, but he knew he had learned to trust at least once—he reached out and squeezed the other's gloved hand. A firm grasp, loaded with unresolved promises.

He remembered a pair of eyes, one green and one blue, and the warmth of a kiss given too late. He didn't know anything else for now. But he knew he wouldn't give up. The man named Niklas, who also had a promise to keep, walked into the snow.

And Winter followed him.

www.ingramcontent.com/pod-product-compliance
Lightning Source LLC
Chambersburg PA
CBHW030626190726
48286CB00008B/2418